THE OUTRAGE FACTORY

A. A. GUNN

Copyright © 2018 A. A. Gunn
All rights reserved.
ISBN: 1720925283
ISBN-13: 978-1720925286

In memoriam D. P.

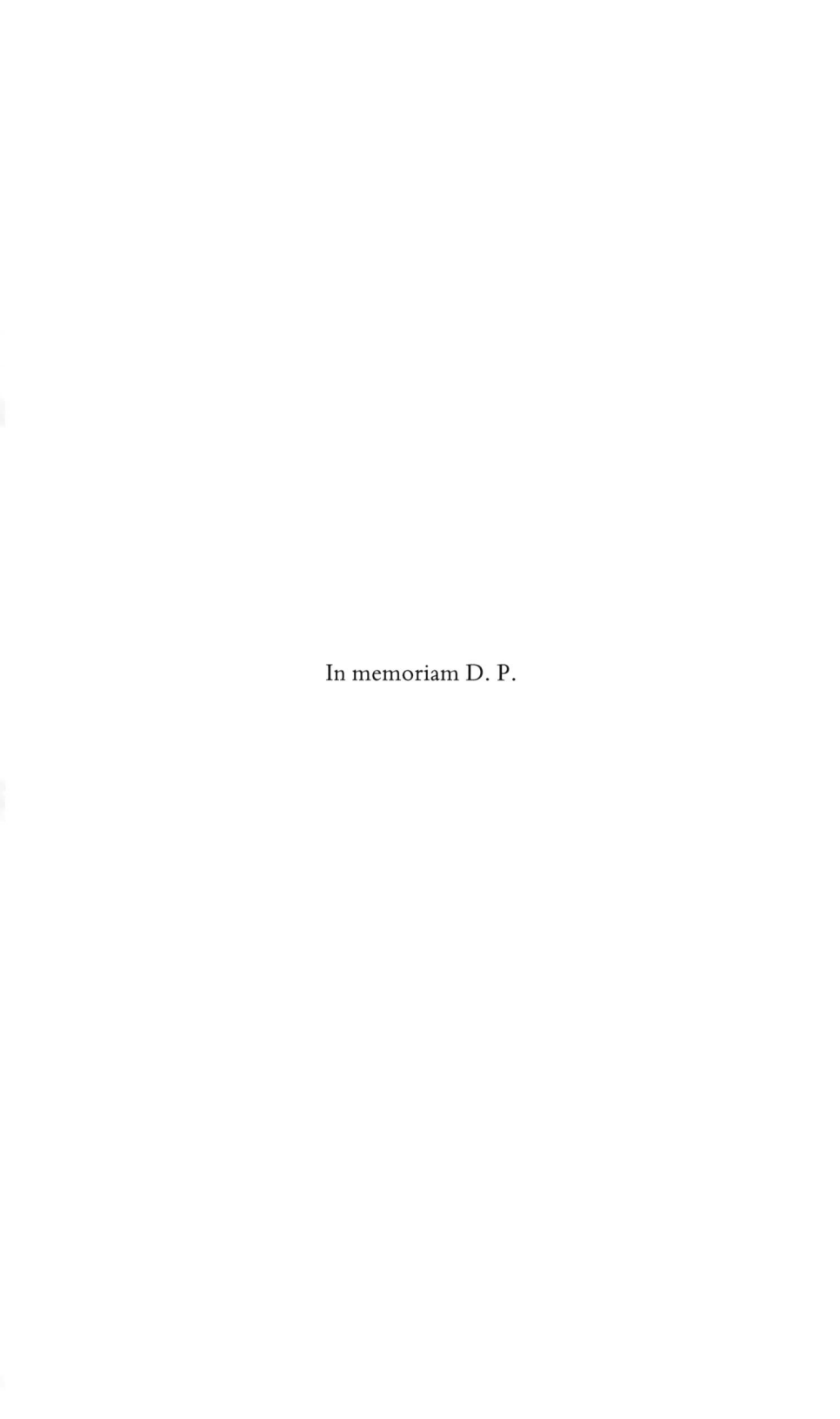

Oh, what a tangled web do parents weave
when they think that their children are naive.
— Ogden Nash

When small men begin to cast big shadows,
it means that the sun is about to set.
— Lin Yu Tang

ACKNOWLEDGEMENTS

My deepest thanks go to: my mother and sister, for their patience, care and navigational skills; E., my first and truest friend; G., for encouraging my fictional baby steps; R., the font of all optimism; S., my cheerleader, encyclopaedia and de facto if not de paid editor; and M., for all the faith.

CONTENTS

Trollr	1
I care because you do	20
Thor	37
International Women's Day	53
Nip it in the bud	69
The Quick Brown Fox	88
Fire	105
And there you have it	129
Informa/McKenzie	146
You are about to share with the world	164
Where Else?	183
International Men's Day	208
The Amish	233

TROLLR

Craig Rupple defiled a Qur'an. He only did it because someone made him do it; he wasn't trying to become an internet sensation, or get the school burnt down. But after the smallest speck of time had passed, the distinction didn't seem to matter. He was the one who did it, and everything else was irrelevant.

At the end of the second Tuesday of November, after double Sex And Relationships, God jumped out in front of him from behind a classroom door. Craig had yet to cross paths with God — real name, Dylan Brewster — and wanted to keep it that way. He was the kind of kid you didn't want the teachers to see you with, not because they'd pay you any more attention, but because they'd pretend not to see, telling themselves that you were probably just friends, leaving you at his mercy. The whites of his eyes were stained with small pink rivers, which meant he was stoned. 'Evening, ladyboy,' he said.

Eyes down, thought Craig: I do not consent to this. That was what he was supposed to say in these events, but the only time he'd heard anyone say 'I do not consent' was on a Fabble post by Grace Cliverton from Pre-Advanced Maths, whimpering and moaning it as she fingered herself, moistening her fingers with her tongue between protestations, pushing her other hand against the cubicle wall. He opened his mouth, and a few noiseless syllables dropped out.

'I said *evening*, you little twunt,' said God.

That's when Craig saw what he was holding: 'The Holy Qur'an', fine gold lettering across the dimpled green cover, and in his other fist, his phone. Not that, Craig thought. Please not that. He turned, to make a break for it down the corridor towards Interfaith Studies; and there was El Jaw, lumbering towards him, suddenly taller than he seemed from a distance, all teeth and greasy skin. Craig could hear his pulse surging up into his head. How could two of them have been waiting to ambush, without him even noticing?

'Answer, gringo,' growled El Jaw, raising his arm. Craig tried to duck underneath it, but then El Jaw slammed him playfully into the doorframe, wedging Craig's nose into an armpit hot with the smell of deodorant. Right away, Craig could feel the bump throbbing, an angry conker just behind his hairline. He froze, his escape route sealed off; as the cheeks of his arse clenched, El Jaw rested his thumb on Craig's throat, and stretched his fingers out across his neck, fixing him in place.

'Fuck off,' said Craig.

'Don't be like that, baby,' said God, holding up the phone. 'Obey your Lord and Saviour.'

Craig looked into the lens hovering a few inches from his face, a black circle swimming below glass, a cow's eyeball, wet and infinite. God was going to make him piss on the Qur'an, or worse: certainly a hate crime of some sort, that was obvious. He closed his eyes. Please not anything to do with the toilet, he thought. 'Fuck off,' he said again, at half the volume.

And then, there was a ripping sound.

'Eat this,' God said. He'd put the Qur'an down on top of a radiator, and was holding up a crumpled page, and smiling. It was a smile Craig had seen before, a victor's smile, a bored demon millimetres beneath the surface. Something about it seemed so reasonable.

Craig looked at the page, grey text on oily yellow. It didn't look edible, but it didn't look that inedible, either; and he'd rather eat it than do anything which involved dropping his pants in front of Dylan Brewster and Jordan Donaghy, the entire internet waiting behind their shoulders. '*You* eat it,' he said, weakly.

'That's no way to talk to the man who's gonna make you famous,' said God, twirling the scrunch of paper slowly in his fingertips. 'You don't wanna be a movie star?'

El Jaw was looming over him, huffing through his nose like a bull. There was a piece of sweetcorn trapped in his metal braces, like the tiny yellow tooth of a vestigial twin. 'Go pick the food out of your braces,' Craig said.

'Fuck YOU!' yelled El Jaw, so loud and so sudden that Craig jumped backwards and banged the other side of his head.

'Easy, champ,' God said. He leant into Craig's ear. 'I'm gonna put you on Trollr. Four more followers and I'm a messiah. Don't pussy out on me.'

So I'm going on Trollr, then, Craig thought. At least it wasn't Fabble; Trollr hadn't been mentioned in assembly yet, so maybe the teachers didn't know about it. 'What's wrong with you, gringo?' asked El Jaw. 'Do as you're fucking commanded.'

Craig stared into the cow's eyeball. Maybe it was being livestreamed, and his stupid, sweaty face was already out there, cowering in a doorway. How many people could be watching him? Two? A hundred? You look like a wuss, Craig thought. Man up.

He straightened his shoulders. 'I'll eat that,' he said. 'No problem, man.'

'Attagirl,' said God.

Shit, Craig thought. Bullying wasn't supposed to work so easily. There was some step he'd missed out, some magical, de-escalating strategy he'd failed to initiate. He reached out his hand for the page.

'Ah-ah-ah,' said God. 'Say *me hungry*.' And then, a small green prick of light came into the corner of the cow's eyeball.

He hasn't been filming, thought Craig, but he is now.

Craig smiled. He wasn't sure why. Maybe it was just having a camera shoved in his face, or maybe the smile made the whole thing less serious, somehow: less of a desecration, more of a prank. Maybe people would think he was the troller, and not the trollee. 'Me hungry,' he said, and grinned.

God stepped back, squinting, and repositioned himself in the doorframe, for focus. 'Say *me want food*,' he said.

So this is how the game works, Craig thought. You win by not looking bothered; that's all you have to do. 'Me want food,' he said. 'Nom nom.'

'You want Qur'an?' said God, zooming in on the gold lettering. 'Here, here's some Qur'an.' And then, he backed up, to get Craig's face and the Qur'an lying on the radiator in one high definition shot.

And Craig took the page, because that was at least better than having it rammed down his throat. The paper was waxy in his fingers, and felt even thinner than it looked: there was hardly anything to it. He crushed the page up into a tight little ball, and chewed it.

'Yeah, that's it, baby,' said God. 'Chow down.'

Fuck you, thought Craig. The paper stuck to the top of his mouth in a big, warm clod, and made him want to retch. 'Nom nom,' he said, and laughed. It was quite a convincing laugh, better than he'd feared.

'Nice food?' asked God.

Craig was trying to dislodge the clod of paper with his tongue, so he could swallow it. He looked at the phone, and did a double thumbs-up.

'How's it taste?' asked God.

'Like shit,' said Craig, the word 'shit' turning into a burp halfway through.

'Dude,' said God. 'Those Muslims are gonna eat you up.'

'You're fucking dead, señorita,' said El Jaw. 'You're fucking yesterdead.'

God flipped his phone over to film himself. 'Suck my balls, trollrs,' he said, 'I am the Lord your God.' And then, he turned off the camera. 'See?' he said, ruffling Craig's hair, right on the bump. 'Told you I'd make you famous.' And with that, he and El Jaw went off down the corridor to Interfaith Studies, leaving Craig propped up against the doorframe, swallowing in dry, empty mouthfuls.

Craig looked up. There was a Sex And Relationships poster mounted on the wall, rounded pink text on yellow.

> Sex is about RELATIONSHIPS
> Sex is about COMMUNITY
> Sex is about SELF-IMAGE
> Sex is about WELLBEING
> Sex is about EMOTIONS
> Sex is about CONSENT
> Sex is about RESPECT
> Sex is about LOVE

He looked from the poster to the Qur'an, and back again. He'd have to get rid of it; he couldn't just leave it there, where anyone could find it, and he could hardly throw it in a classroom bin. He thought about flushing it down a toilet in the changing rooms, but then he'd have to rip out all the pages, as though one page wasn't enough, and the covers looked unflushably thick. So he pulled his lab coat out of his bag, and wrapped it around the cover, knotting the sleeves together to hold it in. Maybe I can lob it into the canal on the way home, he thought.

Craig gave himself a minute to calm down, and then walked slowly out into the playground, where the after-school drama nerds were standing in silent circles. No one was staring at him; the sky wasn't darkening, the birds weren't ominously roosting. He wasn't quite sure any of it had really happened.

•

After a phoneless forty-five minutes of dinner and dishwasher-loading, Craig went up to his room, to reload Trollr's search page every twenty seconds, and to panic, and to tell himself things that he didn't really believe.

Maybe God would have a change of heart, and not upload it. That was the least likely scenario, but it was still possible, Craig reminded himself. More likely was an unexpected file corruption, or a freak battery failure, or a phone dropped in liquid, all hopes which Craig recycled in his mind as he hit *refresh*, over and over. No new results for 'Quran'. No new results for 'Koran'. He was desperately trying not to look at the pictures cascading down the sidebars, one of which had a naked girl on all fours next to what he hoped wasn't a urinal. You won't BELIEVE what these Polish girls will do. Or maybe God would upload it, but Craig could talk him into taking it down, in some way he hadn't figured out yet. Or maybe a minor traffic collision. Was that so much to ask?

The only thing that mattered, Craig told himself, was that it didn't happen twice. He could deal with a single Trollr vid, but not with God and El Jaw coming back day after day for more footage, more sacrilege. He hated the idea of so many invisible eyes on him; under normal circumstances, he was barely the centre of his own attention, let alone anyone else's. He languished among the Pill Heads and the Porn Stars, down, down in the school's social butt crack, with the coders and the kids with inhalers, the boys and girls he could never quite bring himself to talk to, as it might confirm some greater truth about himself that he wasn't ready to admit. Even the Pill Heads had no interest in him, except as furniture during an afternoon comedown. He'd developed a grey mode, eyes front, shoulders hunched; all he had to do was make it to eighteen, and making it to eighteen wasn't actually that daunting, if he broke it up into manageable goals. Make it to Friday. Make it to four o'clock. Make it home. Now, there was nothing to make it to, and he had nothing to do but wait.

And at a quarter to midnight, just when he was about to distract himself with Jerkshuffle, there was one new result for 'Koran'. Sure enough, there he was, with his chin looking weirdly fat on camera, as it always did. But he didn't look sweaty and flushed, at least not in the thumbnail, and the smile was pretty convincing. As the Trollr logo faded to a watermark, Craig heard himself say 'Me hungry'; his voice was surprisingly deep, and he almost sounded relaxed. He studied himself carefully, letting the video play all the way through so he could spot any signs of weakness, but there were none. He tapped *replay* and watched again, this time pausing every few seconds to scrutinize his face. He'd pulled it off. And it was only fifty-seven seconds, he told himself. It was basically nothing.

He was about to close the tab when he saw the thumbnail of Noodle, the short Pakistani kid with the guilty look.

muslim eating bible #holycow #godsquad

So Craig wasn't alone. It looked like Noodle had been cornered in Global Englishes; Craig could just about make out the poster of correctly used, smiling punctuation marks on the classroom wall. He tapped *play*.

'Prove it,' God's disembodied voice said. 'Rip out a page, and eat it.'

Noodle snorted. 'Fine. It's only a fucking *Bible*.' And then, the camera jerked downwards, to show Noodle's fat little fingers tearing a page from the middle of a Bible, and then back up, as he pushed it into his mouth, chewed it, and swallowed it whole. 'See?' he said. 'No one gives a shit.'

'You're a brave little camel fucker, huh?' said God.

'Fuck off, Anglo,' Noodle said.

It was a contest, then: may the best hate-criminal win. Immediately, Craig cared about who had the most upvotes, which pissed him off, because that was exactly what God wanted. So he decided not to check. But somehow, Noodle looked like he was brave and victimised all at the same time; Craig, on the other hand, looked like the whole thing had been his idea, and he was just a bit of a twat.

So curiosity got the better of him, and he checked the upvotes. Noodle had two; Craig already had five. He didn't know whether to be proud, or worried, or both. It was hard to work out.

•

Craig didn't sleep well. He had a nightmare about the Dalai Lama, who he had to show around the playing fields, and who seemed very angry, but wouldn't say why. When he woke up, the sheets were covered in sweat, a wet oval in the shape of the hollow of his back, and two wet circles, one underneath each arse cheek. He checked Trollr: twelve upvotes for Noodle, and thirty-one for him.

He went downstairs to the kitchen, to sit at the table and wait for school, a condemned man, staring into the black outside the window, running his fingers around the doorframe bump to see how much it had grown. By the time his mother came down, a flat, dull fear was growing in the pit of his belly.

'How long have you been up?' she said.

Craig said nothing. It would take him an hour to explain what Trollr was — his parents wouldn't use Fabble until Fabble stopped hating the English, and there wasn't really a way to look stuff up online without Fabble — and another hour to explain that neither he nor they could get Trollr to take anything down. Already, the video was meming away, spreading through the internet like fungus. He'd have to run away, or find a bridge high enough to jump off, and even then there was the danger that he'd mess it up, and end up in a wheelchair, peeing into a bag. He looked up at his mother, and thought: bollocks. She'd worked out that something was wrong, and her help was therefore imminent. Bollocks, bollocks, bollocks.

His mother and father, under the guidance of the local Evanglicans, the Brothers and Sisters of God in Harmony, were following a parenting programme called Straight And Narrow, whose apocalypse-defying tagline was 'Raising a Family in an Age of Darkness'. He'd already decided, with the help of a Fabble search, that this was psychological projection on their part. Usually, Straight And Narrow didn't bother him at all, apart from the sense of disappointment that his parents were trying to get him back onto the rails he hadn't come off in the first place. No drugs: he didn't have enough money for drugs, nor was he at the right social level to have friends who could sell him any. No fraternising with homosexuals: he didn't know any. No use of pornography: well, his parents still thought that was something that had to be paid for. Most of the time, he could ignore Straight And Narrow; he was happy to let his mum and dad scour their credit card bills for signs of porn and narcotics, satisfying themselves that they were radically adjusting the course of his life, and that he suffered for it daily. But staring emptily out of kitchen windows was a sign of deviance of some kind: attention deficit disorder, or acute gaming addiction syndrome, or jihadism, or Marxism, or gender fluidity, or some other monster lurking at the edge of his parents' knowledge.

According to her instructions, his mother adopted the 'Three Cs' approach: confront, challenge, correct. 'Have you taken something?' she asked, confrontationally.

He looked up at her. 'No,' he said. 'I'm not on drugs.'

'Then why do you look so tired?' she challenged. 'Have you been using the internet all night?'

'Seriously. I don't look at porn,' Craig lied.

'Then what is it? What's wrong?'

She looked slightly manic, her hair standing up at the crown, her dressing gown on at an angle. Finally, the devil had come to claim her son. She'd been wondering when that was going to happen. It must be a relief, in a way, Craig thought.

'It's nothing,' he said. 'I just didn't sleep well.' There was no point telling the truth; that would just replace a short term problem with a long term one.

'Please don't snap at me, Craig,' she said. 'You know how I feel about that. Why are you sat down here without the lights on? It's that school,' she muttered, shaking her head. 'It's just not the right environment for you. I really —'

And then, she stopped herself. Right environment or not, exams were looming, and she was stuck with it just as much as he was.

It was decided, after a half-whispered conversation held behind a closed door, that Craig's father would drive him to school, and pick him up at the end of the day. That was how they were going to keep him on the Straight And Narrow. Craig was relieved, because he hadn't been looking forward to walking down the canal towpath. He had visions of Islamic scripture floating on algae. His father seemed less taken with Straight And Narrow than his mother did, as though his heart wasn't quite in it; but he still drove Craig through the suburbs, back seat, passenger side, child locks on, as commanded by the Almighty.

'God bless,' said his dad, as he opened the car door from the outside. Craig had had enough of gods for a while, either heavenly or terrestrial.

How soon would it happen? Would the police come to the school? Maybe he should just hand himself in, and save himself the humiliation; at least then God would be in the shit as well, although God obviously had a way of surviving these things. But nothing happened. The morning classes came and went, information slipping in and out of his brain as normal; by History And Reunderstanding, he was starting to wonder whether any of his upvotes were real people, and not just bots. Or maybe the Rupple clan was so boring that its only son rendered even sacrilegious acts unremarkable. Just get through today, he told himself. If I'm not arrested today, I probably won't be tomorrow. The thought gave him a small burst of relief: normality was in sight. At break time, he sat by himself on the bench by Performing Arts And Self-Expression, and ate his crisps. Teachers walked past, saying nothing; he was his usual, invisible self, and all he had to do to keep it like that was stay out of God's way. He tried to dredge up helpful information from the bottom of his mind. Which bits of the playground were God's territory? Where in the school's corridors and corners could he hide?

And then came a voice, from behind him: 'Ay! Greeengo! Why you hiding out by Perfaggot Arts? I have something to show you, señorita!'

Craig turned. Here it was, then: El Jaw, with Capitán and Tank, two of the other Straight Pride Latinitos, and El Jaw was brandishing his phone, grinning. 'So you wanna see your Trollr comments?' he said, handing Craig the phone. 'Not bad, for a maricón.'

And as Craig watched, the comments began to populate, pinging onto the black space, bubbling with upvotes.

marcus_oralius
wow this dude has nuts

procrasturbator
hehehe yeah do it >:D

cUcUrAcHa
~soo cute~ whr cn i meet this hottie

McFuck
^^^ THIS BOY IS KILLER ^^^

Who were all these people, who thought Craig had nuts, and was killer, and was a hottie? Where had they all been hiding? He'd been imagining something else, something far, far worse. Had he really thought that the head teacher checked the internet every day, sifting through video after video of kids pranking one another? He'd spent the morning working out which flyover to throw himself from. The whole thing felt so ridiculous, now, so dramatic. It was a trolling vid, a joke. And he was a hottie. He was killer. He had nuts.

He looked up at the Straight Pride Latinitos. Suddenly, they didn't seem so unfriendly.

•

Craig had been summoned to see God. How quickly things changed: God knew who he was, and, even more improbably, wanted to speak to him, Craig, and not someone else. The Straight Pride Latinitos were talking to him as though he mattered. People were looking at him, on purpose. He still found it hard to believe.

El Jaw was going to text him by the end of the day. It was

bound to be another prank, which would end up with Craig getting Trollr'd again, or hospitalised, or otherwise screwed over. But there was no question of turning God down. He was important enough to have his own intermediaries, like a prime minister or a prostitute, or Banksy, who they'd learnt about in Visual Art And Cultural Interpretation. It would have been like turning down a speaking part in a movie. And, halfway through Global Englishes, the last lesson of the day, Craig got a text.

unknown number › me
meet ur maker @ g8 by faggot bilding @ 4

It took him a minute to work out that 'g8 by faggot bilding' meant the gate beside the Performing Arts And Self-Expression block. It was brilliant: the use of the word 'faggot' without it referring to Craig. Someone else was a faggot. It was also frightening, but the parts of him which were wary of God's brutality were losing the battle to the parts of him which were curious. He hadn't ever considered kids like God and El Jaw and the other Straight Pride Latinitos as people — more as natural hazards, to be avoided rather than placated. Could he become their friend? Of course, that would come at a heavy price. He didn't want to think about how many holy texts he'd have to defile for that.

So, at the end of the school day, he went to the gate by Performing Arts And Self-Expression, and waited. After two days of chauffeuring, his parents relented, and Craig went back to making his own way home; so he'd be all right, as long as he could think of a Christian, heterosexual, drug- and alcohol-free reason for being late. It was raining, the rain drifting down in a sluggish cloud, the city's lights orange-grey against the sky. All week, he'd been wondering what God would do next; but he tried not to think too hard about it, in case deeper thought revealed that he was about to do something incredibly stupid.

'Hey, pussy,' said God, from above. 'Step into my motherfucking office.'

Craig looked up, to see God sat on the flat roof of the entryway to Performing Arts And Self-Expression, his legs dangling over the side wall. He must've been there before Craig arrived, watching and waiting on high, in silent, divine observation.

'You deaf, princess?' said God. 'Get up here.'

The wall was more than two metres high, with no footholds, and Craig had never climbed anything more challenging than a staircase. He wanted to ask how, but he couldn't think *how* to ask how without sounding like a tit. So he stared up, like a damp dog waiting to be let back into a house.

'For fuck's sake,' God said. 'Stand on the dumpster. Fucking Jew.'

Craig wasn't a Jew, but it didn't seem like the moment to nitpick, particularly as he hadn't noticed the large black dumpster right beside him. He scrambled onto the slippery plastic lid, and tried to haul himself up onto the roof without snapping the flimsy guttering. After a second try, he managed to do it, rolling awkwardly onto his arse.

'Smooth,' said God. Then, to Craig's horror, he hopped up onto the tiles and began to scale the roof. Craig, still out of breath, was going to have to follow; and God was already halfway up, yelling, 'come the fuck on, then, cockwipe!'

On his hands and feet, and then, after a wobble, his hands and knees, Craig climbed the roof of Performing Arts And Self-Expression. What looked from the ground like a normal roof was a perilous precipice, with a drop that could paralyse. He didn't dare to look down, or up; the tiles were cold and slimy, with clumps of moss nestled in between them, and his fingernails couldn't grip them in the drizzle. God made it look so simple, bouncing up like a well-rested cat. By the time Craig got to the top, God had disappeared. He took a second to catch his breath, his legs either side of the roof's apex, trying to find something at eye level to focus on. He'd never been high enough off the ground before to realise how scared of heights he was.

'In here, pussy!'

Craig was quickly getting used to God's voice being disembodied; it was coming from below, this time, and nearby. He looked around. There was an open skylight about a metre from him, on the side of the roof facing away from the rest of the school, even more sharply pitched. I'm going to have to do this all in reverse to get back down, he thought, looking at the expanse of tiles below, trickling with rain. He scuttled down towards the window, arse first, and dropped himself through it, his legs flailing below him.

God was sat in a cushioned swivel chair. Behind him were ranks of black buttons and sliders, dozens of them, and a large piece of glass which had been frosted over. The sloped walls were lined with black shelves, covered in wigs and Stetsons and high-heeled shoes, giant peacock feathers, folded up bits of sequin fabric, old cardboard box files, a fake violin. On the floor was something he felt sure was a bong, if he remembered correctly from Self-Respecting Your Body.

'You like my man booth?' asked God.

Craig realised he was staring. Even though it was school property, it felt rude. 'Sorry,' he said, automatically.

'Perfaggot Arts used to have lighting and shit, before they got all budgetty. This is where they did it from. Look.' He spun around in the chair, and slid some of the controls up and down, to no effect. 'No fucker knows it's here, so I made it my bachelor pad. You like?'

Craig started to think up an answer, but God got bored of waiting. 'What's your name, bitch?' he asked.

'Craig.'

'I know that, prick. Craig what?'

'Rupple. I usually sit on the other side of the room from you,' he added, as though God would've known his surname if only they'd sat a little closer together.

'Fuck me, that's a gay fucking name. What was it again? It's so gay that I forgot already. I have a homophobic brain,' he added proudly, tapping his temple with his index finger.

'Craig R—'

'Yeah, yeah, Clarence Rufflebottom, I got it. Your mummy and daddy must've loved you very much. You seen the killer comments on Trollr? You're still fucking trending, man.'

Craig's heart was thumping. God was smiling at him. God! 'Yeah,' he said, sounding sheepish, 'I did.'

'You got me some good fucking Trollr karma, boy. I'm serious, I'm *this* close to being a maestro.' On 'this', God grabbed his balls in his fist and gave them a squeeze, thrusting his pelvis upwards.

'You're welcome,' said Craig. He closed his eyes, in shame. Everything he said in front of God was bullshit.

But God laughed. 'Thanks, dicksplash,' he said. 'Are you up for another one?'

And here it was already, so quickly. Surely he wouldn't allow himself; if the Qur'an was entry level, God's next idea would be a declaration of war. Maybe he'd have to burn a teacher at the stake, or seduce an ageing bishop. No, he said to himself, I'm not up for another one. And that's exactly what he was going to say.

'Like what?' he said.

He didn't know why, but his thoughts and words had become divorced. It was God's confidence, which didn't come from being accepted, as Craig had learnt that it should, but from the exact opposite. He felt like he was trapped behind his own mouth, his better self screaming silently inside his skull.

'You know that bitch Masood?' God asked.

Craig knew exactly who he meant. Ms. Masood, who taught

him Geography And Spatial Belonging. Kind, funny, young Ms. Masood, who had big almond-shaped eyes and long black hair, and who ended each lesson with a three-minute Why You Can't Laugh Without Geography, and who'd done nothing to deserve whatever vengeance God was scheming up. He couldn't.

'Ms. Masood?' he said, as though he might not know quite who God meant.

'That's the bitch.'

'But she's my teacher,' said Craig, quietly.

'Fuck off, homo,' said God, 'she's one of them. A fucking gimmigrant. I knew you were a twat, but I didn't think you were a fucking traitor.'

'Gimmigrant' was the kind of word Craig's father liked to use when he got back from the pub on Sunday afternoons, one of the words which made his mother raise her eyebrows and purse her lips. What if Craig said no? There would be consequences. Maybe God would wallop him. Or maybe he'd send the Trollr video to a teacher, or to the police. 'What do you want me to do to her?' he asked.

God sprang up out of the chair, re-energised. 'I've got it all planned out for you, motherfucker,' he said. 'It's gonna be mono-fucking-lithic. You're gonna prank that bitch *good*.' He ducked under the slanted ceiling and yanked aside an ancient overhead projector unit which was shoved against the wall, walking it out on its rusted wheels. Then he pulled out a small white cylinder, and tossed it to Craig.

NuHome Scents
Crackling Bacon Aroma

'Stole it off of my mum,' God said. 'She's an estate agent.'

Craig's mum was not an estate agent, but was no stranger to NuHome Scents. She'd line them up next to the cacti on the kitchen windowsill, tiny canisters whose charges of gas were only a finger-twist away in case of company, ready to bomb the air with Norwegian Pine or Cinnablueberry or Cotton Breeze, according to the guest and the time of year.

'You, pretty lady,' said God, 'are going to put this bad boy in bitch Masood's desk, and watch her mental out. And you're gonna film the whole thing.'

Craig knew from the canteen rules exactly why he shouldn't. Was that religiously motivated assault? It had to be religiously motivated *something*. 'Why don't you do it?' he said, without thinking.

'Cos you've got balls, boy,' God said. 'I thought you'd go sick after I Trollr'd you. You've got serious balls, Clarence.'

No one at school had ever told Craig he had serious balls before. Perhaps he did have serious balls, and just hadn't had the opportunity to find them.

'C'mon, you chicken rapist,' God said. 'Be a man.'

And Craig took the Crackling Bacon NuHome Scent, and put it in his schoolbag, because he quite liked the idea of being a man, and having serious balls, and it was better than being a chicken rapist or a ladyboy. It was a simple choice.

The door to the rest of Performing Arts And Self-Expression was sealed shut, so Craig had to clamber back up onto the roof, and scuttle back down the tiles to the dumpster, gathering moss on his trousers as he went. It was almost half past four by the time he left school. He walked home, trying to make up his mind about the Crackling Bacon NuHome Scent, and whether to dump the canister in a litter bin. There were so many reasons not to do what God wanted, and they were so obvious. Detention. Suspension. Permanent exclusion. But every time he tried to focus on Ms. Masood's gentle eyes, his brain shoved her to one side, replacing her image with that of Craig as a Straight Pride Latinito, complete with wonky tie and evil grin. Maybe he could even have a nickname. The Bacon Boy. No, that was shit. But God would come up with something.

•

So he decided to do it. Not right away, but the next Wednesday, when Geography And Spatial Belonging was the first lesson of the day. If he left the house a couple of minutes early, and jogged instead of walking, he could sneak into the classroom before Ms. Masood got there. And he could film it on his tablet, rather than using his phone; Ms. Masood wouldn't accuse one of her least disruptive students of Improper Or Unauthorised Use Of Technology In Class, because she was far too nice for that. With every passing hour, the whole thing seemed easier and easier to get away with; by the time he woke up on the Wednesday morning, he hardly felt nervous at all. A couple of minutes into the lesson, he set his tablet to record, propping it up on the desk, and loaded a Fabble search about coastal erosion in the foreground, as a decoy. And then he sat, watching Ms. Masood draw a cross-section of a coastline on the interactive whiteboard, waiting for the smell to deploy. It didn't take long.

Ms. Masood looked up. 'Can anyone smell that?' she asked. She rolled the chair back from her desk and squatted down onto her knees, checking to see if the smell was coming from the floor. It was exactly like bacon, fatty and appetising, real as breakfast.

Ms. Masood sniffed the air, carefully. 'Can no one else smell that?' she asked. 'It smells like — what is that? Really, can none of you smell that?'

No miss, Craig thought, not me. A current running deep down in his belly had changed direction; he was having far too much fun to feel guilty. He leant back in his chair and put his arms behind his head, like wings.

I CARE BECAUSE YOU DO

When he was little, Rahman starred on a local election poster. It was the spring before he started at Lady Patience, his new school; his neighbour, Mr. Naseem, was running for the unitary authority council, and Rahman was volunteered by his dad to be the face of the campaign. Somehow, his brother Tarek dodged the bullet. When the posters arrived, it looked as though it was Rahman who was standing for election. The top quarter of the poster was taken up by the word 'Naseem', with every possible font effect applied to the text; the bottom quarter said 'I care because you do,' just as bedazzled; and the middle half was Rahman's face, his sticky-out ears pushed right up to the edges of the paper. It was shit enough to be a meme, and it was going to be everywhere, from the lamppost right outside Rahman's house to the windows of the butcher on the main road. He hated it.

Rahman's father was confused, and then became angry, in a way which efficiently replaced the confusion. 'Look at the effort he's put into this poster,' he said. 'Look at how he has put your face right in the middle here, how handsome you look. Lots of boys would love to be on this poster, I'm telling you.'

Rahman knew that wasn't true. But he had cried in front of Mr. Naseem — not just tears, but public tears, tears in front of neighbours. He'd have to apologise, which, in the language of Rahman's dad and Mr. Naseem, meant a Saturday showing Mr. Naseem how to toggle his Fabble settings, or washing his car. And Mr. Naseem had been so pleased with the poster, too, corralling Rahman into the front room and unfurling it theatrically.

Mr. Naseem couldn't see that it was shit, and Rahman was the bearer of shit tidings. He was going to have to do something to make up for it.

The next day, the poster quietly disappeared from Mr. Naseem's front window. His agent-cum-brother-in-law had a rethink, and printed a new one: a portrait of Mr. Naseem, taken by a professional photographer from a forgiving angle, and white teeth edited in. And Rahman was going to lose his Saturday afternoon. He could see it in the grin on Mr. Naseem's face as he opened his front door.

Rahman got his apology in early, and on the doorstep, so his dad was a witness. 'I'm sorry about the poster,' he said. 'I didn't mean to hurt your feelings.'

'It's all forgotten,' said Mr. Naseem, in his perfect Home Counties accent. 'Water under the bridge.' And Rahman felt his dad's grip on his collar loosen. 'So, I hear you're going to be my assistant campaign director today, are you?'

Something about Mr. Naseem — shirt pressed, beard trimmed, trousers ironed into a crease — made him feel like he should say 'yes, Sir,' but he couldn't. Instead, he said 'yes, mister.' It sounded silly, and he looked at the doormat.

'Excellent,' said Mr. Naseem. 'That's the spirit. All hands to the pump!'

Then, Mr. Naseem showed Rahman into his half-empty, freezing house; and Rahman's dad said 'thank you,' carefully and correctly, with a proper 'th' sound, and went home. Mr. Naseem's accent seemed to cast a spell over Rahman's dad, who treated him like a minor aristocrat. He'd have given anything to be the kind of person who came out with things like 'that's the spirit' and 'all hands to the pump' without having to rehearse them first.

Mr. Naseem made Rahman fold one hundred and twenty of the new posters, and put them in little white envelopes, even though half the houses in the neighbourhood had no letterboxes, because who got post when you could just Fabble? So Rahman had to look at the new, Rahman-free poster one hundred and twenty times, being sure not to fold Mr. Naseem's eyes, as he'd been shown. Rahman's father had provided his version of a packed lunch, which was a packet of Monster Munch, eight cherry tomatoes and a can of diet lemonade; and Rahman sat folding the posters, careful to avoid smearing them with grease or spattering them with tomato seeds, and listened to the ambient sound effects made by the waterfall picture above the television, thinking how sad it would be to live like Mr. Naseem.

But once he'd folded all one hundred and twenty, he still didn't get to go home. Mr. Naseem said that he had something that Rahman should see.

'Come and look at this,' he said, and led Rahman upstairs.

On the landing was a big cardboard box, filled with stacks of the Rahman poster, some of them lying flat, some of them rolled up with elastic bands around them. Rahman looked at them, feeling guilty and relieved all at once. He wasn't sure what to say; but he'd have to say something, because Mr. Naseem wasn't going to.

'I'm sorry,' he said. Then, 'they must've been very expensive.'

'That isn't the point, young man,' said Mr. Naseem. And then he did something which Rahman didn't expect. He knelt down by the banister, so his face was lower down than Rahman's, the way adults only do to kids when they're crying, or about to cry. He didn't say anything, but smiled a big, gentle smile.

'Okay,' said Rahman. So what, then? he thought.

Mr. Naseem paused, and then sighed, shaking his head. 'You don't understand,' he said. 'You've humiliated me.'

He didn't sound humiliated. 'Sorry,' said Rahman, again. How else could he say it?

'No,' said Mr. Naseem. 'I'm older than you are. I can see it in your eyes. You're not sorry.'

'I really am,' Rahman said. And he was: the last thing he wanted to do was spend a Saturday folding pictures of Mr. Naseem's faked white teeth.

'No,' said Mr. Naseem again, still looking up at him. 'You don't understand what I mean by humiliation. You think you do, but you don't. I'm going to have to find another way to explain it to you.' And then, he punched Rahman, hard, between the legs.

Rahman fell back. As he did, he knocked the box over, throwing a stack of posters up into the air so the flat ones snowed back down over the landing and the rolled-up ones bounced down the stairs. It was a different kind of pain, not just because of how sore it was, but because he couldn't move his legs properly. His mind went blank.

Mr. Naseem stood up. 'It's not nice, is it, being humiliated?' he asked.

Rahman tried to roll onto his side, but all he could do was crumple his legs up and down. Then Mr. Naseem kicked him, harder, in the same place, and Rahman screamed, his legs jerking upwards all by themselves. The last pile of Rahmans flapped across the carpet, leaving the empty box on its side.

'Do you think you understand, now?' asked Mr. Naseem. He sounded so calm, so friendly. He put his foot on Rahman's ankle, pressing down, the sole of his shoe pinching the skin. Rahman couldn't feel his balls. He put his hand on the front of his trousers; they were warm, and wet.

'Oh, look. You've made a right mess now, haven't you, young man?' said Mr. Naseem, cheerfully. He knelt back down, his face dangling over Rahman. His hair, usually combed so neatly, was flopping down, and his eyes were twinkling. 'Look at the mess you've made of yourself.'

'I'm sorry,' said Rahman. He was trying not to cry.

'And look at what you've done to my landing,' said Mr. Naseem. 'Are you sorry for that, too?'

'Yes.'

'And about the other day?'

'Yes,' Rahman said.

'All right,' said Mr. Naseem, after a pause. 'I think you are sorry, now.' He ran a hand through his hair, pushing the loose strands back into place. 'Let's get you into the bathroom so you can sort yourself out,' he said. 'You can't go home looking like that. Your father will think you've forgotten how to use the lavatory.'

Rahman didn't get it. It was only a poster, and it wasn't even his idea to be on it in the first place. And how could someone look and sound so happy when he was so angry? He let Mr. Naseem help him up by the elbow, and went into the bathroom. 'One moment,' said Mr. Naseem, and disappeared around the corner.

Rahman stood in the middle of the bathroom. He was worried about his trousers — about the smell of them, and that he'd have to take them off. And he was worried how much it hurt when he walked. He'd seen a boy get kicked in the balls before, but that was only online, so it was impossible to know how real it was. What would happen if the pain didn't go away? How could he explain it to the doctor? His dad hadn't ever let him go to the doctor on his own, because his dad had to explain what he thought was wrong with Rahman, to see if the doctor agreed, so they'd know whether or not the doctor was any good.

Mr. Naseem reappeared in the doorway, and handed Rahman a cordless hairdryer. 'Here you are,' he said. 'To dry your trousers. I'll give you some privacy, then,' he added, and closed the door.

Rahman took his trousers off, then his pants, and laid them

out on the side of the bath to dry them. The dark patch of piss stank, but it wasn't that big, and dried up much faster than he'd thought it would. With his other hand, he checked his balls; the pain was more like a normal pain, now, a bumped elbow. He put his pants and trousers back on. They were hot from the hairdryer, and crinkly.

Mr. Naseem was waiting on the landing; he took the dryer and put it on the windowsill. 'All done?'

'Can I go home now, please?' Rahman asked.

Mr. Naseem laughed. 'Of course you can, young man,' he said, and moved to one side so Rahman could get past, spreading his arm and bowing his head. It was like something funny had happened and Rahman had missed it, and it was too late to ask Mr. Naseem what it was. He started to move towards the stairs, big-eared Rahmans scrunching underfoot.

'Ah-ah-ah,' said Mr. Naseem, 'not so fast. You don't expect me to clean all this up, do you?' He gestured to the box and its spilled contents, piece after piece of glossy paper sprinkled across the carpet. So Rahman put them all back. He was under instructions that they should all be facing upwards and neatly piled so the sizes matched, even though it didn't matter because no one was going to see them. Mr. Naseem had gone downstairs and closed the living room door behind him, and was making a weird snuffling noise, so at least Rahman got to do it alone.

They went back to Rahman's house together. Rahman was having trouble walking. It wasn't pain anymore; it was a feeling he'd never had before, like a part of him might fall off. His dad came to the door. Rahman was standing back; he was nervous about his dad seeing the patch on his trousers, still a little darker than the material around it, and about navigating the step up to the house.

'Delivery of one whippersnapper, as promised,' said Mr. Naseem.

Rahman's dad stared at his son, suspiciously. 'Did he behave himself?' he barked, meaning: has he done anything else I'm going to have to apologise for?

'He was a model gentleman,' said Mr. Naseem, and gave Rahman a sideways smile. 'Oh! — I forgot,' he added, holding his index finger up, an idea-lightbulb. He fished around in his back pocket and pulled out a folded up square, giving it to Rahman. Rahman could see what it was straight away, the words 'I care because you do' visible through the thin paper. 'I thought I'd give you a copy,' Mr. Naseem said. 'It might make you chuckle, some day.' And then, he winked, and Rahman's belly floated up towards the sky, like it did just after take-off on a plane.

'Say thank you,' his dad said.

'Thank you,' said Rahman.

'You're very welcome, Rahman,' Mr. Naseem said. 'Well, now, don't keep your father waiting! We can't have you standing out here all day.' And then, he pulled Rahman, hard, by one of the belt loops on the front of his warm, crunchy trousers, jerking him forward. Rahman had never seen anyone do that before. It tugged on his balls, and all the soreness came back at once.

His dad looked funny, as though he was going to burp and was trying to contain it. For a second, he was about to say something to Mr. Naseem; but he must've thought the better of it, because he didn't.

Rahman and Tarek and their dad sat down to eat tea: a microwaved curry that their dad bought at the petrol station, and Monster Munch, again, this time served in cereal bowls. For dessert they had mini meringue nests, also from the petrol station, which had no filling, and stuck to the roof of Rahman's mouth. Food was one of the areas where his dad's efforts to assimilate into English society hadn't worked out very well. His dad was assimilating to a country which only existed in his mind: where it wasn't polite to start fights with the neighbours, and where you should serve snacks in bowls.

•

That was before Rahman became Noodle, as in ramen noodles, which no one at school ate. Rahman had seen Blue Dragon noodles and Pot Noodles, but not ramen noodles. He suspected that Thud — who, in one unthinking second, renamed Rahman for years — hadn't ever eaten them, either; he looked like he lived on energy drinks and battered sausages. Noodle was a pale and flabby name, which was unfair for someone with such handsome, dark eyes as Rahman's. It was the kind of name that would be given to the fat kid who ended up trading his way through the week, taking the blame for everyone else's crimes so he didn't have his SIM card cloned. But the name stuck, as he was stupid enough to protest at the critical moment. He pretended to find it funny the next day, but it was already too late.

Noodle was a pupil at the Lady Patience Okadigbo Inclusive Partnership Academy, wedged between two of the main roads leaving the city, which prided itself on something or other. Lady Patience Okadigbo was keen that children should be educated in a context of blah blah blah, and that a good school should not just inspire the child, but blah the blah — he never really listened. On his first day, he was told that Lady Patience Okadigbo was important to the community, and then died, which made her even more important to the community, and then they put a plaque on the house where she was born, and named a street after her, and she got so important to the community that she became a school.

Lady Patience soaked up the kids whose parents hadn't managed to organise something better, as Noodle's father hadn't: the parents who forgot to declare their religious background on the census; those who'd been caught out pretending to be Catholic to get into Blessed Saint Theodore's — in one case, a father who'd signed an ePetition to ban the Pope from entering the country — and wound up on a council blacklist; those living in unheated, windowless garages, or in Portakabins by the sides of carwashes; the families who hopped from one bed and breakfast to another, or who lived in drained Victorian swimming pools converted into microhomes, with one cubby hole per kid, and communal kitchens in the old changing rooms; the zero hourers whose children never had a hope; the parents who were part of the eMancipated movement, and made their kids bring in tubs of seeds and turnip for lunch, and lived in earnest, wind-wrecked, internet-free communes where the school application forms arrived a week too late; parents who had misunderstood the zoning system; parents who were on their third or fourth child, and were just happy to find somewhere with a high threshold for expulsion. In Noodle's case, the machine gun of his father's disgust took every other option out. When he missed the deadline for the Modern City Grammar where Noodle's brother Tarek went, his dad was left with no choice. The kids at Linda Spinks Secondary were probably all on drugs. And the only thing they taught at the Holmcroft Teaching And Learning Institute For Young People was how to solve richer people's tech problems, and Mr. Mateen's sons were born for greater things than that.

At Lady Patience, he was one of the few Muslim kids at one of the last inclusive partnership academies. Together, the two factors worked as a sort of inoculation; events swerved into other people, not Noodle. And Noodle did fine. He didn't start fights, but he gave as good as he got; the trick was to be neither too interesting nor too boring. And that was good enough for Noodle's dad, who could then ignore the conflicts of interest between the secular governors and the local Evanglican Church, and the stories of kids getting monstered online, and the parent-teacher de-escalation summits, and the toilet turf war between the Transgender Bludfaeries and the Straight Pride Latinitos, and the siphoning of funds to overseas accounts, and the banning of Bunsen burners after an epidemic of kids self-harming their classmates, and the cowboy builders who left the school without a staff room for two years, and the teacher who was given a fat lip by the deputy head and chose, quietly, to resign.

His religion was something that the teachers felt they had to mention, like a special need. It wasn't that it had to be announced; but the teachers were establishing that they knew, and that Noodle *knew* that they knew, and so that made everything okay, not that anything was wrong in the first place, and so on. When the culturally relevant feast days rolled around, his form tutor provided mint tea and dates and baklava for the kids to sample, all the time shooting tight smiles at Noodle, smiles which said 'you'd better be fucking appreciating this.' She'd recognised his faith in a positive setting, which was something that had to be done, like cycling proficiency or maths. It made him a blessing and a curse all at once. He was a tick in a box to keep His Majesty's Inspectorate of Educational Facilities happy, but it was still a box that some poor bastard was going to have to tick. It never occurred to him that Lady Patience might not be normal — that in other schools, no one really cared about faith, especially not in the good ones. He had no idea that most schools had either all their meat Halal, or none of it, and didn't wind up with protests and counter-protests outside the school gates, and an anti-bullying task force sent in by the council to protect the canteen staff. He thought that every school had eight different uniform policies, rather than just one. He bumped along with the nervous eyes of teachers and welfare officers fixed on him, whether he was good, bad, or average. He assumed it was that way for every kid in the country.

'How was it?' his dad would ask, picking him up at the end of the day in their second hand smart car. His lumpy English stressed the word 'it', which made it sound like neither of them was prepared to admit what 'it' was.

'Okay', Noodle would say. And it was. Also, he had to say it was, because his dad wouldn't know what to do if it wasn't. And his dad would smile, then stop smiling, and off they would drive, with Tarek giving Noodle death stares in the rear view mirror, and the back windscreen of the smart car still showing where it used to read 'Madeleine's Hair and Beauty,' with Madeleine's mobile number and followme@ decals still on the bumper.

•

So when God made Noodle rip a page out of one of the school library's Bibles and eat it, it was the first time an event had swerved into Noodle, rather than someone else.

'Fucking hell,' said Tarek, letting himself into Noodle's room without asking. 'You trying to get yourself kicked out of school?'

'Can't you text first, like a normal person?' Noodle asked. 'Or knock? Fuck's sake, I could've been naked.' He didn't like the idea of having Tarek in his room, which hadn't happened for years, much less Tarek coming and going without permission.

Tarek sat on the bed. 'You know how many hits this is getting?'

Noodle didn't know, and didn't want to. 'Who cares,' he said.

'I dunno, man,' Tarek sang, grinning. 'Who'd have thought, my baby brother going viral.'

And then, Tarek's phone said, 'fine. It's only a fucking *Bible*.'

Noodle grabbed the phone. It was Trollr, the grimacing, green slime-blob logo sprawled across the top of the screen; and there, just underneath, God's shaky camerawork, and his own face, chewing defiantly. He dropped the phone down onto the covers, and said 'pff.'

'You reckon?' Tarek said. Then, he put on his finest uptight Anglo voice. 'We awll hev the right to hev ahr religious velues respected, dare boy.'

Don't tell Dad, Noodle thought. His father didn't know how the internet worked, and would assume overnight Islamism on Noodle's part, and then Noodle would have to sit through the lecture about Western values, and how far his grandfather had to walk to school every day, and how his grandmother might still be alive if she'd lived in a country with a National Health Service, and how Noodle and his brother could never understand life in Pakistan, and how easy they had it, and the list of sacrifices they'd never appreciate, et cetera. The thought must have shown on Noodle's face: Tarek's smile had turned to a smirk.

'Don't,' Noodle said.

'What's it worth?'

'Fuck all. Just don't.'

'You know,' Tarek said, with a tilt of his head, 'I could make it go away. For a price.'

Noodle wasn't sure if that was true. His brother's fabled technological knowhow was an unknown quantity, possibly real, possibly a cut-out carrot which Noodle's father dangled in front of him to remind him of his own shortcomings. It seemed unlikely that Tarek really had that much power, and Noodle knew that the price would be anything but an unknown quantity. Pounds per viewer, or pounds per day; pounds per something.

'Listen,' he said. 'I don't give a fuck.'

Tarek picked up his phone, and stood up. 'Your loss,' he said. 'Good luck, though. Glad it ain't me.'

Noodle said nothing. There was no 'it' to be afraid of, he told himself; for all the talk, Tarek didn't want his father to go nuclear any more than Noodle did. Tarek was too close to the exit sign, to life outside of the gulag, and he wouldn't be telling anyone a thing. Noodle stood up to close the door his brother had thoughtfully left open, and then loaded Trollr on his phone. He didn't care about hits or shares or upvotes, or at least he didn't think he did; but he wanted to make sure no one had called him short in the comments, or pointed out his ears.

'No one gives a shit,' his voice said. It sounded like his nose was blocked. And then, 'you're a brave little camel fucker, huh?'

God's nose did not sound blocked. His voice boomed out from the speaker, calm and commanding, like a father to his son — a normal father, one of the fathers with proper cars and polo shirts. I don't care, Noodle thought, and because I don't care, nobody else will.

•

But people did care, although not in the way that Noodle had expected.

Noodle sat next to a girl called Grace Hill. The other Grace in the class, Grace Cliverton, was just Grace, so Grace Hill — shorter, quieter, less pretty, less liable to cry, almost definitely yet to orgasm — had to be surnamed, for clarity. Grace Hill and Noodle got along, mainly because they both understood the benefits of silence. Out of the corner of his eye, he'd watch her doodling out her sketches: bleak, tortured worlds, where neither good nor bad deeds went unpunished; vengeful and merciless villainesses and their ambivalent victims, all female, all with heavy black eyes and thick, straight lines for mouths which she drew with a point-to-point vector. Usually, the victims would perish, wearing large headphones and bored expressions as they were hanged, or drowned, or impaled, or electrocuted, or had their breasts cut off, or were subjected to hours of white noise before finally, still bored, bleeding out. The forces of evil in Grace Hill's world never seemed to enjoy these acts of violence; for her, tyranny was a mundane business. This gave him an insight: Grace Hill was not as bland as she seemed. She was probably more of a threat to the school's moral standing than the other Grace, actual Grace, Grace the genital-urinary time bomb. But Grace Hill's internal world wasn't something he could reveal to anyone else; no doubt she'd been watching him as much as he'd been watching her. Their unspoken rule of non-interference meant that she didn't usually interact with him, so he was surprised when she handed him a note.

> Dear Noodle
> I saw the video of u on trollr. I thought it ws amazing what you did. Most ppl just talk about how shit it is 2 live under the patriarchy but u actually did something about it + I respect u 4 that. I hope ull go on expressing ur identity wherever u r + wherever u go after the exams + never be scared 2 b the person u r.
> Ur friend,
> Grace (Hill)

Noodle looked up at her, but she was busy heating a paperclip under the desk with a lighter, which meant she was about to hold the metal in the palm of her hand until it scorched a small red line into her skin. He decided not to disturb her, and to write her a note instead, except that he never had any paper. So instead, he went to her Fabble profile and liked one of her designs: a row of headless girls, each with her arms folded and her weight resting on one leg, each looking as though her face would have had an eyebrow raised, if she'd had a face. It was as good a way as any to say thank you.

And then, at lunch, came another first.

'C'n I sit here?'

Noodle looked up. It was Ibrahim, from Global Englishes,

who had a fuzzy almost-beard and spoke at half the volume of everyone else.

'Okay,' Noodle said.

Ibrahim placed his tray on the table, and sat down opposite Noodle, looking across at him with his large, brown-black eyes. 'I saw your vid, man,' he said.

'Oh,' said Noodle. He looked down at the heap of chips on Ibrahim's plate, and at the last few chips at the edge of his own, and wasn't quite sure what to say. Then he saw the shadow of Ibrahim's fist, and looked up to see him smiling patiently, his knuckles awaiting a fistbump.

So Noodle bumped fists with Ibrahim, which was the first time he'd ever bumped fists with anyone. 'Didn't know you were a brother,' Ibrahim said.

It was a weird thing to say, Noodle thought. The colour of his skin was an ever-flying flag at Lady Patience; he hadn't realised there were other ways to be a brother, involving doing rather than being. 'What d'you mean?' he said.

'You know,' Ibrahim said, through chips. 'Thought you were a bit of a coconut. I never saw you pray.'

Noodle winced at the thought. He could hear his Dad's snort: *get up off your knees*. 'Yeah,' he said. 'I guess — not.'

'It's all good, man,' Ibrahim said. 'Just never guessed I'd see you on Blackfl.ag. Thought you were a bit too goodboy for that, you know?'

Not Trollr but Blackfl.ag: so Noodle's Bible-chewing was migrating across the internet of its own accord. He'd only been to Blackfl.ag once, and quickly closed the tab because he didn't want to end up being put on a watch list by one of the anti-extremism tsars who did assemblies at Lady Patience once a term. The thumbnails on Blackfl.ag were way too grisly for him, anyway: men being burned alive, or having their hands and feet lopped off with blunt axes, or dragged across the desert from the backs of jeeps. It was hard to picture his face in that list of thumbnails, big ears among the Kalashnikovs.

'D'you see the one from Canada?' Ibrahim asked.

'Which — what?' said Noodle.

'The vid of the brother in Canada, eating a Bible? You started off a whole *thing*, man.' And then, Ibrahim leant back, and pulled his phone out of his trouser pocket. 'Wait. Lemme find it.'

Noodle was about to yell 'don't!', and whack the phone out of Ibrahim's hands; how could he even think about it, in the Lady Patience canteen? He looked at his hand, which was hovering above his plate in pre-whack position, his fingers trembling.

'What?' said Ibrahim.

'Nothing,' Noodle said, and lowered his hand. 'Show me. Just — not too loud.'

Ibrahim grinned. 'Chill,' he said. 'I know. Mute.' And then, he flipped the phone around so Noodle could see.

It was nothing like what God and El Jaw were up to. The camera was fixed in place, and looked like it was way better quality; a guy in his twenties was sat at a desk, slowly perforating a page from a Bible as though he was tearing off the bottom of a form. He ripped the page into small rectangles, lining them up on the velvety black fabric draped over the desk, and then ate them, one by one, occasionally stopping to say something between mouthfuls. We awll hev the right to hev ahr religious velues respected, Noodle thought.

'Nice, right?' said Ibrahim.

'Yeah.'

'What's your ID on there?'

'I, uh — I'd have to check,' Noodle said.

'Add me,' Ibrahim said, glancing quickly over his shoulder before closing the browser. 'I'm fuckthewildwest.'

At exactly the same time, one part of Noodle's mind decided to add Ibrahim, and another part decided never to. He screwed up his eyes. 'Okay,' he said.

So, he wondered, shelving his tray in the stack-o-mat, does that make me an Islamist? 'We are the company we keep,' Miss Waterman-Patterson would have said: but Noodle suspected that she didn't keep much company at all. Maybe he could be somewhere on a spectrum of Islamism. Wasn't she always saying that everything was on a spectrum?

Before lunch was over, Noodle went to the toilet to re-watch himself performing a blasphemous act. Not on Blackfl.ag, which he couldn't join until he came up with some courage and a decent ID, but on Trollr, in the friendlier surroundings of pets spraypainted in rainbow colours and teachers whose dating profiles had been uploaded to interactive whiteboards. He had two hundred and thirteen upvotes in the space of a week, and no idea if that was a decent number or not. He sat on the toilet, and listened to God's voice telling him what to do.

He hated himself for getting hard over God's voice, and for imagining God smacking him between the legs, and for the fact he could never, ever tell a soul what he imagined the Straight Pride Latinitos doing to him, and the names he wanted them to call him. But that feeling wasn't new. So Noodle downloaded the video, and added it to his collection, with the white nationalist preacher from the Deep South with the visible six-pack, and the Martyr of Albion with the FUCK ISLAM tattoo, and the picture of the blonde Royal Marine who pissed on the Pakistani Royal Marine and got dishonourably discharged, and made sure to disguise the file name in case Tarek was actually the genius he said he was and could hack Noodle's phone.

He had twelve minutes before he had to go back to class. Doable, he thought, and unzipped his trousers.

THOR

It was March, the warmest March on record, killing off the daffodils, their trumpets bleached and fried, and Thor was sitting in his bedroom, thinking about how much better it was to be Thor than to be Craig. He hated the word 'Craig'. It was so uneventful, such a sad little noise. It sounded like a technical term in a geological process no one cared about. As a result of the erosion, craigs are formed, which eventually collapse, leaving gaps in the riverbank. Or a tool: pass me that craig over there, would you, I can't get at it from this angle. He particularly hated his mother saying it, squawking the syllable over and over — 'Craig! Craig! Will you answer me, please?' — or drawing out the vowel into a long, nagging whine.

It was annoying that his Qur'an video was technically God's and not his, especially with the number of hits it had. But Thor's own Trollr profile had a decent number of views, for a profile only four months old. He watched his uploads on autostream, one link jumping randomly to the next, which is what he did when he was bored, or when he wanted to cheer himself up. All morning, he'd been hitting *refresh* on his profile page, so he could check his follower count.

Thor has 995 followers
Thor has 995 followers
Thor has 996 followers
Thor has 997 followers
Thor has 997 followers

He was trying not to obsess over it, but the thought of God's face when Thor became a Trollr messiah was too delicious to dismiss from his mind. Soon, he thought, soon. God would be so pissed off, but he'd have to pretend to be impressed, of course. And Thor was impressed with himself. He was adding followers way faster than God was, even though God was uploading more than ever. And Thor's videos got more upvotes than God's, and better comments, which scrolled down the sidebar in smileys and capital letters, user after user. He'd overtake God by the end of the year, and God knew it. Messiah, he thought. Hell yeah.

One of his favourite videos was playing, one he'd stealth-filmed in Global Englishes. He and God had used Flakhak to rig one of the Transgender Bludfaeries' phones so it would play American adverts for conversion therapy at full volume, on Thor's command. FREEDOM FROM HOMOSEXUALITY, the phone blared, its tiny speaker barely coping with the volume, IS CLOSER THAN YOU THINK; and then, the Bludfaerie — Joe something? Joel something? — in full panic, desperately trying to mute his phone, his face going redder and redder, with the snorting sound of God's stifled laughter in the background. Two hundred and forty upvotes. Not bad.

The video disappeared, a quickload circle spinning itself away to reveal the next: another candid camera job, shot in class. At the front of the room was Arianna Clarke — 'just call me Arianna' — one of the external teachers Lady Patience hired for Sex And Relationships. She was pointing at a giant testicle on the interactive whiteboard, her arm looping round in a wide arc to demonstrate the mechanics of ejaculation, bangles clattering as they followed imaginary sperm out of the darkness and into the world of dating and mating. 'Now,' hissed God, out of shot: and then, the testicle disappeared, replaced by a video of two black guys spit-roasting a blonde teenager, the three of them butt naked and pink-eyed; and then, Arianna Clarke trying to see the funny side at the same time as she frantically clicked *Close Window*, over and over.

Thor took another bong hit as the next video loaded, the smoke billowing in his cheeks as he tried not to cough. It was one that never got many upvotes, but still made him smile. God had nicked one of his brother's LSD tabs, and painstakingly grafted it onto the side of a paracetamol, which Thor then sold to one of the Disciples of Hell as a herbal low to get him through Sports And Sporting Activities. God filmed the Disciple of Hell as he stared up at the basketball hoop, holding his hands out in front of him, turning them over and over, his eyes spinning with terror, his teeth chattering. God thought it should've been his upload: he got the LSD, he took the time to graft it to the paracetamol, and he filmed the whole thing, too. But it was Thor who'd risked getting caught in the changing rooms with Class A drugs in his hands. Eventually, they settled it with a game of paper-scissors-stone.

He didn't feel bad about any of it, not anymore. He sort of did, at first; it was one of those things that he knew was a bad idea, but still did anyway, either because all his other ideas were shit, or because he didn't have any other ideas. But right from the start, he knew that he couldn't let God see any sign of weakness. It was like jousting, with God: one blink, and you were fucked. He could never back down, not once he'd become Thor, which was like having his own private militia, or a moat. He couldn't go back to being shitty old Craig. In the space of a few months, he'd learnt a trick, the trick long known to kids like God and the other Straight Pride Latinitos; all he had to do was pretend to be in control, and he would be. It was so simple. He cringed to think of that old, quivering version of himself, sloping from home to school and back again. He had a new skin — not soft, but scaly — and a new wardrobe, too, clothing with an appropriately Germanic vibe, t-shirts with eagles and old Afrikaner

Resistance slogans, and one with a rebel flag on it, 'The South Shall Rise Again' printed underneath. Not this south, he thought: the south coast of England hadn't done much rising for a while, as far as he could see. He smuggled the clothes into the house, getting them delivered to the post office rather than drone-dropped to the door, so his parents didn't start interfering. When he put them on, they looked ridiculous; he bought them in optimistically small sizes, to motivate himself to lose weight, and they stretched over the folds of flab on his torso. But Thor was all about optimism. Thor could shed weight. Craig was a manatee; Thor was a shark.

Outside, he heard the rumble of his parents' car. They were back from the Brothers and Sisters of God in Harmony, their weekly Jesus fix provided. He pulled his metal washing bin out into the hall, hurriedly turning it upside down so he could stand on it to get to the loft hatch, shoving his weed and his bong behind the insulation foam. Running back into his room, he took the extractor fan which God thrinted for him off the windowsill, decoupling the old tumble dryer hose from its front end, and threw them both into the loft, before levering the hatch back into place. He was too stoned to be rushing around, but it still beat smoking down by the side of the kitchen, next to the water butt and the planters, where the neighbour would give him dodgy looks. He sniffed the air, carefully. Most of the smoke had been sucked out of the house by God's patented Weedstink Annihilation System; but he still sprayed his room with air freshener, aftershave and FabriFresh, layering the smells over one another, just in case. The process of covering his tracks always straightened him out, a little; by the time the front door slammed, he was sat at his desk, lightly stoned, watching the crows scuttling on the rooftop opposite, thinking about how hard it would be to be a crow, with the assembling of nests and the finding of worms.

'Craig?' his mother called up the stairs. 'We're back! Would you change your bed before lunch, please?' And then, there was the sound of feet on the stairs, soft and hesitant, as they always were when she'd just had her glass of Holy Spirit topped up. 'Are you in there?' she asked, from the other side of the door.

'Yup.'

She opened the door. 'Oh, your poor eyes,' she said. 'Hayfever again?'

'Yup.'

She tutted. 'It's all this foreign grass they're planting now, is what it is. It's absolutely dreadful, that people are already suffering with hayfever at this time of year. I mean, really.'

'Yup, I know.'

'Will you change your sheets before lunch?'

'Yup, later,' he said.

There was a pause. 'Church was good this morning,' she said, finally. 'Very uplifting. You ought to come, you know. Pastor Colin was asking after you.'

'Yup. Will do.'

'Are you coming down for lunch, in a bit?'

'Yup. In a bit.' He was focusing on his phone, which was lagging, and wouldn't reload his Trollr profile.

'Any plans for today?' she asked.

'Going out this afternoon. Won't be late.'

'Oh that's lovely,' she said, brightening up. 'It's nice not to be cooped up all day. Are you going anywhere special?'

'Nah.'

'Who are you going out with?'

'Just Andy.'

'Oh, fine,' she said, the relief escaping from her nostrils. 'I really do like Andy. He's such a nice boy. Say hello to him from me, will you?'

Such a nice boy, he thought, and so English. 'Yup.'

His mother went downstairs to slam the dishwasher door

shut, and drop other hints, each one louder the longer he procrastinated. He wondered what his parents would think if they really understood the warzone Lady Patience was becoming. One of the Transgender Bludfaeries — luckily, not the one Thor had Trollr'd — had been hospitalised after a suicide bid. All the students were shepherded into a special assembly led by the head teacher, who looked like she hadn't slept in days, her short hair frazzled, her trouser suit crumpled. She started off by imposing an unenforceable Fabble embargo on the students, because some members of the school community had not been taking the matter seriously, and were treating the individual concerned with a lack of basic respect. Q: When does a faerie lose its wings? A: When the doctors turn off the life support. Q: Is it true a faerie dies every time you complain? A: Dunno, but why's it so fucking cold today? Then, the deputy head said that school rankings weren't a substitute for diversity and shared community values, and that he hoped that his message would trickle up to the parents, and all the teachers on the stage nodded thoughtfully, bobbing their disappointed eyebrows up and down. Rumours were flying around about His Majesty's Inspectorate of Educational Facilities putting Lady Patience into special measures, which meant lights out.

And if it weren't for God, Thor might have ended up a gibbering wreck, slouched in a hospital bed like the Transgender Bludfaerie, with visiting teachers bringing coursework and sympathy. Or worse: put on the Straight And Narrow home-schooling pathway. As it was, he was on course to scrape a pass in most of his exams, which was enough to avoid an Academic Concern Summit. Plus, his mum and dad, along with a coalition of outraged parents from Lady Patience, were on the warpath: they were disgusted, *disgusted*, that the exams had been moved, yet again to accommodate the bloody Muslims, who quite frankly shouldn't be starving their children for Ramadan in the first place. So, if he failed, he could just blame it on that, and trust that he'd have his parents' full support. There was always a work-around at Lady Patience, a way to convert a failure into someone else's problem.

•

Andy was a decoy. Thor had stopped talking to Andy months before; he didn't need semi-friends like that anymore, sad little nerds whose voices had never quite broken, not now that he had God. But Andy was a good cover story when he wanted to go out with Buddleia.

He was saving Buddleia as a treat, something to reveal to his parents in a vengeful moment. Mum? Dad? I'm going out with a mixed race girl. Not just mixed race, but half Zulu. Even the word itself was satisfying, looming at the end of the alphabet of his parents' tolerance. Spanish or Greek, they could probably cope with; some type of European, at least. He'd love to see his dad's face, as though he'd said he was dating a dragon, or a chemical element.

He decided to meet her at the food court at Bowled Over, because it was cheap enough that he could offer to pay, and there were so few members of staff that they could smoke in the toilets, all of which fitted in better with his new, post-Craig image. He wasn't going to tell her about being a messiah straight away — it felt like something he should cash in later, when he needed to impress — but then he saw that his latest selfie was her new lock screen, and his eagerness got the better of him. As she exhaled, controlling the flow of smoke from her parted lips, the back of her head pressed against the cubicle wall, he leant into her ear.

'I'm a Trollr messiah,' he whispered.

'Hot,' she said, flashing him a shy smile.

Concentrate, he told himself: they'd banged noses the last time he tried to be manly. He tilted his head, and moved in.

'Yeah,' he said.

'I'm not going to kiss you.'

'We'll see.'

'Seriously,' she said. 'That's actually quite creepy. Anyway, I know what you're like.' Then, she tossed the end of the spliff into the toilet, and flushed it away. 'Are you buying me a milkshake?'

'Yeah,' said Thor, holding open the toilet door as she squeezed past awkwardly, like a stranger in a cinema. 'What am I like, then?'

'You're a terrorist.'

'Yeah, but that's hot. Admit it.'

'I will do no such thing,' she said, in the special voice she only used when she was telling him off, or negotiating curfews on the phone with her parents. 'Your videos are hot,' she added, as they walked past the racks of bowling shoes. 'Not the same thing.'

'It *is* the same thing.'

'Not really. It's just a socially adaptive manifestation of yourself. That's way more interesting than *you* are.'

'Thanks a lot,' said Thor, almost certain she was insulting him.

'I mean it,' Buddleia said, jumping up onto one of the stools at the milkshake bar. 'You know I'm into avatars of masculinity. I find you interesting at a performative level. Red Bull flavour, please.'

Thor put a paper cup under the nozzle, and hit *Red Bull*. 'Yeah, well,' he said, as he watched the pale orange goop curl into the cup. 'I'm still your lock screen.'

'Be that as it may,' she said, for the third time in a day. He still wasn't quite sure what that meant. He ordered himself a corn dog with jalapeño ketchup from the vending machine, checking how much weed was left by pinching the bag in his pocket as the corn dog rotated into view.

'Don't you ever worry about it?' she asked.

'About what?'

'About getting caught. About Trollr. I mean, what if one of the teachers saw your profile?'

'I won't get caught,' he said. 'I take measures to protect myself.' It was true: neither he nor God left digital footprints, not when they could be erased. But it sounded stupid, like he thought he was an undercover agent.

She looked down, and started to pick at her fingernails. 'There was a kid in Scotland last week who got jailed over his Fabble profile. It was nothing, compared to your Trollr stuff. Doesn't that — scare you?'

'Not really,' he said. 'What's the point? Live in the moment.'

'You can't if you're in prison.'

'I'm not scared of prison,' he said.

'You don't *really* believe that,' she said. 'Not *really*.'

She was right, and he couldn't think what to say. He could offer her more weed, just to get her off the subject, but then he wouldn't have enough left for himself. What would God do?

'What are you doing?' she asked.

'Shut up,' he said, and kissed her, too hard. They slightly banged teeth, not enough to hurt, but too much to ignore, and there was a moment when it felt like one of them should speak, but neither did. It was a terrible kiss, and he was sure that it was his fault, but she was nice enough not to say anything.

'Are you walking me home?' she said, eventually.

'I — didn't think that was an option?'

'It *could* be an option.'

•

The walk to her house was perfect. He showed her his profile, and his thousand and one followers, and the new halo over his username; and she brushed her hand against his leg in a way which might have been accidental but seemed deliberate; and they stopped in the park to coat one another in a layer of deodorant, and she kissed him; and he suggested they crawl under a tree so they could do it properly, which they did. A car crawled past, and stopped, leaving its engine running, and they both had to sit motionless until it pulled away, in case it was the police. Then, he put his hand on her thigh, firmly, to see if he could seem dominant without looking like a wanker, and her skin was surprisingly warm, much warmer than his. She didn't say 'performative' or 'avatar' or 'representation' once, so she must have been impressed by the four-figure follower count; and for the first time it didn't feel like he was pretending to be Thor, but *was* Thor, all thunderbolts and lightning and metal chest plate.

And then they got to her house, and he felt like a tit, because it was four times the size of his. Surely she should have told him. Shouldn't there be some kind of rule, for people like that? And why was she slumming it at Lady Patience? He could already imagine her other friends, girls with wavy blonde hair and oversized hound's-tooth sweaters and strings of black pearls, boys in pink trousers and Ralph Lauren shirts, and their sprawling schools with swimming pools and Mandarin lessons. What made it worse was that he couldn't look surprised, because that would only prove how prejudiced he was, even though he didn't think he was prejudiced at all. You're taking the fucking piss, he thought, as she opened the wrought-iron gates with an app, and a line of LEDs twinkled up the drive, casting puddles of white light up into the manicured shrubbery.

'Relax,' she said. 'No one'll be home for ages.'

Once they were inside, she asked if he'd ever had whisky, and he said that yes, obviously, he had, and took a massive gulp to prove it; but it turned out that Mr. Mbatha's version of whisky was nothing like Jack Daniels, and he spat it out across the floor because it tasted like the smell of petrol, and she had to get a cloth. As he waited for her to come back, he looked around the study, feeling stupider and stupider. The rip in his jeans was starting to look less like a design feature and more like a rip; he zipped up his hoodie to cover his Pay Your Danegeld, Heathen! t-shirt, because he couldn't remember what Danegeld actually was, which suddenly seemed to matter. There were more books on one wall of Mr. Mbatha's study than in every room of the Rupple household put together, even if he stretched the definition of book to include magazines. He could have figured it all out, if he'd stopped to think; she'd given him enough clues. The word 'neurologist'. The skiing holiday.

'Are you ok?'

'Yeah. That was gross. Is it coming out?'

'It will,' she said. 'I thought you said you'd had whisky before.'

'I have. Well, Jack Daniels.'

'Oh,' she said. 'I didn't realise that was actually a type of whisky. I always thought it was a — you know, like Bacardi or something.' And as she knelt at his feet, dabbing at the thick white rug with a brand new dishcloth, an image from Interfaith Studies popped into his head: the Pope, washing the feet of the homeless. Tit, he thought. You massive tit.

'Don't you *want* to meet my parents?' she asked, as though they were a normal boyfriend and girlfriend, rather than a Norse God and his devoted follower.

'What do you mean?'

'You just — you look really uncomfortable.'

'I'm not uncomfortable,' he said. 'I don't mind meeting them.'

'Well, it's only my dad tonight,' she said. 'Mum's in Geneva for the week, again.'

Geneva, he thought. Of course. Why wouldn't she be? Why would she be somewhere normal, like Reading or Guildford, when she could be in Geneva?

She stood up. 'I wonder what he'll make of you,' she said, in her performative analysis voice.

He felt a ripple of defiance pass up through his chest. He was there because Buddleia wanted him to be, not because her father had pencilled him in for an interview. 'What's not to like?' he said.

'Exactly!' she replied, brightly. 'Anyway, you could always — you know. If you're feeling nervous.' And then her eyes drifted down to his pocket.

'In here?'

'Well, not necessarily. We could do it in the garden.'

'You smoke in the garden?' he asked. It felt as though the house ought to have a dedicated room for that.

'I don't smoke,' she said. 'I mean, apart from with you. It impairs cognitive function. You know, they test for it at some schools.'

'So how come you don't —'

And then he stopped. How could he finish the question, without it becoming an accusation?

'Go to a school which does drug screening?' she said. 'My parents don't believe in social segregation. Well, Mum doesn't, anyway. She's really into all that inclusion stuff.'

'Oh,' he said. He'd never heard of anyone being into inclusion. His own mum was into interior design and Christianity, in that order, and he suspected that 'inclusion' was one of the words she'd ask him not to use in the house.

'Don't *worry*,' said Buddleia. 'He'll think you're great. Just don't call yourself Thor. He'd think that was — you know.'

It was all a big joke, then. That's what performative masculinity meant: laughing at Craig and his silly nickname behind his back. He jumped up; he had to get out of the house, or at least the study, and certainly the chair, which felt like it was sucking him downwards. 'Okay, then,' he said, fishing the weed out of his pocket. 'I'll skin up.'

So she led him through the kitchen, which didn't seem to have any appliances, only large flat surfaces with small glowing lights built into them, chunks of his armour falling off with every step he took, revealing the wibbly Craig beneath. As they walked out onto the patio overlooking the garden and the low hill beyond, he realised that he probably wasn't her first boyfriend, which hadn't occurred to him before, and felt a rush of envy. So what happened to that guy? Which stage of the Mbathas' interview process did he fail? Bad grades? Bad teeth? The wrong attitude to inclusion?

'I can see what you're thinking,' she said, perching beside him on the sun lounger. 'But I'm still *me*.'

'Trust me,' he said, trying to roll the weed evenly into the paper in the weak light of the LEDs. 'You don't know what I'm thinking.'

'I do like you,' she said. 'I mean, not just the Trollr thing. I think you're really authentic.'

'I don't want to be authentic.'

'I didn't mean it like that. I meant that you're really — you're *you*. No one else is like that, with me. Everyone's always — pretending.'

Craig looked at the spliff, which was half as good as the spliff Thor would have rolled, and which God would have called a fucking abortion. 'Maybe,' he said to his clammy palms, 'if everyone else is pretending, then you're the one who's making them pretend.'

There was a silence, the real kind of silence that you could only hear if you lived far enough from the motorway. Craig held the lighter in one hand and the spliff in the other, trying to decide what to do. He could stay, and get stoned with Buddleia, and hope that Mr. Mbatha saw his authenticity and not his ridiculous t-shirt; or he could walk all the way back home through the rows of houses, each smaller than the last, as though he were becoming a giant, or un-becoming a dwarf. He turned to Buddleia. 'Do you really think this is a good idea?'

And then, she grabbed his knee, and jerked her neck up. 'Ssh,' she said. 'That's him.'

He rammed the lighter and the terrible spliff into his pocket, and sprang off the sun lounger. One by one, the kitchen lights began to glow, a warm yellow spreading out from the belly of the house and into the garden. He could see a tall man's back by the fridge, the leather strap of a satchel slung diagonally across it.

'Sweetheart?'

'I'm out here, Dad!' she called.

Mr. Mbatha turned around, and strode out onto the patio; he was handsome, with a big square jaw and a perfectly fitted shirt, and Craig felt his hand rise for a handshake, the interviewee's vital first impression. 'Hello,' he said.

Mr. Mbatha took one look at Craig's hand, his neck recoiling; then, he looked up, and closed his eyes, as though he'd seen mould on fruit. 'Absolutely not,' he said. 'Absolutely not.'

'Dad!'

'Darling,' said Mr. Mbatha patiently, 'absolutely not.'

'*Why?*'

Mr. Mbatha snorted. 'Look at him, Buddleia. He's *stoned*.'

'Dad! Why are you so judgemental? Jesus —'

Craig hadn't even got to say 'pleased to meet you', and already they were discussing him as though he wasn't there. 'Sweetheart,' Mr. Mbatha said, 'I'm a surgeon. Really? Did you really think I wouldn't notice?'

'He's not — it's not like that, Dad. He's — we're dating,'

Buddleia said.

'Pleased to meet you,' Craig said, finally.

'You're absolutely not,' said Mr. Mbatha. 'I can tell you now, young lady, that you and he are *not* dating.' He looked at Craig, and gave a tight little smile. 'Yes,' he said, sighing, 'you too.' And then, he turned back towards the house, pulling the satchel off his shoulder as he went.

'Wait here,' said Buddleia, following her father into the kitchen. 'Dad. *Dad!* Wait —' And the huge glass doors closed behind her, their black frames smoothly flumping into place, and she disappeared into the living room.

Craig shut his eyes. She'd be pleading and gesticulating and possibly crying, and Mr. Mbatha would be calm as a rock face, explaining how disappointed he was, and how Craig would impair her cognitive function, and how even social inclusion had its limits. It all felt like a mistake — the botched kiss, the whisky spat across the study floor — a mistake which his own father would have greeted with an I-told-you-so of an eyebrow, which his mother would have soothed with a didn't-we-tell-you-so of a hand on his shoulder. It was wrong, wrong in that horrible way which couldn't be neatly pinned on someone else, and would be even more wrong when he woke up tomorrow.

Along the side of the house was a meandering pathway in varnished wood decking, a line of recycling bins tastefully concealed behind fans of bamboo. Tomorrow was Monday, and International Women's Day, and Craig had to write a presentation about the role of women in tech, and he was an hour's walk from home with nothing but an unsmokable spliff for company. So he quietly made his way along the path, letting himself out onto the herringbone brick of the front drive, where the gates opened as though they'd been waiting to get rid of him as soon as he arrived.

mum › me
what Time are you coming home ?Do you need a lift ?

mum › me
Going to bed now ,Call if you need

mum › me
Please don't go to bed without changing sheets ,Love youX

He looked out on the broad crescent of three-storey homes, the narrowed eyes of their loft windows opened and closed, light and dark, sleeping and awake. It would have been nice if one of them could have been his house. Just for a night.

INTERNATIONAL WOMEN'S DAY

Everything in Noodle's life seemed to be getting more and more complicated, and it was starting to show on his phone. He had two HideAway apps, one which Ibrahim downloaded for him so he could use Blackfl.ag, and one which he'd cloned so he could access the videos of hot guys stored on his secret cloud account, the account he was terrified of Ibrahim or Tarek seeing. Except that the video of him eating the Bible ended up on the hot guy account, because God sounded hot telling him what to do; and there was something so wrong about seeing his own face in a carefully curated column of race baiters that he had to make another secret cloud account, which then needed another cloned HideAway app. And on top of all that, he had no idea where to put the Trollr video of Thor eating the Qur'an. Did Thor belong with Noodle, or with the skinheads and the white nationalists? The first, obviously, because they were classmates, except obviously the second.

Even with his precautionary measures — the secret accounts, the clearing of caches — he still had the nagging sense he could be found out. He could feel his history silting up in the recesses of the web, scoured from his phone but never entirely forgotten, the pictures and the videos all recorded in some faraway place, stocking up like bullets in an armoury, encrypted in binary but no less damning, the data breeding in the space between love and hate. The whole thing was just too massive to contemplate, too much like looking directly into the sun, too full of truths which he'd always known, but never been able to agree with.

Noodle had been taught about consent and assault, in Self-Respecting Your Body, and in Sex And Relationships. He knew that he could get help from a trusted elder, and had filled out the card where he'd named his three trusted elders, and provided reasons he could trust them. Together with everyone else in his half of the alphabet, he'd sat in class and practised saying 'I do not consent'. He had a peer mentor in the year above, whose job it was to make sure that he wasn't subjected to bullying or discrimination. He knew not to trust anyone — family, friend or other — who made him feel threatened or violated, and had been tested, successfully, on identifying behaviour that was threatening or violating, and had a digital certificate to prove it. He knew everything that Lady Patience wanted him to know about consent and assault.

But what God and Mr. Naseem did had nothing to do with Self-Respecting Your Body, because Self-Respecting Your Body wasn't about real life. Noodle knew how to be safe: steer well clear of your peer mentor and your state guardian, so you didn't look like a pussy, and end up as someone's punch bag; avoid the jonesing methhead kids; avoid the guys who sat around in parks. But it was the two things together, the poster and then the Bible: obviously, it must be something about *him*. So what was he doing wrong? And why did it make him so angry whenever he had to sit in History And Reunderstanding with all of the Straight Pride Latinitos monkeying around in front of him, and Interfaith Studies with God and Thor pink-eyed and giggling in the back row, and Social Networking And Communication Strategies with Deth and Ragnarök and the other Disciples of Hell trying to take out passing traffic with their laser pointer apps? Other than God and El Jaw, none of them had actually done anything to him. It was the fact they were there, the fact he couldn't tune them out, the fact he cared what they thought of him when they'd never even given him a second glance.

'Thank you very much, Grace H., for that wonderful presentation on equal pay,' said Miss Waterman-Patterson. 'A round of applause for Grace H., please, class.' And Grace Hill slumped back down into the seat beside Noodle, and dumped her scrunched-up chaos of notes back onto the desk, lists of pay brackets and web addresses and actresses' names and statistics, each page with the word 'BURN' written over and over in a column down the right-hand side. As Noodle clapped, she looked up at him through night-sky-black mascara. 'Well done,' he mouthed.

'And now,' said Miss Waterman-Patterson, 'Craig is going to give a talk on the role of women in tech. A round of applause for Craig, then, please.' And she installed herself behind her desk, propping up her tablet on its fuchsia-patterned case, and gave Thor a supportive raise of her eyebrows as he walked to the front of the class. Me hungry, thought Rahman.

Thor cleared his throat, and fiddled with his phone to bring up his notes.

'Cough cough faggot cough,' said God, from the back row, not even bothering to fake the coughs.

'Quiet, please,' said Miss Waterman-Patterson. 'Craig? Are we ready?'

Thor looked up at the class.

'Everyone has the right to express an opinion,' he said, 'even though some people think they have more right than other people, but they are wrong because we should all be equal so we should recognise that we have a right to say what we want and that right is a legal right and shouldn't be —'

He paused, and squinted at his phone. 'Ab — rogated,' he said. And then, he glanced over at Miss Waterman-Patterson, who smiled and nodded encouragingly.

'In this presentation,' Thor said, 'I will be expressing opinions which are based on data and other people's opinions which are expert opinions and so many of the things I am saying cannot be questioned because they are statistics and none of us have got the right to our own statistics. Also, my opinion is protected by the law because the law is there to protect everyone's opinions even though there are some people who wish that it wouldn't.'

And he looked across at Miss Waterman-Patterson again, who nodded again, although slightly less encouragingly.

'Research has proven that there are fundamental differences between men and women which you cannot just pretend don't exist because you wish they didn't when they do. For example,' he said. Then there was a long pause, and Thor swallowed. Noodle studied him. He was sweating, but it wasn't fear sweat. He almost looked angry.

'For example,' he said, finally. 'Last November, a study by the University of Shanghai found that for every woman going into tech there were fourteen men. Some people have said that this figure should be ignored because it is from China, but this is obviously racist because China is an ethnic minority country and so for every woman in tech there's fourteen men.'

Noodle looked over at Miss Waterman-Patterson. She'd stopped smiling, and was staring ahead, blankly.

'In this country,' Thor said, 'some universities have introduced positive discrimination to get more women into tech. However.' And then he stopped speaking, and pawed at his phone with his massive fingers.

'However?' prompted Miss Waterman-Patterson.

'I — lost my — okay, I got it back,' said Thor. 'However. Positive is a value judgement and so it is an opinion, and so some people may not think that it is positive even though it's called positive, and it's wrong to dismiss an opinion. Also, many people think that discrimination is wrong because we shouldn't discriminate against one another on the basis of gender according to the United Nations and also according to many experts on gender.'

He stopped to wipe his nose on his blazer. 'So in my opinion we shouldn't say positive discrimination but discriminating against men, which is a less part — partisan? — partisan way to say it. Also, it hasn't worked, because if it had worked there would be lots more women in tech than there are now.'

Miss Waterman-Patterson was biting the corner of her lip, and rubbing her thumb against her index finger.

'Even if you are not a Christian you have to respect the viewpoints of Christians and other religious minorities who say that there are fundamental differences between men and women. I will now elu — elucidate some of these differences using a visual aid.' And then, Thor turned around to face the interactive whiteboard, and loaded a graphic of two pie charts, with illegibly small labels for each slice of pie. Miss Waterman-Patterson squinted at the board with a frown, and started tapping at her tablet.

'As you can see from this chart,' Thor said to the board, 'women have different personalities from men because of motherhood and other factors. Even though some people pretend that there are no differences between men and women, women are less entre — entrepreneurial than men and men are nearly always the people who start companies especially in tech. Even though some people think we shouldn't be able to say this because they don't believe in freedom of speech, we should be able to say this even if some people find it offensive because it is true.'

Miss Waterman-Patterson cleared her throat, and pressed her chin down into her neck, as though she'd eaten something too fast.

Then, Thor turned around, and stared at Buddleia Mbatha, who was sitting in the front row. 'A lot of women mistreat men and treat them like they're not equal and don't have any rights and it's very hypocritical, especially when sometimes those women are only successful because they have rich fathers even though they say they don't want to rely on men. Some women who succeed in technology only succeed because their families have lots of money and everything is biased in their favour even though they pretend to be nice people who believe in equality. People who are hypocrites should never be trusted and they shouldn't be allowed to work in any industry until they stop lying and being unkind to men who haven't done anything to deserve it. That is why I think we shouldn't just say there should be more women in tech, and we should listen to dis — dissenting voices before it is too late and there aren't any jobs left for decent working families because of policies which discriminate against men.' He looked up, and said, 'I hope you enjoyed my presentation, are there any questions, thank you,' then locked his phone, and slid it into his trouser pocket.

'Well,' said Miss Waterman-Patterson. But before she could say anything else, Buddleia Mbatha jumped up out of her chair, hiding her face in her elbow, and ran to the door, snivelling loudly; as she went out into the corridor, Amelia Brink sprang up after her, shouting 'Buddy! Wait! Miss, can I —'

'Go on,' said Miss Waterman-Patterson. And Amelia Brink grabbed her tablet and blazer and ran out of the classroom, slamming the door behind her.

Thor looked down, and started to shuffle past the desks to the back of the room. 'Well,' Miss Waterman-Patterson said, again, 'I think —'

And then, something unusual happened. As Thor walked past Grace Hill, she screamed 'FEMPATHY!' at the top of her voice, and stabbed him in the outer thigh with a pair of compasses.

'Jesus, fuck!' Thor yelled, clasping his leg.

Miss Waterman-Patterson jumped up. 'Grace! No!'

'What the fuck!' said Thor. 'You fucking — bitch — what the *fuck*!'

'FEMPATHY!' Grace Hill shouted, brandishing the blood-tipped spike in the air victoriously.

Thor raised his hand, either because he was about to hit Grace Hill, or because he thought she was about to stab him again; and then, she plunged the compasses into the palm of his hand. Thor yelped, and there was a collective drawing in of air through teeth.

'Ooh, *fuck*,' said God, from the back row. 'That's gotta hurt.'

'Put it down,' said Miss Waterman-Patterson, who was standing in front of the board, legs apart, eyes wide. 'Put it down, Grace.'

'You fucking freak,' Thor said, pressing his thumb into the palm of his hand. 'You fucking — weirdo —'

Grace Hill turned to Noodle, dropping the compasses onto the desk with a clatter. She was grinning, almost laughing, her breath shallow, her tongue sticking out between her teeth. 'Fuck the patriarchy,' she said to Noodle, and raised her fist for a fist-bump.

•

The rest of the morning was a bit weird, and didn't have much to do with International Women's Day. After Thor went off to the school nurse, the head teacher, Mrs. Flores, arrived, and interviewed various people in the corridor, while Miss Waterman-Patterson sat at the front of the room looking betrayed. Everyone had to sit in silence and learn about the core tenets of Judaism, which Miss Waterman-Patterson had suddenly decided there was going to be a test on. Fifteen minutes before the end of the period, Buddleia Mbatha and Amelia Brink came back in; they'd both been crying, and both shot God evil looks as they walked across the front of the classroom to their desks. Then, after another ten minutes, Thor came back in with a plaster on his hand, stomping past Noodle and the space where Grace Hill had been sitting, his face gnarled into a furious knot.

Noodle wanted to turn around and stare at him, but it didn't seem like a good idea, because people were getting yelled at for things that wouldn't normally have mattered, like whispering or texting or looking things up on Fabble. He was interested: would Thor still be sexy when wounded? Or maybe even sexier? Or was he secretly glad that Thor had been stabbed in the hand, and hoping that it hurt?

So, just before the bell rang, Noodle turned around. Thor was slumped in his chair, sulking, his eyes seething at a point in the middle distance. He looked up, and saw Noodle.

'Cocksucker,' Noodle mouthed, and smiled.

'Paki,' mouthed Thor, and gave him the middle finger, his fingernail peeking over the top of his desk.

'Right,' said Miss Waterman-Patterson, looking at the clock. 'With the exception of those of you who still have to talk to Mrs. Flores and fill out an Incident Report Form, the rest of you can go. Dylan, I will not tell you again to put that phone away.' She stood up, balancing her coat and scarf on her arm as she squeezed her tablet and the stack of Incident Report Forms into her bag, and trundled out of the classroom.

Noodle waited as the other students filed out, one by one; as God walked past, he accidentally-on-purpose banged his bag into the back of Noodle's head.

'Sorry, porky,' said God.

But Noodle said nothing, because he had an idea. He wasn't sure why it hadn't occurred to him before; it was an open goal, begging him to score.

'Miss?' he said, in the corridor. 'Miss?'

'Yes Rahman,' said Mrs. Flores. 'Do you need an Incident Report Form?'

'No,' Noodle said. 'But I think there's something you should see.' He handed Mrs. Flores his phone, with Thor's Trollr profile loaded on a fresh tab.

'All right,' Mrs. Flores said, putting her reading glasses back on.

Down the hallway, Noodle could see God and Thor, both walking backwards. God was staring right at him, drawing his index finger silently across his neck. 'You're fucking dead,' he mouthed.

Noodle looked at Mrs. Flores, who seemed appropriately shocked. 'I just thought you'd want to know,' he said.

•

'Oi, camel fucker!' God shouted at Noodle, after Pre-Advanced Maths. 'What the fuck was *that*?'

Crap, thought Noodle. Grace Hill, who usually walked with Noodle to the school gate, hadn't been in any of the afternoon classes, and everyone else had already gone home. He was all alone with God and Thor in the dismal basement which Pre-Advanced Maths had tried to cheer up with a colourful mural of square roots. Noodle turned around, and then realised that it was a dead end.

'Nowhere to run, bitch,' said God. He tried to grab Noodle's head, to smack it against the square root of eighty-one, but Noodle dodged under his arm.

'Fuck off,' said Noodle, starting to panic.

'What did you say to Flores, huh?' said Thor.

'And you,' said Noodle. 'You can fuck *all* the way off, you pasty piece of shit.'

'*You're* the piece of shit,' said Thor.

'Nice,' Noodle said. 'Nice comeback.'

Then God lunged at Noodle again, this time getting him, a hard slap around the side of the head. Noodle went to push him, but Thor smacked the other side of his head when he wasn't looking; then Noodle turned around to hit Thor back, and God slapped him again. They had him backed up against the wall, and they were both taller than he was, and broader, too. He could feel himself scowling.

'*What* — did you *say* — to *Flores*?' Thor growled.

'I told her about your dad's prosthetic dick,' said Noodle. He'd had enough, now. His head ached, and he wasn't scared of God, or his sidekick. Then, Thor punched Noodle hard, in the stomach. It hurt, because Noodle wasn't braced for it, and he had to pretend it didn't. 'Is that it?' he said, controlling his voice so he didn't sound winded. 'Is that all you've got?'

Before Thor could answer, Miss Waterman-Patterson appeared at the end of the corridor. God and Thor jumped back, and all three of them stood in the corridor, as though they were waiting for instructions.

'What's going on down here?' she asked.

Noodle and Thor looked at one another. It was obvious what had to be done: Noodle, as the shortest kid in the corridor, and the one backed up against the wall, would have to speak first. 'Nothing, Miss,' he said. 'I was just asking how Craig's hand was, is all.' Thor's eyes narrowed.

'Yes, well, I think we've all had enough drama for today,' said Miss Waterman-Patterson. 'Do you need to go back to the nurse?' she asked Thor.

'It's fine,' Thor said.

'Well then. In that case, I'd suggest we all go home and try and make tomorrow a better day than today.' She touched Noodle on his shoulder. 'Salaam alaikum,' she said, softly.

'Alaikum assalaam,' said Noodle, still staring at Thor.

There was a pause. None of them could be the first to move, and certainly not Noodle; he was in standoff mode. 'On you go, then!' Miss Waterman-Patterson said to Thor.

'See you tomorrow, *Rahman*,' Thor said, his voice ominously cheerful.

Noodle waited silently at the bottom of the bright blue staircase which led up to the ground floor. Finally, when the footsteps were out of earshot, he walked up the stairs and out of the gates, where his dad and brother were waiting in the second hand Toyota, which had fake number plates and smelt of cigarette smoke.

'What have you been doing in there?' his dad snapped. 'I've had enough of you keeping me waiting. Last week you were late, and today again. What are you doing in there that's so bloody important?'

Noodle said nothing. He was looking at the patterns of the twigs on the trees, and the streaks of rain on the car's windows, the twill of the seats where it met the plastic headrests, the half-peeled-off stickers on the moulded fittings. The car moved through the city in fits and starts as his dad fought with the clutch, leaning forward in the seat at every junction before launching out into the oncoming traffic. Noodle felt sick. It wasn't from the motion of the car, although that didn't help. He looked in the rear view mirror.

'Wanker,' Tarek mouthed, from the front seat.

•

After dinner, Noodle felt like he had cats fighting inside his head. He couldn't stop thinking about Thor belly-punching him, which was the most annoying, most brilliant thing that had happened to him in years. So eventually, he cracked. He checked that the curtains were fully drawn, and that his browser was set to incognito mode; then, he logged on to Sleazydoesit, and navigated to the local ads.

anon-7ymqUL4
taxi driver gives free rides to hot girls under 21

anon-t2HSj8e
need fuck NOW (tues am) girls only be POLITE

anon-99ef8og
spunk in ur pussy or up ur ass no time wasters

anon-8k29f31
paki boy needs beating up by white guy, cant accommodate

anon-rR3pHRw
buy/sell used underwear dirtier the better

He hadn't checked the site for days; there was a danger that someone had answered, and then lost interest. But he guessed that the guys on Sleazydoesit were used to disappointment — from what he knew of the internet, most of the responses would be data-miners, or Trojan zebras, or some other threat wiggling its way through the web, gobbling up information to sell on to third parties — so they might be prepared to wait a bit for the real deal. When he saw his ad in the list, it didn't seem any worse than the others. He wondered what the people who used Sleazydoesit did with their incredibly precise desires, before the internet came along. Noodle could hear his dad's voice, screeching with disbelief: 'Underwear? Why does this person want someone else's underwear?'

Would he really go through with it, he wondered, if he got a response? There was a risk it would be God, or Thor — but the risk was tiny, and he'd be able to recognise them one way or another. And if it was: perhaps he'd agree to meet, and then go to the police. But that was a fuzzy scenario, a fantasy he didn't really know if he wanted to become a reality.

And he did have a response.

anon-a54C04m › anon-8k29f31
Sounds good. When?

It wasn't Thor, nor God. Neither would've missed the opportunity to throw in a quick insult, a drive-by 'fuck you'. He looked as his tablet, his heart quickening. He'd posted the ad as though he were offering up someone else, and watching the result from a distance, but it was his body on offer. He would be the one meeting a stranger — where? In his home? In a car, parked in some tucked-away lay-by? He was giving himself up, dropping into a void. It was stupider and more exciting than anything else he'd ever done.

So he agreed to meet at midnight, by which time he could sneak out of the house without being heard, as long as the swelling and gargling of his father's snoring was still going. The man hadn't given a name, and nor had Noodle; all he knew was that there'd be a red car at the end of his street. He could see it from outside the house, sitting on the corner by the dropped kerb, engine running, parking lights on. He walked towards it quickly, his head down, past his neighbours' houses, dark under the sleeping hats of their roofs. As he got closer, he could see that the man was bald, and much older than he'd imagined — older than his dad, almost the same age as Mr. Naseem. He wasn't just bald; he looked totally hairless, even eyebrowless. He rolled down the window on the passenger side.

'In,' said the man.

So Noodle got in. The car stank; there was a little green cardboard tree hanging from the rear view mirror, with *Nordic Forest* written on it, which smelt of toilet cleaner. The man put his hand on Noodle's knee, and gripped it. Noodle did nothing.

They drove south, and then east, into the narrow streets of terraced houses, the man only lifting his hand from Noodle's knee to change gear. The white bones between the knuckles were too long, making Noodle's leg look stumpy; so Noodle tried not to look at the hand, and instead watched rows of homes flicking past, their windows open in the heat. He thought about remembering the route, leaving a trail of mental breadcrumbs; but somehow that would ruin it.

'This is us,' said the man, and parked up outside a flaking house with an old satellite dish on the front. 'Out you get.'

Noodle got out. He wondered how long he was going to let himself be bossed around; it couldn't last forever, and yet here he was, silently obeying. The man showed him into the house, which had no hall, the front door emptying straight into an over-lit lounge, the smell of air freshener masking another, mustier smell. There was a huge, dirty aquarium stretching the length of one wall, with ragged plants behind the algae-stained glass, and sluggish yellow and purple fish gulping for air at the surface. On the other side of the room was another tank, even bigger, with a bright halogen lamp baking the wood chippings and straw at the bottom. Noodle had a horrible feeling that it was housing a snake.

'It's a vivarium,' said the man. 'You scared of snakes?'

Noodle nodded.

'Don't worry. She can't get out.' The man was standing a few centimetres in front of Noodle, his thumbs tucked into the pockets of his jeans. 'Lift your shirt up,' he said.

Noodle still hadn't said a word. The longer he went without speaking, the less possible speech seemed. He lifted his shirt up and hooked it over the back of his neck, avoiding the man's eyes, which he could feel running over his body, the brown of his skin yellowing in the brightness of the room. Then, the man slapped Noodle on the belly, lightly. It didn't hurt at all; it almost felt friendly. Noodle looked up. The man had raised his eyebrows — which did exist, only just, two lines of fine white hair — which was his way of asking without asking. Noodle said nothing.

'Harder?' asked the man.

And Noodle still said nothing. So the next slap came; and it was harder, quite a lot harder, the flat of his hand ringing out against Noodle's stomach. Then the man closed his fist, and waited, holding Noodle in his gaze, the fist hanging just in front of his skin. Noodle nodded. He tried to make it the smallest nod he could manage, to minimise the treason his neck was committing against his torso. 'Put your hands behind your back, then,' the man said.

The punch made him topple backwards, and he had to steady himself on his feet. As soon as he did, another punch came, a little harder; and then a third, a lot harder. Noodle heard himself grunt. He closed his eyes, so a small part of him could pretend it wasn't quite happening.

'No,' said the man. 'Eyes open.'

But Noodle didn't open them.

'Open your fucking eyes,' the man said, louder, and slapped Noodle's face. 'Look at me.' He was staring at Noodle intently, his hand raised to the level of his ears, ready to smack him again, his eyes smouldering in the pale field of his skin. 'So you like being called a Paki, do you?' he asked.

Noodle nodded his minute nod.

'You look like an Arab. But then, you people all look the same to me.'

He was saying it as a challenge, but Noodle couldn't work out if he'd pass the challenge by speaking, or by staying silent. He stayed silent.

'What else do you like to be called?' asked the man. 'Goatfucker? Taliban?'

'Talib,' said Noodle, 'not Taliban.' He was barely audible, his voice high-pitched and feeble.

'Eh?'

'Talib. Taliban is the plural.'

The man looked at him, halfway between delight and disgust. 'You fucking correcting me, Taliban?'

'No,' said Noodle.

'Sure about that?'

Noodle said nothing.

'Stand with your legs apart, Taliban,' the man said. 'I'm gonna give you a proper smack.'

Noodle stepped back, his shoulders banging on the glass of the fish tank. Suddenly, it felt real; he'd spoken, breaking the spell. He opened his mouth to say 'no', but nothing came out. Without knowing it, he'd taken his hands from behind his back and was holding them in front of his crotch, the fingers cupping one another, shaking.

The man lowered his hand. 'This isn't really for you, is it?' he asked, disappointedly.

Then, Noodle ran. He bolted past the man, who barely had time to turn around, so fast that he almost threw himself into the Perspex of the front door, yanking at the handle and jumping over the doorframe, hurling himself out into the street and pelting down the pavement, not looking back. He'd never run so fast before, his feet powering him along between the houses and the hatchbacks, dodging the manhole covers and the broken paving slabs. Once he hit the corner, he stopped, his hands leaning on his knees as he tried to catch his breath.

He was standing by a small square of grass, with a dog poo bin in the middle, and the silvery-yellow light of a lamppost above, his chest still bare. In the sky, a dry flash of lightning jumped between the clouds; there was a soft crumple of thunder, moving the warm of the night along the ground. Around him, there was nothing he recognised, no landmarks and no street names, no way to navigate back home. He'd scrubbed his movements from the city's streets, a deleted history, a purged cache. It could've been anywhere in England.

NIP IT IN THE BUD

'What I'd like from you,' said Mrs. Flores, 'is a sign that you're taking this seriously. Because these are very, very serious allegations.'

It all happened within twelve hours. The first sign that something was wrong was the night before, when Thor wanted to see how many followers God had, and found that God's Trollr profile had been deleted. He checked the link, twice, and stared at the screen.

Error 404
Seek and ye shall find, muthafucka!

Then he checked his own, and that was deleted, too. Just like that, Thor was gone, eradicated by the internet, a small, rocky planet eaten by a supernova. All signs of his existence — his trollings, his devotees, his upvotes — disappeared. That was when the ball of dread appeared in his chest. It was still there when he woke up.

According to the school's policy on bullying and relationship management, an Early Intervention Panel was arranged for half past nine. There were ten of them in the room: Craig, God, El Jaw, Noodle, Grace Hill, Buddleia, Amelia Brink, Mrs. Flores, Miss Waterman-Patterson, and someone called Ivana Applethwaite, who was apparently the designated welfare officer for Craig's year, and had a Slavic accent so strong that no one had any idea what she was saying. The school administration set aside a conference room, usually off-limits to students, given what Mrs. Flores called 'the scope of the situation'. Craig suspected that she was secretly having fun, with her colour-coded to-do list of justice loaded on the interactive whiteboard, so everyone knew the order in which they would disappoint Mrs. Flores and Miss Waterman-Patterson and Ivana Applethwaite with their behaviour.

'I *am* taking it seriously,' said Craig. '*I'm* the one who got stabbed in the leg. And the hand.' For evidence, he held up his palm; he'd deliberately forgotten to change the plaster, to maximise the bloodiness, but the small spot of brown in the centre of his hand wasn't very impressive.

'We've dealt with that,' Mrs. Flores said, 'and Grace has apologised. This part of the session is about *you*, Craig, and what *you* did.'

It was true: Grace Hill had apologised, first in an awkward-jokey sort of sing-song voice, and then, after stern eyebrows from Mrs. Flores and some mystery words from Ivana Applethwaite, with snivelling, a choreographed apology, complete with sad, bored, tears. It was all very half-arsed; she was still semi-detached from the whole thing, interested but powerless, like a weather forecaster apologising for grey skies. So now it was his turn.

And then, Craig realised he had a decision to make, one which was desperately simple. He could do what Noodle had just done, and blame God and El Jaw for his blasphemous savagery; then he'd be classified as a victim, which might at least mean he got out before lunch. Or he could take the blame himself, which had other consequences, consequences which were further off and harder to define. It was impossible to pick. She was asking him to choose between losing his only friends and admitting Islamophobia. He looked across at God and El Jaw; they were both staring at the floor.

'I know it was the wrong thing to do,' he said finally. 'But it's only a book.'

'I can't believe you'd say a thing like that, Craig,' said Miss Waterman-Patterson. 'I really cannot believe you'd be so naïve. You know that's not true. It's *not* only a book, is it?'

'You must have known the gravity of what you were doing, Craig,' Mrs. Flores said. 'Did you feel — pushed into it? Because if that's what's going on here — if Dylan and Jordan *made* you do it, like Rahman, then you need to tell us. We can't help you if we don't know the truth.'

And then, God looked up at Craig. He had a sad face on, and hunched-up little shoulders, a bunny rabbit in an animal rescue shelter. The eyes were surprisingly convincing; but Craig knew him well enough to see the sniper's lasers powering up in his pupils.

'No one made me do anything,' he said.

'Is that true, Dylan?' said Mrs. Flores.

God shrugged.

'Jordan?'

El Jaw looked at the ceiling. 'Dunno,' he said.

'Because it looks to me — and I'd never seen this Trollr site before — but it looks to me like this was some kind of — perverse — competition. I'm right, aren't I, Dylan?'

God said nothing.

'Was that the idea? To see who you could get into more trouble? Rahman or Craig?'

God sniffed, because he was a good bunny, and all he'd ever wanted was a warm hutch and some carrot to nibble.

'Why would you do that, Dylan?' said Miss Waterman-Patterson.

Question by question, Craig could feel his friendship with God crumbling apart. This was the point where he had to take the hit, to dive in front of the bullet like the goons in the movies did to protect their supervillain bosses. Otherwise, only God knew the vengeance which would be rained down on Craig's head.

'I'm telling you, Miss,' Craig said to Miss Waterman-Patterson. 'No one made me do anything. It was meant to be a joke.'

'And you, Jordan?' said Mrs. Flores. 'What do you have to say for yourself?'

'Not much,' said El Jaw. God sniggered, and tried to disguise it as a cough.

'Yes,' said Mrs. Flores. 'Well. We'll see about that this afternoon, won't we? Because I'm not finished with you three boys. I am extremely, *extremely* disappointed.'

Craig stared at Noodle's feet. That was it, then: Noodle had neatly excluded himself from the category of 'boy', and was in some other category, which involved Buddleia and Amelia Brink and listening and nodding and the tender clasping of knuckles.

'There's something else that Mrs. Flores and I want to discuss with you, Craig,' Miss Waterman-Patterson said, 'which is your behaviour in class. When you gave the talk.'

'Oh,' Mrs. Flores said, dropping her voice and turning to consult the interactive whiteboard. 'Is that — do you want to do that now?'

'If that's all right,' said Miss Waterman-Patterson.

'Er — fine,' said Mrs. Flores, and opened her tablet to move Craig's neon yellow block of shame up two rows.

'I think it's part of a more general — *pattern* of behaviour,' Miss Waterman-Patterson said. 'And I think that it would be positive for everyone if we could explore that.'

So then, Buddleia got to talk. She'd been humiliated by Craig; Craig had exploited International Women's Day as part of a vendetta against her; then he'd bombarded her with texts, and she was so upset about it that she was skipping meals. She was scared of coming back to class, because everyone was talking about her. She felt unwelcome. Craig realised with growing horror how well prepared she was, as though she were giving a speech which she'd rehearsed and honed. Humiliated. Exploited. Vendetta. Bombarded. He wasn't allowed to interrupt her, to point out how much hotter Thor was than vendetta-free Craig; and all the way through, she was clutching hands with Amelia Brink, who'd managed to promote herself to Buddleia's chief of staff overnight.

'I have to say,' Miss Waterman-Patterson said to Mrs. Flores, 'that it was — quite nasty. I was very disturbed by some of the things Craig came out with.'

'I'm the one who got stabbed,' Craig mumbled. 'Twice.'

'Craig,' Miss Waterman-Patterson said. 'We've moved on from that. Your behaviour is a big part of this situation. A *big* part.'

'And you have to take responsibility for that,' added Mrs. Flores.

'Can I say something?' asked Amelia Brink. 'Because I think that this has all had an impact on *me*.'

•

At lunchtime, Craig, God, El Jaw and Grace Hill had to take their food from the canteen and eat it in one of the Geography And Spatial Belonging classrooms, under the supervision of Miss Waterman-Patterson; Noodle, Buddleia and Amelia Brink were allowed to sit in the canteen, with the other human beings. Lunch was only half an hour, because the morning session overran, and the next stage — reflective self-development — would take at least an hour. Beyond that were stacked darker clouds, looming into an afternoon storm: community representatives; interviews conducted in the head teacher's office; parents. Craig had lost his appetite.

'You need to eat, Craig,' Miss Waterman-Patterson said. 'None of this is going to get any better on an empty stomach.' And then, she gave him the fakest smile he'd seen in his whole life.

Craig closed his eyes. He decided to visualise a more satisfying version of Miss Waterman-Patterson, just to spite her, building an image against the blackness of his eyelids. He started with the shape of her body, like a lemon that had collapsed, then selected the clothes piece by piece: the loud paisley top she wore at prize-giving, which pinched at the armpits; the denim floor-length skirt which rucked up over her arse, showing her wide, pale ankles. He added jewellery: a low-hanging necklace with lumps of fake coral looping down, and jumbo beads in primary colours, with matching earrings. He draped a floral scarf over the paisley top, and imagined it flapping down over her breasts. Then he thought about the wrinkles which branched out underneath her jaw, and the fat around her neck. He thought about how it would feel to touch that part of her, which looked cold and a bit clammy. He thought about her hair, which looked like someone had knitted it, not quite brown, not quite blonde, not quite grey, the colour of swept-up dust. He thought about the way her hair would feel if he touched it, like a scouring pad; how it would give way as his fingers went into it, and then spring back, but slowly. 'Salaam alaikum,' he had her say. And then he gave her worse teeth than in real life, her gums receding when she smiled. It made him feel a tiny bit better.

'Suit yourself,' the real Miss Waterman-Patterson said, from the other side of his eyelids.

Miss Waterman-Patterson walked Craig, God, El Jaw and Grace Hill back across the playground with their lunch trays in silence, a line of ashamed ducklings behind an exasperated mother. Outside the canteen, Buddleia was sitting on a bench, Noodle to her left, Amelia Brink to her right, like a reality TV star with her entourage, or a medieval queen at court.

Craig stared at Noodle, who stared back. What had he done, to make Noodle so angry? What *was* it?

•

Reflective self-development lasted until three. Everyone had to roleplay different scenarios, which would encourage broader understandings and reunderstandings and the sharing of perspectives. Then, everyone had to submit a written statement proving that the experience would lead to reflective self-development, and Amelia Brink asked lots of questions about what she should put in her written statement, and how long it should be, and whether she'd be able to submit it for her coursework, which Mrs. Flores said she almost certainly wouldn't be able to, but would check. There was an extra person at reflective self-development, a man no one had ever seen before called Dr. Braveman, who was there as a representative of the unitary authority, and sat at the back of the room making lots of notes. Every now and then, Mrs. Flores would walk in and out, and whisper things to Dr. Braveman, who would smile and say nothing. Craig stared at his tablet, wondering what to write; no one else seemed to be stuck for ideas like he was. It was difficult, because he was usually given a list of key points to make whenever he had to write anything. How could he know what was right and what was wrong? In the end, he didn't write much at all, and made sure not to mention anyone else by name, which seemed like the safest option.

Then Dr. Braveman stood up, and walked to the front of the classroom. 'Does anyone here know what Moodulate is?' he asked.

Amelia Brink raised her hand. 'It's an app,' she said. 'For people with bulimia. And to help you if you're thinking about self-harming and stuff.'

'That's one of its applications, yes,' said Dr. Braveman. 'But Moodulate can help you with much more than that.' And then, he turned around, and started demonstrating how Moodulate worked on the interactive whiteboard. Then everyone had to download Moodulate onto their phones, and type in a special code so that Dr. Braveman could access their user data, which he explained would help the unitary authority to develop its anti-bullying strategy. Craig looked at the screen, which was asking him to pick a word which best described how he was feeling.

yaass
owningit
omg
yikes
grr
bleurgh
sadness
meh

'Don't overthink it,' Dr. Braveman said. 'There are no wrong answers. Just be honest with yourself.'

'Can I pick more than one?' Amelia Brink asked.

'You can pick as many as you like,' replied Dr. Braveman, with a smile.

So Craig picked *meh*. It turned out that he wasn't just being honest with himself, but with everyone else in the room as well, because then Dr. Braveman loaded everyone's answers onto the interactive whiteboard in a word cloud, a giant *meh* at its centre.

'Very good,' said Dr. Braveman, studying the word cloud, his chin cupped in his hand. 'This is excellent.' Then he turned around, and asked: 'So, now you've all seen this, can anyone tell me when Moodulate might be able to help you?'

'If you're feeling marginalised?' Amelia Brink suggested. 'I mean, like people aren't listening to you when you have a problem?'

'Yes, but not just that,' said Dr. Braveman. After a long silence, he held his hands up in mid-air, for emphasis. 'It can help you at any time. *Any*. That's the point of it. You can use it whenever you need.'

Craig scrolled up and down on his phone, but the words only jiggled around a bit; he had to pick a mood to get back to his home screen. He looked at the word cloud, and the tiny *owningit* at its edge, and tried as hard as he could not to wonder who the fuck felt like they were owning it, and what the fuck they were owning.

•

And then his parents arrived. 'Shit's getting real,' said God under his breath, as he passed Craig in the corridor.

'My son,' said Craig's mum, 'has been stabbed. At *your* school.'

'I understand,' said Mrs. Flores. 'But what he *did* —'

'No no,' Craig's mum interrupted. 'My son — has been stabbed — at *your* school.'

Craig felt quite sorry for Mrs. Flores, who was trying her best to interrupt as his mother fired 'welfare' and 'physical assault' and 'consequences' across the office at Mrs. Flores, like poison-tipped darts. After half a minute, Mrs. Flores gave up, letting the tirade wash over her, which Craig could sympathise with. Finally, when his mum stopped for breath, Mrs. Flores reached for her tablet.

'There's something I think you ought to be aware of,' she

said, and handed it to Craig's dad.

'FREEDOM FROM HOMOSEXUALITY,' said the tablet, 'IS CLOSER THAN YOU THINK.'

Craig sat in the itchy chair, watching his parents' sails deflate of all wind. 'And this one,' said Mrs. Flores, leaning forward to tap the next link. Craig shut his eyes.

So they've got it all, then, he thought, the whole profile, every last prank, downloaded and archived. 'Come on then princess,' said the tablet. 'Show me your titties.'

'From the school's perspective,' Mrs. Flores said, 'we're way beyond pastoral care, here. *Way* beyond.'

Craig had a horrible feeling he was going to cry. He could feel the rage emanating from his mother and father in the seats beside him, thrumming with a dangerous energy, two miniature power stations about to blow. He looked at his dad, and then looked down instantly, because he'd never seen that expression on his dad's face before.

'You'll be aware that there are usually options around Feeling Focused Therapy and inclusion classes,' Mrs. Flores said, taking the tablet back from Craig's dad. 'But those are off the table, in this case.'

Craig started to cry.

'Don't bloody snivel,' his dad snapped. 'And sit up straight, for God's sake.'

Mrs. Flores stood up. 'I'm sorry to have to do this,' she said, 'but we really have no choice. I've — contacted the anti-social behaviour unit, because — well, there are some questions that Craig is going to have to answer.' And as Mrs. Flores walked across to the door, Craig's dad took his mother's hand, and Craig realised that his mum was crying, too, and he hadn't been able to hear it over his own sobs.

'It's okay, Carla,' his dad said. 'Just let them do their job.'

'I — I don't want —' his mum stammered.

'I know,' said his dad.

Constable Hudson didn't look like the kind of person who wanted to talk about reflective self-development. He was scary, mainly because he didn't blink, or look at anyone other than Craig. He also called Craig 'Mr. Rupple,' which no one had ever done before. He explained to Craig that the anti-social behaviour process was entirely separate from the school's disciplinary process, and that Craig should bear that in mind. His role, he said, was not confined to the Early Intervention Panel; the panel was only preliminary, meaning that further measures might follow. He stressed the word 'measures', and left a pause after it.

'Okay,' Craig said.

Then Constable Hudson started to ask questions. He asked Craig about his relationship with Mr. Brewster. It took Craig a few seconds to realise he was talking about God, who suddenly sounded a lot less powerful as Mr. Brewster. Craig said they were friends. He asked about Ms. Masood, and the Crackling Bacon NuHome Scent, and whether Craig put it in her desk, and Craig said he did. He asked whether Craig had ever used school technology to hack into other pupils' phones, or tablets, or Fabble accounts, and Craig said he had. Then, he asked how many times, and Craig said 'a few'. He asked how many times a few was, and Craig said he didn't know. So then, he asked Craig to estimate. Five? Ten? A hundred? Craig must have some idea.

'A lot,' said Craig.

Constable Hudson wrote something down in his notepad, something much longer than 'a lot'. Then he asked about the Transgender Bludfaerie, and the gay conversion therapy. He asked about the girl with hydrocephalus whose Fabble profile Craig and God hacked so it claimed that she was the regional director of Mensa. He asked about the Disciple of Hell and the basketball hoop, and the boy in the year above with mild cerebral palsy whose surname had been changed to 'Spacker' on the school register. He asked about the supply teacher Mr. Beame, whose laptop had been seized by the Child Safeguarding Authority on an anonymous tip-off which turned out to be malicious. It went on and on, and it was terrifyingly methodical, following the timeline of Craig's Trollr profile, video by video.

Then, he asked about a whole bunch of things that Craig had nothing to do with, or didn't even know about. He asked whether Craig had been involved with Grace Cliverton's Fabble uploads, which, he reminded Craig, were indecent footage of a minor, and therefore illegal. Craig said he hadn't. He then asked about Peter Ukwuoma, who'd shattered his kneecap when he fell down the stairs outside Music And The Auditory Arts. Craig had completely forgotten about that, and said that he hadn't even been there at the time, which was true. Then, the constable asked about the minor outbreak of food poisoning three months ago, which led to the school canteen being inspected by the Food Standards Agency. Craig said he had nothing to do with it. He wanted to throw up.

Next, Constable Hudson asked Craig what a messiah was, and why he and Mr. Brewster kept talking about messiahs, and Craig realised that the constable had been reading their texts, and felt even sicker. So Craig explained about Trollr status, about minnows and maestros and messiahs and metatrollrs, all of which seemed to make the constable even angrier. He leant forward in his chair.

'You're many things, Mr. Rupple,' he said, 'but you are *not* a messiah.'

After more silent note-taking, Constable Hudson read three paragraphs out to Craig, slowly and clearly, which told him about his rights, and who would and wouldn't be able to access his case file, and what he could expect to happen next; the words moved indifferently around Craig's ears, a shoal of grammar swimming between rocks. Mrs. Flores had to read the paragraphs, and agree that she'd understood them, and Craig's mum and dad had to do the same, and Ivana Applethwaite too, which took forever. Constable Hudson then shook everyone by the hand, apart from Craig, who got a solemn nod of the head, and told Craig's parents he'd see them tomorrow. Then he left.

Craig wouldn't be coming back to school. That was how it was phrased. The implication was that no one — especially not Craig — should dare to ask whether that decision was permanent or temporary, so Craig assumed it was permanent. His mother said that she was too upset to speak — which obviously wasn't true, as she had, after all, managed to say it — and his white-knuckled father said he had nothing to add, and Craig was sent out into the corridor to wait on the blue seating, next to a thirsty cheese plant. He stared at the wall, which had a poster of a teenage girl with her head in her hands, so she looked as though she was about to cry.

> Don't ignore the early signs of self-harm
> Join our campaign to #nipitinthebud
> @moodulate

It was weird to think that it was his last day at Lady Patience, and there was no one else to share it with. He almost felt sorry for himself. After a minute, the door opened, and he was asked to come back in. His mum's make-up had run all down the sides of her face, making her look like a rainy window.

'Now,' Mrs. Flores said to him, 'I need to ask you whether there's anyone you'd like to name as a peer mentor. Anyone we can put down as supporting you? Of your friends, I mean.' She turned to his parents. 'Just for the pastoral side of it,' she said.

But Craig couldn't think of anyone. God and El Jaw were out of the question; presumably, they were going to be permanently excluded from Lady Patience, too. And he could hardly say Buddleia, not anymore. He was about to check the list of contacts on his phone, but then it dawned on him that he didn't really have any other friends.

'No,' he said.

'All right. Well,' said Mrs. Flores to Craig's mum, 'you've got my email, and you know where I am.'

His mum looked tearfully into his dad's eyes, and then at Mrs. Flores. 'Do you mind if we say a prayer?' she asked.

Mrs. Flores's lip curled, involuntarily. 'Do you think — I mean — if you think it would help?'

'I do,' said his mum. And his dad nodded.

'Fine,' Mrs. Flores said.

So Craig's mother asked the Good Lord to provide guidance, and to shepherd the Rupple family through these darkest of times, and to help Craig and the people whose lives he'd made an utter, utter misery, even though he knew better, and to help us, Carla and Michael, to love our son as well as we can in the circumstances, and everyone said 'amen', except for Mrs. Flores, who said 'thank you' instead, and Craig, who said nothing.

'Thank you,' said his dad, 'for being so understanding.' He shook Mrs. Flores by the hand, and she puckered her mouth in sympathy. So Mrs. Flores, the woman his father used to call 'that pinko head teacher', was now his ally. Then, he turned to Craig, and barked 'car.' Craig went to walk through the double doors out into the playground beyond, but his dad yelled at him that he should let his mother go first, which was apparently a rule he should have known, even though it had never been mentioned before.

They drove home, the car buried deep in a snowdrift of silence. With each silent roundabout and silent junction, silent red and amber lights turning a silent green, the ball of dread in his chest knotted tighter and tighter, twisting his organs inwards, closing up like a fist. He really wanted to text God, although he wasn't sure what he'd say: something between 'u ok?' and 'go fuck urself'. God would get away with it, one way or another, as he always did, and Craig would be the one left with a criminal record and parents who hated him. It was so unfair.

'Why don't either of you care what the Muslims did to me?' he asked the backs of his parents' heads.

'For God's sake, Craig,' said his father.

'No, I mean it. You're always going on about how they're ruining this country, how they won't be happy until they get to make all the decisions. And all I did was fight back, and what you're doing is —'

His dad did an emergency brake in the middle of the road, jolting Craig out of his sentence, the seatbelt chafing on his shoulder. He wrenched up the handbrake, parking the car in the middle of the traffic, and turned around. He was baring his teeth.

'You made a false report to the Child Safeguarding Authority,' he said, slowly. 'You changed a disabled child's name to *Spacker* on the school database. You humiliated a girl with a birth defect. All for that bloody Troll website —'

'Trollr,' said Craig.

'I don't *care*. This has nothing, *nothing*, to do with the Muslims.' His father was staring, his body entirely still. It went beyond anger, beyond disappointment: it was betrayal.

Craig could feel his eyes heating up. 'But they're still —' he started.

'You've been taking drugs. We've told you a hundred times about the dangers of drugs, and you've been taking drugs. You gave drugs to a boy without telling him. You *damn* near came close to poisoning someone. You're lucky he didn't die.'

'He already had drugs, I just swapped them over. I didn't poison —'

'You pushed a boy over and broke his bloody kneecap. You do realise that if your mother or I had done that when we were at school, we'd have been sent to a young offenders' institute? You do realise that, don't you?'

'I actually *didn't*,' said Craig, 'he just fell, it wasn't me. Why are you —'

'I don't believe you. How am I supposed to believe anything you say? What are your mother and I expected to think? You've turned into a criminal.'

'You're the ones who are always saying we should do something, and then when —'

'SHUT THE FUCK UP!' screamed his mother. 'JUST SHUT THE FUCK UP!'

No one spoke. Behind them, an elderly woman in a little yellow hatchback had been waiting for them to move off, her indicator winking patiently. After a moment, she must have decided that they were lost, and drove carefully around them, raising her crabby hand in a 'thank you', the tight curls of her hair flaring white in the headlights.

Craig had never heard his mother swear before, except for one time when she said the word 'crap', and then apologised. He wondered which of the universe's rules might be broken next. Perhaps gravity would stop working, and the car would detach from the road and float up into the atmosphere. Perhaps there would be an unscheduled solar eclipse.

•

The next day, as promised, Constable Hudson arrived at Craig's house. He was shown in to the front room, where Craig's mother had laid out biscuits on plates; her house was now a house where snacks came with crockery, indicative of other changes happening beneath the surface, a new regime implementing order on its restive citizens.

'I'm going to be honest with you,' said Constable Hudson. 'In my view, in an ideal world, we'd be talking about pressing charges, now. And that's probably what would've happened five years ago, before they brought in the Early Intervention Panels. As I say, if I had my way — but that's how it is. You've been lucky. Very, very lucky. If this had all happened a year later, you'd have been too old to qualify for the panel, and then — well. It's really saved your bacon.'

Craig looked at him.

'A poor choice of words,' said Constable Hudson. 'It's made your life a lot easier, is what I meant.'

So, no charges were going to be brought. Craig was given a Social Responsibility Contract, which had a number of terms. His father attached it to the fridge.

Craig would be going to church with his parents, at least three times a week, as part of a series of measures to deal with his behaviour. He didn't put up a fight. He went, and listened to the readings and the sermons, and shook hands with strangers so that peace would be with them. Everyone in the congregation knew what had happened. None of them said anything, but their eyes had dirty twinkles, and their voices had nosy, sympathetic edges. Peace be with you; and also with you. From what I've heard, you'll need it. The Brothers and Sisters of God in Harmony were going to take him under their copious, collective wing; as if the private hell of his family weren't enough, Craig was going to be smothered by Evanglican feathers. He'd never done anything as boring in his life as sit through the services of the Brothers and Sisters of God in Harmony. It went beyond punishment. He couldn't work out what sins his fellow churchgoers must have committed, to put themselves through it willingly.

As well as going to church, he'd attend counselling sessions with Pastor Colin — when did Pastor Colin become a counsellor? he wondered — who'd then liaise with Craig's parents, as well as with Constable Hudson. The sessions with Pastor Colin took place in the front room, which was turning into Craig's personal office; he had bleak thoughts about putting his name on a brass plaque on the door. Pastor Colin asked him lots of open questions in his soft, low repentance voice, and made Craig pray to God, silently. Dear God: fuck you, you two-faced twat.

He wasn't allowed out on his own, under any circumstances. Every Wednesday morning, he'd go to the GP with a parent — to be determined — where he'd give a urine sample, to test for drugs and alcohol; and every Wednesday afternoon, he'd meet with Constable Hudson, who'd assess his progress, and who had the right to impose further conditions, if and when he saw fit. And he wouldn't have access to a phone, or to the internet. They may as well cut off my feet, Craig thought.

In the interests of providing him with what Constable Hudson called 'continuity of education', the Lady Patience Okadigbo Inclusive Partnership Academy agreed that Craig would still be entered for his exams. However, it was felt best by all concerned that he should sit them off-site; his presence on the school grounds could be disruptive to the other students. So, Constable Hudson would arrange for Craig to take his exams by himself, in a small room at the Barratt Centre, where the local social services department was based, under the constable's supervision. Craig began to wonder if he'd wake up one day to find an addition to the contract: perhaps he'd no longer be able to take a crap without Constable Hudson sitting on the edge of the bath to oversee the process. Every night, Craig would have to be tucked into bed by Constable Hudson, who'd sing him the special lights-out song; failure to comply would result in further sanctions. In the meantime, his parents had to make sure he worked to the curriculum, so he was ready for exams. In other words, he was still at school, but they were his teachers.

He was fucked.

There was no point trying to talk to them. They were immersing themselves in the Social Responsibility Contract, expressing their fury clause by clause. His father only spoke to him in one- or two-word sentences; his mother wasn't speaking to him at all. It was such hypocrisy. Suddenly, he, their only son, was the only person in the world who'd ever done anything wrong. Never mind that he'd been called 'whiteboy' and 'Anglo' and 'gringo' and 'pasty' day after day. Apparently, that didn't matter. No one else was having to praise Jesus three or more times a week; no one else was having to live without the internet or a phone. Why should he be singled out? It wasn't right.

Thor was a six-month holiday from reality; and now, God was gone, and Buddleia was gone, and he was all alone. There was no point blaming Trollr. He'd done it to himself, all to become a messiah, whatever that meant. He should never have listened to God, telling him he had balls, telling him not to be a chicken rapist, not to be a ladyboy, shaping and reshaping him in his warm, clever palms.

In the darkness, Craig walked out onto the landing, trying to make his footsteps inaudible, and looked up at the loft hatch.

Fuck it, he thought, and went back to bed.

THE QUICK BROWN FOX

In the head teacher's office, Noodle's father was acting like he knew all along that this would happen someday, and was doing his bit to represent Noodle's interests, halfway between a dad and a lawyer. For some reason, his main concern seemed to be money.

'And how in the hell am I going to *get* him to the counselling sessions?' he boomed. 'Drive him myself, I suppose: more petrol. It's just more, more, more with you people. It's too much. It's money I don't have.'

'With respect,' said Mrs. Flores, 'let me state once again that the sessions are —'

'No,' his dad went on, 'no more stating once again. If *you're* going to make him see a counsellor, then *you're* agreeing to pay for it. I'm not going to listen to any more of your nonsense. You put him in this situation, with these ridiculous — boys — and where are their families? Where are their parents? Do you see *my* boy making people eat Bibles? Let *me* tell *you*. I am a widower. I am a single parent. I am working full time. I am buying the food, cooking the food, washing and ironing the clothes. And do you see my boys behaving like this?'

'I take your point, Mr. Mateen,' Mrs. Flores said, 'but Rahman still —'

'*He*,' said Noodle's dad, pointing for emphasis, 'does not need counselling. You think he needs counselling? Half of your students can't decide if they're boys or girls! And you think *he* needs counselling?'

'It's part of our policy,' she said, sounding unconvinced.

'Then change your policy,' Noodle's dad concluded.

'Mr. Mateen. I can see that you're angry —'

'You're damn bloody right I'm angry. I will not have my boy blamed for this.'

'We're — we're not blaming Rahman for anything. It's a complex situation,' she said.

'Then make it less complex. Pay for the petrol. If you're going to make him go to some bloody awful counsellor, pay for the petrol. And don't expect me to be dropping everything in the middle of the day to ferry him around all over the place. You break it, you buy it.'

Noodle was surprised. He hadn't expected his father to stick up for him; it was always other people's parents who were appalled, and mentioned the school's so-called reputation, and the legal advice they were seeking, and used the phrase 'cross community' as a threat.

Mrs. Flores sighed, and typed something. 'I'll do my best,' she said.

'Your best?' he snorted. 'Is that what you were doing when these boys were running around with their Bibles and their — Trollr?'

'We can't be everywhere, Mr. Mateen.'

'Why not?' he said. '*I* have to be.'

'What happened with Rahman,' Mrs. Flores said carefully, 'was extremely unfortunate. But — please, just let me say this. Please.'

And Noodle's dad sat down, and folded his arms, like a sceptical parole board officer in front of a burglar who'd found God.

'Rahman was a victim of bullying, yes. I accept that it happened on my watch, yes. But the video has been taken offline —'

'As far as you know.'

'As — we — as — yes, all right: as far as we know. But

there's no reason for this to become — acrimonious. The individuals involved have been permanently excluded. Look, we are weeks, *weeks* from the exams. I would strongly urge you not to do anything which would harm Rahman's chances.' And she turned to Noodle for backup.

'I don't care,' Noodle said. He was enjoying this new version of his father, respawned with an undepleted energy bar and a full magazine of ammo.

'So you want me to send him back into this — bloody —'

Noodle's father paused, searching for the correct word.

'Dump! To sit his exams? And what? Hope this doesn't all happen again? You have *no* control, woman. Even on the way in, I see girls wearing makeup, I see boys with tattoos all the way up their arms, I see —'

'Please don't address me as *woman*, Mr. Mateen. I am a head teacher. There's no need to bring gender into this.'

'Fine,' Noodle's dad said. 'You have no control, *person*.'

Mrs. Flores slumped down in her chair, and put her hand over her eyes. Suddenly, her shoulders started wobbling up and down, and Noodle realised she was crying.

'I don't know what I'm going to do,' she whispered.

And then, Noodle's father surprised him once again. He turned to Noodle, and winked. 'I understand,' he said, his voice a little softer, his tone a little gentler. 'Maybe I can suggest something.'

•

The next day, Noodle's father made a Big Decision. He phoned in the middle of lunch to announce that a Big Decision had been made, but that he didn't want to say what it was over the phone, and that Noodle would find out soon. The thin layer of rage which was usually draped over his father had lifted; he almost sounded cheerful. Noodle spent the afternoon speculating. His dad had made Big Decisions before — he was going to retrain as a lawyer; they were going to move to the Midlands; he was going to build a conservatory onto the back of the house — and they all ended up buried under an avalanche of failure. Noodle decided not to take it too seriously, whatever it was; hopefully, it wouldn't need him to do anything.

He'd developed the habit of leaving school later and later, principally to annoy his dad. But the Big Decision was so Big that his dad didn't seem to care; he was more interested in building up the suspense. Tarek was getting the bus home by himself, he explained, and they'd be driving a different route back. And so they set off into the traffic, a smile sat on his dad's face like a friendly alien who'd been dropped, unsuspecting, onto the surface of a hostile planet, gazing at the acidic fauna and the steaming sinkholes with wide, benign eyes. At the Holding Hands With The Future monument, his dad took a left, and started to drive more cautiously, crawling past each junction, studying the road names, stacking impatient cars up behind. They went past a parade of shops, with a brightly lit dentist's surgery and a vaping store and a Sikh Community Outreach Centre; then past some playing fields that Noodle had never seen before, and a Vietnamese restaurant surrounded on all sides by its own car park, topped off with a colossal pagoda roof, red lanterns dangling above the sliding glass doors. Finally, they turned down a newly tarmacked road which ran along the edge of the sea, where the air stank of low tide. His dad pulled up abruptly at the side of the road, and switched off the engine. He turned to Noodle.

'I have a surprise,' he said.

Diagonal parking is not a surprise, thought Noodle. He looked at his dad, and then out of the window. And then he worked out what was happening.

Noodle would be attending the Liaqat Khan Bhatia Madrasa

And Centre For Community Excellence. He knew about Liaqat Khan Bhatia; Ibrahim had a cousin there, and the kids at Lady Patience sometimes mentioned it, although never by its real name. They called it the Quick Brown Fox, which is what the Martyrs of Albion called it when they were petitioning to stop it getting built, because its name used every letter of the alphabet at least once, even though it didn't; or they called it the Pakiversity, because the Pakistanis outnumbered all the other students, even though they didn't; or they called it the Megamosque, because it was the largest Muslim school in Europe, which Ibrahim said wasn't true, and never had been. It was all very sudden. For a start, it was spring, when Noodle was supposed to be exam-ready, and no one changed schools in spring. But, in their infancy, his dad's Big Decisions never had downsides. It was an act of heroism, as though he'd pulled Noodle out of the wreckage of a burning car, and was modestly retelling the story to a local news channel. Noodle would have two more days at Lady Patience, and pick up his new uniform on Saturday morning, and start classes on the Monday, and everything was going to be fine. Apparently, his dad cared much more about schooling than he'd been letting on.

'And no more of that bloody Lady Patience with the trans fairy blood bollocks,' he announced, triumphantly. And with that, his father's semi-professional anger vanished. Everything was resolved.

Noodle was pissed off. He hadn't even been consulted; and now there was going to be a last-minute one-hundred-and-eighty-degree handbrake turn in his education, which would almost certainly mean even more revision. Plus, it was an all boys' school — would that make him more likely to get a girlfriend, or less? Presumably less. And what about Ibrahim? He was the first proper friend Noodle had ever had. It was Ibrahim who'd taught him what black hat hacking was, and the basics of nineties-style breakdancing, and how to do parcours on the railing outside Global Englishes, and forwarded him 3D porn, and shown him how to route around the anti-plagiarism filter so he could submit essays downloaded from homeworkskank.com without being caught; and it was Ibrahim's dad who dropped Noodle back home after Sports And Sporting Activities in his BMW, which growled when he accelerated, and let Noodle sit in the front seat. Now, Ibrahim would be all the way over on the other side of the city, and Noodle would never get to see him.

But a much bigger part of him was delighted. He hated Lady Patience. It was a shithole, from the smell of painted-over smoke to the drafty Jenga of Portakabins which passed for classrooms; a damp, dark, poky shithole, the all-rounder of shitholes. He looked out of the car window at the grounds of Liaqat Khan Bhatia, which a shaft of sunset had helpfully bathed in gold and yellow, an oasis of calm shimmering in the grainy desert of the city beyond. He said nothing; he wasn't ready to show gratitude, not yet. But, irritatingly, not even silence could deflate his dad, who patted him on the knee — a first — and beamed at him. 'It's the right thing to do,' he said. 'You'll see.'

It turned out that Noodle's dad was a better negotiator than Noodle ever imagined. Up against the threat of legal action, Mrs. Flores contacted the head of Liaqat Khan Bhatia, and, by the sound of it, begged them to take Noodle at the last minute. And Noodle's father miraculously dropped all his objections to organised religion, and conveniently forgot who wrecked his beloved homeland. Exams were the only events that mattered, and Noodle was going to medal.

So Noodle said goodbye to Ibrahim, who pretended not to care, which meant that Noodle had to pretend not to care either. On Noodle's last day, Ibrahim sulked; but then he got over it, and shook Noodle's hand and hugged him, and suggested that Noodle should come round for dinner with his parents, who had so far been off-limits, like plants which had to be kept out of direct sunlight. They agreed that they'd text one another — but not every day, because that was gay — and that they'd meet up at the weekends, and still send one another links to Blackfl.ag videos, and to porn, but only if it was good porn. Then, he said goodbye to Buddleia Mbatha and Amelia Brink, who'd started being nice to him since International Women's Day, and to Grace Hill, who cried. He didn't say goodbye to the Straight Pride Latinitos or the Pill Heads or the Transgender Bludfaeries or the Porn Stars, or any of the tribes to which he'd never belonged. He was free of the Disciples of Hell and their aluminium manacles, free of the memory of Thor and God, Heil Hitlering behind him when the teachers weren't looking. His last day at Lady Patience was the first day in months that he could remember leaving on time.

And as quickly as Rahman became Noodle, Noodle became Rahman. As he walked out of the school gate, he vowed to himself that he'd never respond to that word again, ever. If anyone even offered him noodles, he'd punch them in the fucking throat.

•

At Liaqat Khan Bhatia, Rahman wasn't a curiosity anymore. It shouldn't have come as a shock, but it did. His brown skin, rather than being interesting, was normal; it was the white kids — a few English, a few Albanian and Kosovar — who stuck out. On his first day, he learnt that there was even another Rahman in his year group, so he was Rahman M., rather than just Rahman. He was unremarkable, compared to the kids who'd recently arrived from Eritrea and Nigeria and Libya and Syria and Egypt, squeezed out by war, or hope, or both, bringing outlandish tales of courage and despair, which they'd tell, either solemnly and quietly, or loudly, complete with comedy accents. Rahman was just another someone, his outside brown, his inside hopelessly, overwhelmingly, irreversibly white, the colour of the avenues and crescents of England's eventless south coast, where there were no wars or famines or outbreaks or coups. Not even white: colourless. He didn't know how to feel about being one of many, rather than one of few. It was like losing a superpower, but gaining an army.

All of his lessons at Liaqat Khan Bhatia had different names: geography was just geography, history just history, English just English. And either Rahman knew the correct terms or he didn't; rather than having differently valid opinions, or alternative narrative analyses, the teachers had facts. If Rahman's facts didn't match theirs, he was simply wrong. It was terrifying, especially because everyone else seemed so used to it.

'Lots of English words actually come from Urdu,' said Mr. Hadid, in English. 'Like *thug*.'

Rahman put his hand up. 'Isn't that racist?' he asked. 'To talk about Urdu and thugs at the same time?'

'No,' said Mr. Hadid. And that was that.

Other things were different, too. Rahman could tell when it was class and when it was break time, just from the level of background noise. The other boys were worrying about their grades, and their parents' reactions to their grades, and had favourite subjects — not based on how lenient the teachers were, or how many classes they could get away with skipping, but on what they were good at. They even showed signs of pride in the school: when the white kids from Linda Spinks called them 'bhatty boys' on Fabble, they bothered to come up with stinging comebacks about Linda Spinks, rather than just laughing along with them about how shit their school was. Even though he'd only be there for half a term, Rahman was given an initial report card, to identify areas of academic strength and weakness; and his dad, instead of just snorting 'propaganda' at it, read it slowly, digesting it subject by subject, making notes on his ancient laptop, tapping at the keys with his index fingers.

It almost seemed a little too quiet, as though there had to be some scandal heading the way of Liaqat Khan Bhatia that was late arriving. The boys Rahman sat next to never broke any rules, and spoke so little that he only knew their names from the register. But then, he realised that was normal. More than normal: good. It was how school was supposed to be. Teachers weren't supposed to ask if you were all right five times a day. You weren't supposed to worry about the number of friendly faces around you, in case of an incoming barrage of thrinted missiles. You weren't supposed to practise parcours. You were supposed to be focusing on your schoolwork, and your grades. It dawned on him that he might actually be quite clever, in an environment where that possibility could be explored.

On the second day of his second week, at lunchtime, Rahman got a text.

ibrahim › me
y r u not textin

It was unfair. He hadn't been texting Ibrahim, but Ibrahim hadn't been texting him either. And Rahman's teachers weren't like the teachers at Lady Patience. They didn't coax the pupils into obedience; they required obedience, and it was forthcoming. If Rahman started texting in class, there would be consequences.

ibrahim › me
r u 2 gd 4 us @ lady pateince now ur @ madrasa

He knew that if he didn't answer right away, he never would; but he had to study, anyway, not goof around watching the 3D porn and Blackfl.ag videos that Ibrahim sent him. He ignored the text, and forgot about it. Then, just before he had to go back into class, he got a final message:

ibrahim › me
prick

Brotherhood didn't last long, then, he thought. He looked out at the sea. It was high tide, and the sun was bouncing off the grey hills in the distance, turning them silver. Away from the deeper currents, the water at the shore was lighter, stiller; all along the concrete seafront he could see clumps of dirty seafoam, a creamy yellow, a toxic shampoo, lapping up and down. He thought about all of the tiny particles in the water, each one the same as the next, a nation of sea. Suddenly, Ibrahim seemed very far away.

•

'Right, then!' said Noah, who was wearing his usual lumberjack shirt. 'How's it going, Noodle my man?'
'It's Rahman, now,' said Rahman.
'New school, new name, eh? *Nice*.' And Noah gave Rahman a conspiratorial wink, like Rahman had just told him he was banging a movie star. 'Hokey dokey,' Noah said. 'Early Intervention, meeting three. Let's *nail* this bad boy.'
'How many more of these do we have to do?' Rahman asked, trying not to sound too impatient.
'Number three's the third and final, my man. Return of the Jedi, Return of the King. I mean, as long as I can say we've ticked all these boxes, you know?'
'Okay,' Rahman said.
'Brill,' said Noah, navigating somewhere on his tablet. 'Bril-

liant, brilliant stuff. So.' He looked up. 'Tell me about this place. Culture shock, right?'

'It's not that bad,' Rahman said. It would be better, he thought, if he didn't have special meetings with victim counsellors in staff-only rooms. He was already conspicuous, turning up at the last minute, taking exams the other boys weren't; he didn't need another neon sign hanging over his head.

'Looks pretty sweet to me,' Noah said. '*Massive* playing fields, m'I right?'

'Massive.'

'Yeah, we didn't have those in my day,' Noah said. 'Back in the dark age of dial-up.'

Rahman didn't say anything.

'Bit soon to have made any friends, I'm guessing?'

'A bit,' said Rahman. Then, he realised that *making friends* was probably one of the boxes which Noah needed to tick, so he added, 'but I've got a couple. I mean, in class.'

'Perfick,' Noah said, and typed. 'Still in touch with Ibrahim?'

'Yeah,' Rahman lied.

'Perfick perfick,' said Noah, and typed some more. 'How's your dad? Same old?'

'He's fine,' said Rahman.

'Just fine?'

'Yeah, he's good. Really good.'

Noah let the tablet rest on his lap, and leant forward. 'Happy to have you out of Lady Patience, m'I right?'

'Something like that,' Rahman said. A giant hypocrite for suddenly falling in love with a faith school: that was a type of 'happy to have me out of Lady Patience', Rahman thought.

'All righty,' Noah said. 'All righty in Blighty. Still using Moodulate?'

'Sort of,' Rahman said.

'Gotcha,' said Noah, picking his tablet back up again, and

swiping to a different page. 'Got — cha. One sec.' He pushed his glasses to the top of his nose. 'Right,' he said. 'I'm gonna lay it on the line for you, mate. There *is* — one outstanding concern. That's the wrong word. Issue.'

'Okay,' said Rahman.

Noah breathed in, and then held his breath for a few seconds as he decided what to say. 'Here's the thing,' he said, finally. 'I — just wanna be sure that you're in a position to defend yourself. If something like that happens again, d'you know what I mean? It's like — I mean — I don't think it's *gonna*, but if it did.'

'You mean if someone videos me eating bits of a Bible and puts it on Trollr again?' Rahman asked. It didn't seem likely at Liaqat Khan Bhatia.

'Well, not — that, necessarily. Just, you know. Look mate, I've got a box here that says *assertiveness*, and I wanna put a tick in it for you, d'you get me?'

A thought occurred to Rahman, one he'd never had before: he was a case, one case among many. Noah did this all day, trolling from school to school, to interview kid after kid. In some database, there was a folder with Rahman's name on it, which probably had the Trollr video in it, too. Maybe it would never be deleted; maybe he'd be unassertive for the rest of all time.

'How about if I told you to fuck off?' Rahman said.

And before they both laughed at his assertiveness, there was an awkward, empty half-second when all the air rushed up to the top of the room, and Rahman could imagine himself kneeling down in front of Noah, the way adults did to children when they were about to cry.

•

Rahman had a class called Islamic Studies: five whole hours a week, just learning about Islam. It was a world away from Interfaith Studies with Miss Waterman-Patterson, where they had to debate whether or not the popularity of the Taj Mahal was a sustainable example of faith-tourism, or watch presentations on the interactive whiteboard about the sociological origins of the Pastafarian movement, or find points of cultural commonality between the world faith groups that Miss Waterman-Patterson randomly selected using her home-made Wheel Of Faithtune board. 'Now spin that wheel! Protestants! And spin it again... Hindus! Ready, and... *go!*'

It seemed so pointless. Lady Patience didn't teach Islamic Studies, so Rahman was the only one in the class who wouldn't have to sit the exam; he was only there because he had nowhere else to be. But, for some reason, he cared. There was a whole vocabulary he hadn't learnt, and it made him look stupid. The other boys could define words that Rahman couldn't even spell, words like 'hejira' and 'hadith' and 'adhan', and Rahman was supposed to sit there silently, just like he sat silently at the edge of the assembly hall as the other boys prayed, pretending he knew what was going on. Only a few miles down the road from Lady Patience, the kids at Liaqat Khan Bhatia had been absorbing all this stuff for years, while he'd been learning about the history of ethical diversity and finger-painting his emotions onto his tablet. It was embarrassing.

Mr. Ayoob, the Islamic Studies teacher, looked up at the class. He had an expression on his face which Rahman recognised, the look that teachers got when they were about to make him discuss things with the person next to him, and then present his ideas to the class.

'Someone tell me what makes you a Muslim,' he said. 'No need for hands up. Just shout out.'

If Rahman had been asked that question at Lady Patience, he'd know what to say — being Muslim was a dialectically established narrative — but he had a feeling that wasn't quite right anymore.

'Community,' he said, tentatively.

Mr. Ayoob paused. 'What do you mean?' he asked.

Rahman faltered. It was like someone had asked him what legs were.

'For example,' said Mr. Ayoob, looking at Rahman, 'is England a community?'

'Not really,' Rahman said. 'It's lots of different communities put together.'

'All right then. Which communities?' Mr. Ayoob asked.

'Like, Muslim is a community, the Muslim community, and then there are — other ones. Like Christian people. And London.' It was coming out all muddled, mainly because it was so basic that it *couldn't* be explained. How could Mr. Ayoob, a teacher, not know this?

Mr. Ayoob appealed to the other side of the classroom. 'Why wouldn't we call the whole of England a community?'

'Because people in England come from different places,' said Suleyman Qureishi, from behind Rahman.

Mr. Ayoob pointed over Rahman's head at Suleyman. 'Good,' he said, 'but let's be more specific. We can say it's about — not community, but what?'

Silence.

'Could we say background?' he asked.

'Do you mean, like Bangladeshi?' said Suleyman.

'Good! So we could say background. Could we even say identity?'

'Yes?' said Suleyman. He didn't sound too sure.

'Yes, we could,' said Mr. Ayoob. He turned to the whiteboard, and wrote IDENTITY; then, he stood to the side, so everyone could copy it down onto their tablets.

'But anyone can be a Muslim,' said Suleyman, after a pause.

'Ah! Now that's interesting, isn't it?' said Mr. Ayoob. 'You're right; anyone can be a Muslim. But in England, most Muslims are — what?'

'Socioculturally marginalised?' Rahman suggested.

'Asian,' said Suleyman.

Mr. Ayoob didn't say anything, but instead went back to the board. (MINORITY), he wrote, underneath IDENTITY.

Rahman was all out of ideas. He was sure he'd been saying the same as Suleyman, more or less. It was impossible; every answer he could give would just create another question. He wrote down (MINORITY).

'What else?' said Mr. Ayoob. 'What else does it mean, to be Muslim?'

'Belief in Allah and his prophet Muhammad, alayhi s-salaam,' said Suleyman.

'Okay,' said Mr. Ayoob, 'but let's make that more general, because it's believing in more than that, isn't it? It's believing in the Qur'an and the Hadith and the Sharia, too. We believe lots of things, don't we? So we could just say *belief*.' He went back to the board, and wrote BELIEF next to IDENTITY.

Rahman knew that Muslims had to believe certain things. But if you wrote 'belief' in an assignment for Miss Waterman-Patterson, she would underline it, and write 'Really?' or 'What do you mean?' or 'Culture(s)?' or 'Not necessarily!' or 'Careful!' or 'This is problematic!' in the margin. He was the only boy in the class who'd be examined on Interfaith Studies, so he was the only one who had to understand dialectically established narratives; it had always sounded like bollocks to Rahman, but it was obviously teachable bollocks, which made it hard to distinguish from, say, algebra. But now, in class, the chances of guesswork providing him with the correct answer were vanishingly small. There were no magic words: 'cross-community' and 'wave-based' would get him nowhere.

'So, it's more than one thing, isn't it?' Mr. Ayoob said, finally, standing back to look at the board. 'We could say that we're Muslims not just because of who we *are*,' — he underlined IDENTITY — 'but what we *believe*, too.' And then he drew a line below BELIEF, for symmetry.

It got Rahman thinking: not about being a Muslim, but about being non-white. Somehow, that was different from not being white, which was the absence of a thing, rather than a thing itself. Maybe that's why God and El Jaw had picked on him in the first place: because of what he was, not what he wasn't. Maybe that's why his dad hadn't said anything to Mr. Naseem that afternoon, on the front door step. Maybe the intersectional analysis of communities and faith groups was bullshit, and it was actually all just the colour of his skin. It might explain a lot.

And maybe, if he untangled all the words and laid them out in front of him so they made sense, other things would become possible. Maybe he'd be able to stop thinking about Thor all the time, even though he never saw him anymore. Maybe he wouldn't feel so angry.

He wrote BELIEF on his tablet, next to IDENTITY, and drew a circle around the two words, labelling it MUSLIM, as Mr. Ayoob had done. He still wasn't sure it was true, but it was pleasingly symmetrical, and something he could understand, for once.

•

Rahman was trying to sleep, but it wasn't working. Every time he drifted off, his thoughts circled back to the same thing: the snake in the tank, and whether it could get out, and what would happen if it did. It was horrible to think that he was sharing a city with a snake, which might be slithering out of its cell and along the gutters towards him at any moment. Then he started thinking about earthworms, and eels, and electric eels, and centipedes, and any other long animal which had the ability to creep; and then, how near they might be to his bed, and whether he'd even know it. Grace Hill once told him that he was never more than two metres from a rat, even if he was on a plane. Surely, that figure could be halved, for something as small as a worm?

He got up, and went downstairs to get a glass of juice. Maybe, he said to himself, he was thinking too much. Maybe the dreams about the snake tank would go away, eventually. Maybe it was what Arianna Clarke would call a natural part of his development.

FIRE

Craig didn't have to remind himself to make it to eighteen, anymore; it had gone from a helpful mantra to an all-consuming philosophy.

As his Social Responsibility Contract demanded, he took his exams at the Barratt Centre, with Constable Hudson sitting across the table from him, glancing up from his casework occasionally, to stop Craig copying answers from a non-existent neighbour. The staff at the Barratt Centre smiled coolly at him, and called him 'Mr. Rupple', which he guessed Constable Hudson had told them to. The exams were nightmarishly complex, mostly because he hadn't bothered reading Lady Patience's revision guides, which his parents had forwarded to his schoolwork-only, police-supervised email account, in messages with barbed titles. *All the stuff you've missed since last month. What you would have done in Geography. Maths (do not ignore). Read if you actually care about passing English.* And so on. He'd forgotten half of the terms he needed to know, and the others seemed hopelessly vague, describing everything and nothing all at once. He couldn't even check the answers online afterwards, or talk to anyone else about what they'd written; he tapped *submit* at the end of each paper, and his mistakes swivelled off into the wiring. Success didn't seem likely.

He failed exactly half of his subjects. Of the exams he didn't fail, he only just scraped through; and they were the useless ones, the modern languages and the arts, the subjects which wouldn't even get him unpaid work. His parents almost seemed happy. His performance had demonstrated some deep truth about him which they'd known for some time, but hadn't been able to prove.

'Well, maybe that's the best you were ever going to do,' said his mother. 'Of course, if you'd revised —' And the sentence tailed off.

'Hmph,' his father added. 'It's a good job you didn't have quadratic equations to solve, like your mother and I did. I can only imagine —' And his dad looked at his mum for approval, his own verdict dutifully following hers into the sad silence of judgement.

He didn't have anything to say back to them. Any conversation dredged up God and Trollr and Peter fucking Ukwuoma, and then his dad yelled, and his mum cried. No one from Lady Patience was going to arrange any re-sits; the school only agreed to enter him for exams under duress. So that was that. He'd failed, totally and irreversibly. He'd have to live at home forever, with his parents and their well-sharpened sorrow, trudging to church and back, his youth eating itself one sermon at a time. He had no idea how to get what his dad called a 'traditional job'. How could anyone make money without the internet? Not that Trollr ever earned him anything; but he and God used to hack apps from other kids' smartphones, and sell them on at bargain prices on aarr-me-hearties, which at least kept them in weed money. His parents' suggestions weren't much help. He couldn't do gardening for the neighbours, because none of their gardens had any grass or flowerbeds, only decking and water features. He couldn't work in a bookshop like his dad did when he was seventeen, because there weren't any.

One by one, the parties interested in his case — the welfare officers, the state guardians — had lost interest, demoting themselves to stakeholders, which meant they'd be informed of his outcomes by email, and could do something better with their afternoons than pretending that his future could still be plucked from its plughole-vortex. Constable Hudson had nothing to say, other than to talk about what would have been done in his day, to which Craig's dad would answer that the constable's day was far more lenient than it should have been, and that, in *his* day, there was none of this wishy-washy PC nonsense about anti-social behaviour, the two men trying to out-grandpa one another over the marble-topped coffee table.

So Craig sat in front of the family desktop, and started to apply for jobs — three per day, as his contract required, a number conjured from some recess of Constable Hudson's mind. He focused on the positives, which is what Pastor Colin had encouraged him to do, and got his parents to order an e-book called 'Making money in the post-social network', which told him that he needed to build his brand continuity when applying for positions, and that success was picking himself up one time more than he'd fallen down. There were jobs to be had — tutoring South Korean schoolkids in conversational English over Fabble, 'no knowledge of grammar required'; cold-calling pensioners, to sell them eFraud insurance — but none he'd ever get, not with eight Es and eight Fs. And the constable could, in theory, examine his applications, so he couldn't even get away with lying.

Rejection after rejection plopped into his inbox, with every company from the smallest cottage industry to the most heartless multinational thanking him for his interest, but unfortunately declining to progress with his application at this time. Craig asked himself what he had to lose, and decided that the answer was nothing. So, trading realism for ambition, he applied to be an apprentice technician for Interrobang, the people who sold microphones that claimed to make you sound seventy-five percent more trustworthy, even though he didn't meet a single one of the requirements. He applied to be a Transhuman Resources Sub-Manager for Fabble, even though the job was in Colorado

Springs and he knew nothing about sub-managing resources, human, transhuman or other. With luck, Constable Hudson would take it as a sign of a new, go-getting attitude, and leave Craig alone, which was probably the best that he could hope for.

Until everything changed, when God burned down the school.

•

Craig's dad put his head around the bedroom door. 'You need to come downstairs,' he said.

'Okay,' said Craig. He was trying not to use question words with his parents: 'what' and 'why', in particular, tended to start fights. He pulled on a t-shirt and a pair of jogging bottoms, and went down into the living room, rubbing his eyes. His mum was sat on the armchair, rather than the sofa, which meant news. He looked at the TV: and there was a blackened, windowless Performing Arts And Self-Expression block, the roof which Craig once scaled now mossless, licks of dead flame around the edges where the gutters used to be. The news channel had scrambled its helicopter; as the camera gained height, he could see where the fire had spread through the school, block by block. Between Biology and Global Englishes, a small cluster of luminous dots walked back and forth between fire engines, stepping over the red hoses snaking across the playground.

'— started in the performing arts department,' the TV was saying, 'and moved out in a north-westerly direction, helped by unusually high wind speeds, leaving building after building charred beyond recognition. Lady Patience Okadigbo has been mired in controversy in recent months, ever since the unitary authority hinted that its inclusive partnership academy contract might not be renewed. But this is the first incident where an inclusive partnership —'

So it was definitely an act of God, Craig thought. He could picture God running a line of petrol along the auditorium seating, trailing it down the carpet of the central corridor, circling the whole building with characteristic attention to detail, a ritual sacrifice, and finally watching his creation from on high, probably from a roof, and seeing that it was good. But it made no sense. It was an overreaction, even by God's standards. And why now, when he'd already been excluded? What was the point?

Craig's dad had a newspaper, because the print media was the last bastion of something or other in this godforsaken country. 'Here,' he said, passing it to Craig. 'I went to the corner shop.'

Craig took the paper. Immediately, one word jumped out at him from the middle of the second column of text: Trollr. His eyes screwed up tight, all by themselves. He dared to re-open them.

> have named Dylan Brewster as a person of interest, although not yet a suspect. Brewster, whose whereabouts are described as unknown, was permanently excluded from the Academy after posting abusive videos of other students on the controversial website Trollr, including racially and religiously motivated bullying. Police say their investigation will focus on whether the attack was intended to target a specific member or members of staff, and

There was no mention of Craig, and nothing else about Trollr. He started again at the top of the page, re-reading the article word by word, his heart dropping down through his body like a pebble thrown into a pond.

And there, on the TV, was Mrs. Flores, flanked by the school's governors, who themselves were flanked by police officers. She was using her assembly voice, which was like Pastor Colin's sermon voice, only much, much louder, and talking about her deep pride, her deep regret, her deep sadness, swimming further and further into deeper and deeper emotions, away from the oxygen at the surface.

'That woman has some stamina,' his dad said.

Craig's mother sat forward, and smoothed down the front of her dressing gown. 'Well. It's a good job we got you out of there, then,' she said, as though Craig's parents had decided to withdraw him from Lady Patience when they realised it was failing to live up to their meticulous standards. 'Before you got burnt to a crisp.' She picked up her coffee mug, and walked out to the kitchen.

'Was it that Brewster lad, then?' his dad asked.

Craig looked at the TV. Parents had gathered at the edge of the cordoned-off area, bringing their children with them as props. It's just not what you expect, not here. No idea what we're going to do. Nothing from the council, nothing from anyone. Absolutely devastated, devastated. Except that the children didn't look devastated at all; they looked like they were about to go on a day trip, to somewhere sunny and fun.

'I don't know,' Craig said. 'Maybe.'

And his dad turned around, and looked at Craig over the back of the sofa.

'Yes,' said Craig.

'Jesus.'

And then Dr. Braveman appeared on the TV screen, his hands clasped behind his back. 'I can't answer that specifically,' he said, 'because this is all under investigation, and I'm sure you wouldn't ask me to pre-empt the results of that investigation. But what I can definitely tell you is that we are one hundred and ten percent focused on —'

'Well, that's today out,' Craig's dad said, turning off the television. 'Put some proper clothes on. That prick of a copper will be paying us a visit, mark my bloody words. About as much use as a condom machine in a nunnery, that one.'

•

The biscuits were laid out on their plates, ready for inspection. But Craig had to wait in his bedroom, because Constable Hudson needed to talk to Mr. and Mrs. Rupple first, without Craig present. Eventually, after ten minutes of sitting on his bed, staring at the wallpaper and wondering what people used to do before phones, he was summoned downstairs.

'First things first,' Constable Hudson said, and opened his notebook.

He asked Craig if he knew where Mr. Brewster was, and Craig said he didn't. Then, he asked if Mr. Brewster had made any attempt to contact Craig, and Craig asked him how anyone could contact him when his parents had confiscated his phone. Then Constable Hudson pointed out that Mr. Brewster might have tried to contact him on social media, and Craig had to remind him that they'd taken away his tablet, too, and wondered exactly which carrier pigeon Constable Hudson thought was delivering secret messages to Craig's bedroom window. The constable asked whether Mr. Brewster had ever mentioned burning down the school, or attacking the school's premises in any other way, or its staff, or instigating any other acts of violence, and Craig said no, not that he could remember. Then, Constable Hudson said that it would be extremely helpful if Craig had any suggestions as regards Mr. Brewster's current whereabouts in terms of his location at the present time, even if Craig didn't definitely know for certain; and Craig said that God never even told him where he lived, so he couldn't really say where God would hide if he were on the run from the police.

'As you may know,' the constable said, 'Mr. Brewster has been named as a person of interest in relation to this incident, so it's imperative that you do let myself know if he tries to contact you.'

'I know,' said Craig.

Then the constable closed his notebook, and turned to Craig's parents.

'As I was saying before,' he said, 'in my judgement, your son fell into the path of what I would call a sociopath, or certainly a young man with what I would call sociopathic tendencies.'

'Really,' Craig's mum said. It wasn't a question.

'So I would urge you to be vigilant as regards your family domicile, and anyone approaching you, and just to keep an eye out for anything untoward,' he added.

'Isn't that *your* job?' Craig's mum asked.

Constable Hudson looked at her blankly.

'To keep an eye out for anything untoward? I thought that's why we paid tax: so *you* did that.'

'It is,' he said, slowly. 'I'm simply suggesting —'

'I understand what you're suggesting,' she interrupted.

The constable hesitated. 'Good,' he said, eventually. 'So let's turn to the matter of the Social Responsibility Contract.'

Astonishingly, Constable Hudson changed his mind about Craig's results, which he suddenly made a point of examining, certificate by certificate, with duly impressed facial expressions. He'd been sure, he said, that Craig was going to fail them all, so sure that he'd have laid money on it, had he been a betting man, which he wasn't, and neither should Craig be. However, Craig had done well, and should be very proud of himself. Here, the constable looked at Craig's parents for reinforcement, and got a modest amount. Constable Hudson had been around the block a few times, he went on, and most lads in Craig's situation ended up with a pile of crap, if the Rupples would pardon Constable Hudson's French. So Craig had really turned a corner. The constable then said that the words 'turned a corner' would be appearing in his summary of the meeting; then, he wrote something in his notebook, which was presumably the words 'turned a corner'. Craig began to suspect that the constable didn't understand the grading system as well as he thought he did. It was sad, really, that none of them realised how fucked he was, in the academic and professional senses. He didn't have the heart to tell them. He was protecting his parents, in an odd sort of way, by not explaining to them how meaningless his so-called passes were. It was his gift to them.

To Craig's further surprise, his Social Responsibility Contract was going to be amended to reflect his eight gallant Fs and eight triumphant Es. His meetings with the constable would be fortnightly, not weekly, and he wouldn't have to supply urine samples anymore; the church attendances were scaled back too, to Sunday services only. And Craig would finally be allowed to use the internet again. Before he got too excited, Constable Hudson said, his internet usage would be supervised, because there was a need to keep a close eye on his online activity, and Constable Hudson had already had a long chat with Craig's parents about which internet-enabled devices he could and couldn't use. Unfortunately, limited resources meant that the constable wouldn't be able to monitor Craig himself, although in an ideal world, the constable said, that would be the best option. So it would be Craig's father, under the constable's guidance, who was in charge of watching over his internet use; and the constable had every faith that Craig's father would be more than able to prevent him from lapsing into his old ways.

To prove that he would be more than able, Craig's dad folded his arms, and raised a single, stern eyebrow, and leant back in the armchair. Constable Hudson had shown him how to use a special app which would record the websites Craig was looking at, even if he used a different device within the house, his dad said, because it worked on something called IP addresses. He said 'IP addresses' as though he'd recited a Russian tongue twister; he looked so proud. Craig felt like he should congratulate him.

He had to control his face. His dad was in charge of monitoring his internet access. His dad, who said that he didn't trust the cloud, even though it was the cloud which regulated the Rupples' central heating. His dad, who still plugged the printer in with a wire. His dad, who had CDs. The only obstacle between Craig and his freedom was his father's technological prowess. He had to be careful: he couldn't look too happy, as he didn't want Constable Hudson working out how much his dad had exaggerated his abilities; nor could he look too miserable, or they'd all return to the favourite topic of conversation, which was how lucky Craig was, and how different things would be if various people had their way. So he tried to stay deadpan, staring at the constable's tie. Suddenly, the idea of escaping from his parents' house didn't seem so outlandish.

'So,' said the constable. 'Your mother has something to give you.'

And Craig's mother disappeared into the hall for a few seconds, and retrieved his phone and his tablet from wherever she'd been hiding them, and gave them back to him ceremonially, her fingers momentarily reluctant to unclench.

After rattling through the usual paragraphs and getting the usual signatures, Constable Hudson handed Craig a leaflet on the Phoenix Programme, and told him that it had been helpful for some wayward young men, and might be able to stop Craig falling back into bad habits, although he might want to ignore the bits about achieving positivity through social media, given his circumstances. Craig couldn't remember what wayward meant, but took the leaflet anyway. Then the constable shook Craig's hand, and called him 'Craig' rather than 'Mr. Rupple', to mark his re-entry into society.

'I'll be in touch,' said Constable Hudson, standing up.

'Don't feel you have to be,' said Craig's mum, and flashed him the smile she usually reserved for receptionists.

Both the tablet and the phone were out of battery, and Craig had to wait as they charged back up, which seemed to take twice as long as the forever it usually took. His first instinct was to text God: but then, when he finally got into the messages pane, he looked at the list of unanswered texts, and wondered if there was any point; then he imagined Constable Hudson asking him what he'd intended to achieve by contacting Mr. Brewster, and scribbling down Craig's inadequate answer in his stupid little notebook. Nope, he thought, not this time. So instead, he swiped away the weeks of messages and updates, scouring the guilt from his phone, freeing its memory up for newer, happier megabytes. As he did, his news feed flashed up trending fire after trending fire: a blast at a fireworks factory in Vietnam; a bush fire prowling around the outskirts of Melbourne, finally leaping into the suburbs, killing eight. There were streaming pictures of uncooperatively chipper Australians offering one another camp beds and second hand clothing, setting up firebreaks and pooling their childcare while the networks hunted for signs of looting. The police suspected arson and were already looking for culprits, even as the nearby hills still crackled.

'Happy?' his dad asked.

'Yeah,' said Craig. And his dad grunted, and went back to reading the newspaper.

Craig went upstairs, logged on to the Brothers and Sisters of God in Harmony's website, and navigated to their Bible study section. Then, he went into his tablet's settings, and restarted his parents' router remotely, Flakhaking the identifying features of the Bible study page onto an incognito browser tab. He set up his usual proxies, jumping his connection from Thailand to Argentina, from Argentina on to Iceland, masking his user credentials and crossing his fingers for good measure. He didn't have God's technological omnipotence, but he could at least remember the basics. He contemplated sneaking out onto the landing to get his stash of loft weed, but it felt like pushing his luck. It had probably gone off, anyway.

With no phone and no tablet, he'd had no way to hook up with girls for months; without even thinking about it, he was navigating to JerkShuffle, the reassuring chessboard of unknown females dangling in front of him, mesmerising in its beauty. He'd forgotten how addictive it was, watching the estimated connection time dropping down second by second, waiting to see who he got. It didn't matter. She could be old, or fat, or frigid — for all he cared, she wouldn't even have to get her tits out. Nor even speak English. He was happy to let Fabble translate; he wasn't a racist, after all. It felt wonderful, to have it all back, like the first drop of rain after a great drought, the coolness of the water absorbed so lovingly by the baked, baked earth.

Time for some Bible study, he thought, undoing his flies.

•

And the next day, someone burned down Linda Spinks Secondary. It wasn't as successful — only maths, and some of the science blocks — but that didn't matter to the local news channel, because once was a crime, and twice a crime wave, and crime waves trumped crimes. Then, the Martyrs of Albion accused the Islamists of doing it, as revenge for the Islamophobic videos on Trollr, and that was a news cycle in itself.

So *was* it God, then? wondered Craig. He felt like a bit of a shit; even if God was technically a sociopath, Craig could have waited for some evidence. It was, of course, possible that God was on a spree, moving across the city by night with jerry cans of petrol and a balaclava; but that was a stretch, even for God, a little bit too much like organisation.

'Whole country's gone mad,' Craig's dad said. 'Mad.'

The Rupples sat in the lounge, in front of the forty inch television which Craig's mum had tried to stop his dad buying, watching the rolling news, which was left on twelve hours a day so no one would miss the latest instalment of the world's descent into pandemonium. To protect the schools which were yet to be torched, the local branch of Students Against Fascism formed human chains around them, and declared them to be safe spaces; then, the Martyrs of Albion accused Students Against Fascism of restricting access to schools, and discriminating against Christians, which Craig's mum said was almost certainly the case, and was despicable, even though she seemed delighted about it. So Students Against Fascism sent activists from across the south coast to the Quick Brown Fox and the Holmcroft Teaching And Learning Institute; and then, when the vloggers and TV crews turned up to film them decanting from their buses, the activists declared that the media were untrustworthy, and started covering their faces; and then, the Martyrs of Albion arrived, because someone had to protect the good people of England from the useful idiots of communism, if the police wouldn't; and then, the police were sent in, to separate the useful idiots of communism from the forces of nativist xenophobia, and it kept on going, consequence after consequence, reaction after reaction, until everyone was refusing to comment because no one knew what to do.

Finally, after three days of that, someone was arrested at the port of Dover, and charged with arson. The police wouldn't say who it was, and said nothing about Dylan Brewster.

And then Craig *really* felt like a shit.

'I'm telling you,' his dad said, through a mouthful of macaroni cheese. 'Usual suspects. Why do you think they're not naming names?'

Unbelievable, thought Craig. When he'd needed his dad's reliable rush to judgement, he got nothing; and then, at the exact moment it no longer mattered, the Muslims *were* to blame. 'How do you know?' he asked. 'They haven't named him. He could be anyone.'

'Bloody hell,' his dad said, dropping his fork. 'After everything you put us through with that school, and now you're —'

'Enough,' said Craig's mum. 'We're not going down that road.' And his parents spent the rest of dinner giving one another weird looks.

So Craig decided to spend less time downstairs. He was getting sick of listening to politicians interrupting one another in terse, shouty battles, and people fighting about who could and could not draw a stripe of coloured marker pen under their eyes to show that they were on the side of the schoolchildren being denied an education, and journalists talking about the same bits of recycled footage, dialling the rhetoric up and up with each repeat, and debates about cordons and peace walls and facial coverings and who may or may not have attempted to bomb Students Against Fascism's head office, and his mum and dad stamping around the house saying how appalling everything was, and how everything was falling apart. He decided to watch cartoons, instead.

•

Pastor Colin was a new man. He could have predicted all of it years ago. He was like a kid who'd discovered where his parents kept the sugar, and was secretly shovelling it into his face with a dessert spoon while the babysitter watched TV in the lounge. He walked up the two steps leading to the altar, and turned to face the congregation.

'All I see is outrage,' Pastor Colin declared. 'From the masked student — to the Martyr of Albion — from the newsreader's desk — to the school gate — outrage!' And then there was an arse-shiftingly long silence before he roared, 'OUTRAGE!'

It was a lot more theatrical than normal, and even Craig, who only just passed History And Reunderstanding, could tell he was copying Martin Luther King, and must have been practising for hours. The delivery was exactly the same, from the quavering heights to the thundering depths, to the great, swelling, God-filled pauses; Craig could imagine Ms. Burton lip-synching along with closed eyes. On the altar, a purple cloth was draped over something small, which meant that the pastor was gearing up to use a visual aid, like the time he gave a sermon on moral compasses and revealed an ancient satnav halfway through, the wires dangling down through the fingers of his upturned palm.

The pastor walked from one side of the raised platform to the other, and back again, his hands cupped behind his back. 'I see fury in our streets,' he said. 'I see rage in the eyes of strangers. I see pain — pain in the hearts of my brothers and sisters, pain where there should be love.'

It might have worked better, thought Craig, with an American congregation, which might have been readier to gasp, or cry 'no!' and 'no Sir!' in the gaps, like they did in films. Out of the corner of his eye, he saw his dad slump forward in his seat, pinching the bridge of his nose.

'The lost sheep,' the pastor said, '*deserves* — to be lost. The prodigal son *deserves* — to be turned away from his father's door. The traveller *deserves* — to lie beaten and naked at the side of the road. And I have the *right* to forgo the lost sheep, to turn away the prodigal son, to cross over the road. *I*,' he said, thumping his chest with his fist, 'have a right. *My* right.' And he gave his chest another thump. 'What *I* want. *Me*.' For a second, the pastor paced from side to side, and it looked like he might have lost his train of thought, until he swivelled on his heel, and shouted, 'MY OUTRAGE!'

The sun passed behind a cloud, thinning the light drifting down onto the pews. Someone behind Craig coughed, briefly denting the tension.

'We have forgotten the *we*,' Pastor Colin declared, switching to his softer voice, the voice of the thoughtful philosopher, the tender moderate to subdue the guerrilla of his own creation. 'We have forgotten the flock to which that sheep belongs. We have forgotten the family which raised that son, the town through which that traveller was passing when he fell, broken, at the side of that road.'

Craig looked across at his mum. She was praying, her hands pressed together, her neck stretching upward.

'Brothers and sisters, we must rediscover that *we*. We must lift — up — our — eyes.' And then, he walked to the altar, pulling away the purple cloth to reveal a phone. Here it comes, Craig thought. The pastor turned, and held the phone outwards for the congregation to see, its innocent grid of icons facing out into the nave. 'And it is this,' he said, 'from which we must lift them.'

'Yes,' a woman's voice said, quietly. 'Yes.'

'Our children,' the pastor went on, 'our children have lost their sight. Their eyes, their eyes are cast downwards.'

'Yes,' the woman repeated, louder, 'that's right.'

'And we must lift them up. We must divert their eyes to the heavens, we must take these devices from their hands —'

'Yes!' Except this time, it was Craig's mother, her widened eyes fixed on a point above the pastor's head, a smile growing across her face.

'— and help them to see — once — again,' the pastor said. 'For this is *nothing*,' he proclaimed, thrusting the phone upwards, 'but a factory for outrage, a farm for fury, nothing but despair and falsehood, a shackle and a cell. Yes, a cell.' He turned his head to the side. 'Even the word itself: a cell phone. A *cell* — phone.'

The pastor left a moment of silence for wisdom to float down through the air. And then Craig realised that the pastor was looking at him.

'In this very room,' Pastor Colin said, 'sit young men and women whose eyes have been pulled down from the heavens, pulled down into the darkness. Whose futures, whose very futures —'

Craig stood up. 'Excuse me,' he whispered to the woman beside him, 'can I —?' And then, squeezing past her, he made his way along the edge of the nave to the gents.

'— souls have been caged in these cells, whose —'

Closing the main doors behind him softly, Craig stood for a moment in the foyer, and wondered if he'd lost his soul. It wasn't something he'd ever considered in detail; he wasn't really convinced that anyone even had a soul in the first place. Five minutes, he told himself; a shit takes five minutes. That would be enough time for the pastor to get back to the battle between I and we. He let himself into the small toilet, with its black spores of mould growing up the baby-boy-blue skirting boards, and sat down on the lopsided seat. He was about to pull out his phone, which was what he always did on the toilet. There were still updates downloading, still queues of backlogged videos to watch or delete; even though he'd had no choice, he felt guilty about the weeks his phone spent unattended, like a pet he'd forgotten to feed. But then, he decided to leave it in his pocket, just in case Pastor Colin was actually right. So he sat on the toilet, watching shapes through the frosted glass, squirrels chasing one another through the trees, defending and advancing the borders of their territories, scuffle by scuffle, bite by bite, waiting for his five minutes to be up.

Even though it was a waste of water, Craig flushed the toilet for the benefit of anyone lingering outside, and went back into the foyer. On the wall opposite, there was a new poster for Straight And Narrow, with the coordinators' followme@ and Fabble addresses lined up across the bottom, in pews.

•

'We're not leaving you in the house by yourself,' Craig's father said. 'Out of the question.'

'Why not? It's a house, not a school. No one's gonna burn it down.'

'Don't get clever,' his dad said. 'You're still on probation.'

His parents decided that someone needed to do something, and if no one else did, they would. So they were going to the Community Hive, the meeting held once a month in one of the buildings off Ottawa Square, usually attended by no one but local planners and their intended victims. As they drove into Ottawa Square, there were already dozens of parked cars, and his dad had to circle around twice to find an empty bay. 'Disgraceful,' his mother muttered, looking up at the abandoned council offices leaning overhead, drifts of litter collecting in their corners. 'Look at the state of it. Absolutely disgraceful.'

Maybe, Craig thought, trying to see the positives, it was a good idea for him to go. He wasn't a Martyr of Albion, but it would be useful to know exactly which buildings were going to end up off-limits. If it spread to train stations and bus stations — so far, no one's assumption but his father's — he'd have to learn to drive. And where would he find the money for that?

The Hive wasn't what he expected. Inside, the auditorium

was already half full, bubbling with noise like a St. George's Day street party on a supermarket advert. Craig had pictured a little room with a horseshoe of desks, thinly scattered with never-to-be-eaten snacks; by the time the meeting was due to start, there were people lining up along the walls. A week and a half of bomb threats and school barricades had given everyone something to talk about, a reason to go to a Community Hive which wasn't just bitching about property developers. But it was more than that, he realised; the anger had been there much longer, tucked underneath the city like an egg beneath a bird. Before the panel was even assembled beneath the council's inexplicable whirlpool logo, there were chants and whistles; even the sound guy who crept onstage to test the microphones was slow-clapped. When the panel members finally took their seats, there was a crescendo of boos, until the chair threatened to call the whole thing off unless there was silence.

'Thank you,' he said, finally. Then: 'We're going to start with a statement from the mayor.'

'RESIGN!' someone shouted. There was a vigorous burst of applause, which went on for almost a minute; after some muttering behind hand-covered microphones, the Chief Inspector sitting to the mayor's right intervened, only to be yelled at to resign himself. And then Craig saw Grace Hill.

She was sitting beside the Chief Inspector, behind a sign which said GRAY HILL; and she had a boy's haircut, spiked at the front and sides and shaved up the back, and was wearing a skinny t-shirt which made her look way flatter-chested than Craig remembered. Without the mascara and the ratty fringe, he could see how blue her eyes were, and how wide, even with the line of marker pen underneath each eye. Thank fuck she can't see me, Craig thought; or at least he hoped she couldn't, in the glare of the lights pointing at the stage. He wondered what this new version of Grace Hill was. A second-wave hipster? A guy? That would be perfect: Grace Hill joining the patriarchy, like Kent becoming part of France.

Eventually, after more threats of cancellation, the chair managed to establish an acceptable level of uproar, over which the panel members could be heard. Then, the mayor said that there was no evidence that Islamic extremists were responsible for the arson attacks.

'Wash your face!' someone shouted.

The mayor, sporting the same red and green cheekbone-stripes as Grace Hill, wasn't going to be derailed by a heckler. 'I want to be absolutely clear about this,' he declared. 'There is a vast majority of Muslims in this country who —'

'Where?' Craig's mum asked, loudly.

Even in the light-hubbub-with-snacks scenario he'd imagined, Craig hadn't expected her to speak. Everyone turned around to look at her. Surely she'd lose her nerve?

'Where are they?' she said, her voice shaking, but still loud. 'Where is this vast majority that you keep telling us about?'

Grace Hill leant into the microphone. 'They're out defending their religious rights, is where they are,' she said. 'Do you realise what they're facing? There are people spitting on them in the street, ripping off their veils, defiling their holy scriptures —'

Craig dropped down a couple of inches in his seat.

'Bullshit!' a man yelled, from behind. 'Fake news!'

'No!' she cried. 'This is real! I can tell you the names of —'

'Don't,' the Chief Inspector said, flattening the air in front of her with the palm of his hand, 'don't let's — use anyone's names. If there are crimes taking place —'

'If?' Grace asked, turning to him, her voice incredulous. 'What do you mean, if?'

'When, or if,' he said: 'either way, nothing is going to be solved by going into individual cases. Please,' he appealed; and she slumped back, pouting.

But Craig's mum wasn't finished. 'If they don't like this country, they need to leave,' she said.

'Let's, now, let's not say things we might regret later,' the Chief Inspector said.

'I don't intend,' his mother said, 'to sit here and have a man tell me what I can and can't say. This isn't Saudi bloody Arabia yet, no matter what you or His Majesty might think.'

The room reverberated with applause: stamping feet, even, and a couple of whoops. 'Damn right!' shouted a voice, from the corner.

'Look,' said the Chief Inspector, 'what we want to do here is de-escalate the situation.'

'How d'you de-escalate arson?' the voice yelled.

'So send in the army,' said Craig's mother.

The mayor and Grace Hill both snorted at the same time, firing off another volley of boos. 'That's hardly proportionate,' said the mayor, struggling to raise his voice over the crowd.

'No-go areas?' said the man in the corner. 'In your own country? Shame on you!'

'Powerful city mayors!' shouted the man behind. 'We were told we'd get a powerful city mayor! Where's your power, mate? Where's your fucking power?'

'We are responding to all these issues,' the Chief Inspector said, flashing the mayor a guarded look. 'Including the discrimination Ms. Hill is referring to —'

'And what about the discrimination against us?' Craig's mum asked.

'My job, Madam,' said the Chief Inspector crisply, 'is to address the needs of *all* communities. If you feel you've been subject to discrimination — if *anyone* feels that — then it's my job to investigate that and to stop it. And that's what I do.'

'When?' someone yelled. In front of Craig, somebody else laughed, right from the belly, almost a shout.

The Chief Inspector ignored it. 'The bottom line,' he said, 'is that we have to follow the law. The police service can't start acting unilaterally, not when —'

'Then you're helping them, aren't you, you prick?' shouted a different voice from the back of the room.

'All I'm doing,' the Chief Inspector protested, 'is explaining the framework —'

'Absolutely pathetic,' Craig's mum cried out.

'We follow the law,' he said, firmly. 'If we're not following the law —'

'Just following orders?' shouted the voice at the back.

'— then we're acting against government policy. You must understand —'

'Like a nazi?' the voice shouted.

Grace leant forward in her seat. 'Godwin's Law,' she said. 'Fail. You lose.'

'Please,' said the chair, 'this is getting a little out of hand. Let's all take a moment to calm down — and if I could ask you to let the panellists respond, Madam — if you could allow them to answer —'

Craig's mother folded her arms, her back rigid. Craig looked at his dad, who was staring ahead with thrilled, terrified eyes.

The mayor whispered something to the Chief Inspector, who whispered something back. 'I think we can all agree,' the mayor said, 'that there are many concerns to be balanced, here.'

'You're a fucking genius, mate,' said the man at the front.

'Sir,' said the chair, 'let's just address one another civilly, shall we?'

'Why should we be civil to people who burn down schools?' Craig's mother asked. She'd missed the point; but the arms were already folded, which meant that she'd be deciding what the point was, and not some council flunkey.

'Please, Madam.'

'I've calmed down,' his mother said, with mock patience, 'as you asked, and I'm perfectly civil. I'm asking a simple question.'

'I appreciate that,' said the chair, 'but we don't want this meeting to be dominated by —'

'Patriots?' suggested the man in front.

'*I'm* a patriot,' Grace Hill said, 'and —'

'Not so much,' said Craig's dad.

'— I will never, ever let the so-called Martyrs of Albion win. We *have* to find a way to protect ourselves from this hate, from the trauma it causes. Students Against Fascism —'

'Students Against Fascism,' Craig's mum snapped, 'is nothing but an outrage factory. Manufactured outrage. What do they want? Enclaves? Different laws for different people? Ridiculous. We all have to live under the same law!'

'Which is *exactly* what you people did to the indigenous Australians!' Grace Hill yelled. 'Look at what your democracy did, look at the tyranny —'

'You're not an indigenous Australian, and neither am I,' Craig's mum interrupted. 'We cannot have — schools and God knows what else — policing themselves! Where will it take us? This is like living in a bloody war zone! And who is this *you people*, anyway? You sound remarkably English to me.'

'I'm European,' said Grace, 'not English.'

'Yeah, good luck with that,' muttered Craig's dad.

The chair rolled his eyes, and sighed. 'This tone,' he said, 'isn't getting anyone anywhere. Hives are about constructive dialogue, not shouting at one another.'

'*Thank* you,' Grace Hill said.

The chair ignored her. 'We are here,' he said, 'to try and find a common ground, a consensus position.'

The consensus position, to be put to a vote, was that all communities should have freedom of movement, but that all discrimination had to be addressed swiftly and effectively. No one voted against the motion, but no one voted for it, either; by the time the panel members agreed on the wording, no one was really listening. The audience had split into different groups: some people had left in disgust; some had restarted the slow-clapping; some were talking to one another about what to do, outdoing one another with the ferocity of their suggestions. Craig's mother was loudly dissecting the Chief Inspector and the mayor and 'that dreadful young woman', a dozen people turned round in their chairs to listen. They said 'hear, hear' when they agreed, which Craig had only heard on Fabble clips from the Parliament. The next time he looked up at the stage, the panel members were gone.

In the car, Craig's mum had unspent adrenaline. She veered from raising the voting age to jailing all the politicians, her monologue plundering English history for ammunition: Isambard Kingdom Brunel, the invention of the train, Florence Nightingale, Queens called Elizabeth, the Industrial Revolution. No thoughts were unspeakable; no potential solutions to the crisis could be disregarded. We were English, she said, not European. We were pragmatic; we were engineers, we were inventors; we could solve anything. She started to flag after a few minutes; but then, the car ran into a cordon draped across the road, where the police had created a safe space around a safe space, a level of absurdity his mother couldn't cope with, and the tirade restarted with a new vigour. Craig was trying to work out how to tell her that the dreadful young woman was, in fact, the same dreadful young woman who'd stabbed her son with a pair of compasses on International Women's Day. But then he realised that it might tip her over the edge into violence, or madness, and decided to keep it to himself.

In the driver's seat, Craig's father sat silently, listening with a cheeky half-smile. Yep, thought Craig: the world *is* going mad. His mum was a revolutionary, and his dad was her chauffeur.

AND THERE YOU HAVE IT

The summer after the exams was sweltering. Day after day, thunder rolled in off the Atlantic, snapping overhead rainlessly, drying up the grass, leaving the parks cracked and dusty, the hill overlooking the city turning a Californian yellow. Rahman sat upstairs in his pants, with the curtains drawn against the heat, surfing the internet, eating Yee-Haw All-American one-minute microwave burgers and drinking GoGo energy drinks. He used the weather as an excuse to cut off all his hair, which made him seem older, the edges of his body more distinct. He started to grow a beard, too; it came pleasingly quickly, and was wiry, a deep, night black. For a week, mirrors surprised him: he'd gone from fourteen to twenty-one, overnight. He liked it, because it made him feel taller, and like his shoulders were a little wider.

'Fucking hell, Gandalf,' said Tarek, 'what's with the beard? Are we off to join the Caliphate, now we're a big boy?'

'Piss off, coconut,' said Rahman.

'D'aww. I like it. It's cute. Do something wizardy. Summon a dragon or something.'

'Go fuck yourself with a cactus.'

Why shouldn't I have a beard? Rahman thought. Everyone else was changing. Grace was Gray; the Quick Brown Fox had a new perimeter of mask-wearing students living in yurts; Lady Patience was going to be rebuilt as an ice hockey arena. Why should he stand still, when everyone else was hurtling into the future?

'Beard,' said his dad.

'What about it?'

'Cut it off,' he said. 'Every bloody day it's on there, I'm going to say *beard* until you cut the bastard off.'

Rahman went to the bathroom and trimmed it. With luck, the noise of the clippers would get his dad's hopes up.

Just when he was starting to wonder if the beard was worth the hassle, Rahman passed all his exams, which left his dad no option but to be proud of him, and shut up about his facial hair for a day or two. The results came as a surprise; he'd expected to fail at least one. He was the only kid at Liaqat Khan Bhatia taking inclusive partnership academy exams, and all his revision had to be done without the web-based resources Lady Patience would have provided: the coaching apps, with their mnemonics; the TraceMe diagrams that could be saved as templates and copy-pasted in on the day; the downloadable lists of terms, helpfully categorised by emoji. ☹ Definitely in the exam. ☺ Probably in the exam. ☺ Only if you're unlucky!

His dad didn't take it as proof of Rahman's intelligence, but of his own foresight, a tale of one father pitted against a faceless bureaucracy, with his son demoted to a bit part. But Rahman must have been fairly intelligent, because his grades were good enough for the University of Southern Wessex — 'now among the top fifty percent of English universities' — and at least got him out of the exciting opportunities for personal growth, code for unpaid. He applied for a community representative position which he probably wouldn't get, the kind of job that would go to kids whose parents had been fluffing up their CVs for years, the kids who'd been class presidents and student volunteers and junior community heroes. He put in for a job at a thrinting company, mainly because he liked the idea of having access to a thrinter; with no Ibrahim, he didn't know anyone who owned one. Rahman didn't really care that much what he'd end up doing, and there were always ways to make money in the meantime. He could guinea-pig for a tech company testing out its security protocols; two minutes of selecting palm trees in stock photos and he'd have enough credit for a bus ride. Jobs were for people without imagination, like his dad.

But his dad had different ideas.

'What are you doing to look for a job?' he asked, over dinner: Golden Saffron MicroRice, tipped out onto the plate, still in the oblong of the plastic tray, served with herb-encrusted roasted-style potatoes, also microwaved.

'I've got a job,' Rahman said. 'I'm a security protocol consultant contractor.'

'Pff,' his dad snorted. 'The thing clicking on street signs? That's not a job. You need to be applying for real jobs, not these bloody internet social networking things.' On 'real jobs', he prodded Rahman twice in the shoulder for emphasis, one prod per word. 'I can't pay your way forever. And what are you doing up there all day, by yourself?'

'Research,' Rahman said, which was sort of true.

'Job research?'

'Yes.'

'And?' his father asked.

'I've only just started applying for stuff,' said Rahman. 'I won't hear anything for weeks.'

'Then call them. You're always carrying that bloody phone around: use it. Call them.'

'It doesn't work that way,' Rahman said.

'Then tell me how it works. Tell me how you're going to get a good, steady job.'

Rahman didn't want a good, steady job. He wanted to be a photojournalist, documenting the war in Chad, or possibly a fighter pilot, although that was looking less and less realistic, and he wasn't sure which country he'd be doing the bombing for. 'By applying,' he said, 'online. The normal way. I can't just show up at someone's office.'

'Not looking like that, you can't,' his dad muttered. 'I'd take one look and say: what's he doing with *that* all over his face? Can't his family afford to buy bloody razors?'

'Loads of Muslims my age have beards,' Rahman said. His dad couldn't argue with that; it was the truth.

'We're not Muslims. Muslims go to mosque. Anyway, look at that nice man who does the cricket on the television, Mr. Islam. His face doesn't have this bloody beard nonsense all over it. And his bloody surname is Islam, his bloody surname!'

'He needs to be aerodynamic,' said Rahman. 'I don't need to be aerodynamic.'

'You need to be slapped on the head, is what I think,' his father said. 'Bloody idiot. How are you going to find a nice girl, if you can't even get a job?'

Rahman didn't want a nice girl, either; and even if he changed his mind about that, he certainly wouldn't be going to his father for dating tips. His father, who called all women 'ladies', even though half of them were obviously nothing of the sort; his father, whom he suspected of stashing alcohol somewhere in the house, and getting rat-arsed at night, alone.

'Maybe she'll like it,' he said. 'Maybe she'll think it looks manly.'

'Maybe she'll think you're a terrorist.'

Rahman smiled. He quite liked the idea of looking like a terrorist.

•

Buddleia, Amelia, Gray and Rahman were all on a train to London, although it turned out that Solar Garden City was nowhere near London, and Gray called it London anyway to make it sound more exciting. Solar Garden City was almost halfway between London and the south coast, only forty-five minutes away, and had none of the mazes of aborted streets and gated apartment complexes and noisy construction sites which London had. He'd never heard of Solar Garden City before, so he looked it up on Fabble, which told him that it was London's largest and newest dormitory town, and had Europe's biggest arboretum. It had the highest number of public bikes per person in the country; its motto was 'Above us only sunlight', which was something to do with John Lennon, who Rahman guessed must have had something to do with solar power. He clicked 3D, and wandered around the streets for a while; all along them, solar trees had been planted, their glassy leaves feeding the homes. He tapped down Solar Garden Way, the main road which spiralled outwards from the centre. At the intersections with the other roads — Andromeda Avenue, Mercury Boulevard, Ganymede Close — there were large corner plots with turreted homes on them, each with its own three-car-wide drive, and broad grassy strips between the pavements and the kerbs. It was more like America or Australia than London, or at least what America and Australia looked like on TV.

He'd never been on a protest before, and didn't know what to expect, other than a plot of land earmarked for a mosque, and a mob of Martyrs of Albion singing 'Land Of Hope And Glory' as the bulldozers moved in. It wasn't that he was *only* going so he could admire the Martyrs of Albion, although there was something fascinating about them, especially when they had shaved heads and tattoos. He did care about the mosque, just not as much as the others seemed to.

'If they can picket a mosque, then we can picket *them*,' Gray said. 'Bunch of racist twats.'

They walked together through Solar Garden City, following Solar Garden Way clockwise, curling between vast homes with swimming pools and double garages, and sculptured gardens with bounce-safe play areas. As they came closer to the junction, Rahman saw the building site in the distance, yellow hazard signs up, ready for excavation. But then, when they finally got there, there were only two protesters, and they were both women: one young and overweight with massive breasts and huge sunglasses, holding up a placard with 'NOT IN MY NAME' scrawled across the middle; the other, elderly, wearing a tattered 'MAKE ENGLAND GREAT AGAIN' cap, repurposed for the occasion. Rahman felt let down. Usually, when the Martyrs of Albion showed up, they came in their dozens, pouring out of minibuses wearing matching polo shirts, with plastic masks strapped over their mouths. He felt stupid, in the black shirt he'd carefully picked out to look battle-ready; without the promised xenophobes, he looked like an overemployed bouncer.

'I thought you said there was a protest,' he said to Amelia. 'That's not a protest. That's not even a queue.'

'There'll be more,' Amelia said, not really looking at him.

The four of them formed a line in front of the wire fence, as planned, looking out across the empty homes, For Sale! signs hammered into the lawns, solar trees fluttering leaf-up in front of them. Behind the fence, a contractor in a hi-vis vest was walking backwards and forwards, kicking at the earth as he tapped on his mobile phone.

'Morning!' said the old woman. 'No more mosques!'

'Fuck you,' Gray said.

'Don't you speak to a lady like that,' screeched the girl. 'This is our country too!'

'Not for long,' said Gray.

'Just ignore them, darling,' said the old woman. 'No more mosques!'

'*Loads* more mosques,' Gray said. 'We're gonna put a mosque on every single corner.'

'Over our dead bodies,' said the girl.

'It'd have to be a fucking big mosque to fit over *your* dead body,' said Gray.

'What an unpleasant little — person you are,' the old woman said, raising her chin. 'Didn't your parents teach you not to swear?'

'Yeah,' the girl said. 'Have some manners.'

'This is a Christian civilisation, not some Islamic backwater,' the woman said. She'd stopped looking at Gray, and was glowering at Rahman. 'No more mosques!'

'Islam *is* civilisation,' Gray said. 'It's your precious Christianity which kills people.'

'Islam's evil,' the girl spat.

'Fascist,' said Amelia.

Buddleia touched her on the arm. 'Don't engage with it,' she said. 'There's no point. They're not intelligent enough to understand.'

'Let me assure you,' the old woman said. 'I'm long enough in the tooth to understand exactly what *you* are.'

Buddleia drew herself up to her full height. 'And what am *I*?' she asked.

'You, my dear girl,' said the woman, 'are spoilt. A spoilt little child.'

'You've got no right to judge her!' Amelia cried. 'What gives you the right to talk to her like that?'

'I'm eighty-three years old,' the woman said, 'and I am an Englishwoman. I shall say whatever I please, thank you very much.'

'I don't care what you think about me,' Buddleia said, although it sounded like she really did.

'Why do you hate women of colour?' Gray asked the woman. 'Is it because your so-called white race is dying out?'

'*You're* fuckin' white,' the girl said. 'Go look in a fuckin' mirror.'

'Try not to swear, dear,' muttered the old woman.

'Yeah, try not to swear, *dear*,' said Gray. Outside of the moment of fempathy, Rahman had never seen her like this. But it made sense; all those decapitated girls had to come from somewhere.

'Why don't you,' suggested the woman, in her best childcare voice, 'stand over there, and we can stand over here. And then we'll all be happy.'

'Oh, you'd like that, wouldn't you,' said Gray. 'Segregate the races.'

'Now you listen to me,' the woman said, suddenly animated, raising her index finger. 'I was alive when Dr. King —'

'No one cares,' Gray interrupted. 'No one cares about your stupid white history.'

'Dr. King was —'

'Stop raising your finger at me!' yelled Gray. 'I'm not a child!'

'Then stop behaving like one!' the woman yelled back. She was rearing up like an angry cat, the skin around her eyes crinkling with rage. 'I'm trying to protect you.' And she jabbed the air in front of Gray's sternum.

'Oh my God, that's literally — insane,' said Gray. 'How are you protecting me?'

The woman stood back. 'You're wearing a gay pride badge,' she said, pointing at one of the dozens of badges streaming down the lapels of Gray's coat. 'Do you really think Muslims believe in gay rights?'

'I'm bisexual,' Gray said, and then turned to Rahman, 'and he's a Muslim —'

'Yes,' interrupted the woman, 'your quiet little friend. Odd how he's letting you do all the talking, isn't it?'

'Piss off,' Rahman said. Since when was Gray bisexual?

'Do you think *he* believes in gay rights?' asked the woman.

'Of course he does,' said Gray, furiously.

'Why don't you ask him?' the woman suggested, airily. 'Go on. Ask him.'

'All right,' Gray said. 'Rahman, do you believe in gay rights?'

Rahman wasn't sure if he believed in gay rights, because he didn't know anyone gay; until a few seconds ago, he'd never even met a bisexual. The old woman was staring at him, as though she could see every part of his brain, her eyes like moons in the daylight, white behind blue, sad and triumphant.

And Rahman saw a hundred copies of his own face falling down a staircase, the words 'I care because you do' raining down after them, and a pair of eyebrows so faint they were hardly there, and purple and yellow fish gulping in a dirty tank, and a long-fingered fist in front of his naked belly, and Thor, his line of perfect white teeth in a perfect white grin. Rahman opened his mouth, and nothing came out.

'And there you have it,' the woman said.

•

Rahman was dreaming.

He dreamt that he was standing barefoot in wood chippings and hot straw, the fibres scratching the gaps between his toes. He was lifting his feet, one at a time, to brush them down, but he couldn't get them clean, and the skin on his soles was dimpled where the straw was pressing into it, making it itchy and sore. There were fish swimming slowly through the air around him, some yellow, disc-shaped, with thin faces and papery fins fanning out behind them, others small and translucent, spines glinting as they turned.

He dreamt that he was sat at the edge of the playing field at Liaqat Khan Bhatia, with Mr. Ayoob on the bench beside him. It was sunset, the last rays of light streaming through the gaps between the clouds, drowning the grass in a warm orange puddle. Mr. Ayoob was trying to explain that Rahman wasn't a Muslim, and must be something else, instead. He was insistent, and cross; he'd obviously been trying to explain it for some time. So Rahman started to draw him a diagram. But as soon as he began to write the word 'BELIEF', Mr. Ayoob suddenly got angry, and grabbed Rahman's tablet, hurling it across the playing field, yelling, 'No! No, no no! That's not right at all! You're never going to get it unless you listen!' The tablet landed face up in the grass, the first depths of the twilight above reflected in its screen. 'I'll start again,' said Mr. Ayoob, a little more patiently, doing his best to smile.

He dreamt that he was standing at the top of an empty building, looking out over a war-wrecked city. The front of it had been ripped off, the ends of the walls torn like card; the building opposite was almost destroyed, its floors collapsing onto one another. Somewhere in the cratered roads below, he'd left Ibrahim, who was screaming 'Noodle! Noodle!' from far away. But there was no way to get down to the street; all he could do was shout Ibrahim's name back, his voice reverberating, blasting the dust and grit from the walls.

He dreamt of Grace Hill. They were sitting together in History And Reunderstanding, and she was heating paperclips under the desk, trying to keep them out of Ms. Burton's line of sight. His phone was out on the desk, asking him to pick an emotion — *yaass*, *owningit*, *omg*, *yikes*, *grr*, *bleurgh*, *sadness*, *meh* — but he couldn't choose, his fingers scrolling on the screen, the words rolling up and down. Grace was smiling at him, and he couldn't work out why.

He dreamt he was holding Mr. Naseem's hand. It was plastic and glossy, its fingers hardened, slightly apart, slightly clasped, the lazy wave of dead nerves. Up close, he could see the lines on the palms and the small webs of skin between the fingers; at the wrist, where it had been severed from the arm, there were circles of meat-pink and fat-white. It was warmer than it looked; not dead but asleep.

And then, he dreamt about Interfaith Studies with Miss Waterman-Patterson. He had to give a talk about the core tenets of Judaism, standing in front of the board so that everyone could see him. As he rattled through Rosh Hashanah and Hanukah and Yom Kippur, he could see Thor licking his lips, the way the 3D porn girls did, half as a lure, half as a joke, closing and reopening his eyes in slow motion, tilting his neck, jutting out his chin, writhing a little in his seat. And then, all of a sudden, Thor was right in front of him, so close that Rahman could see the pores on the end of his nose, the layer of thick blonde fur on his forearms, the hairs curling together into knots. He had his fingers on the belt loops of Rahman's school trousers, and was tugging Rahman forwards, gently.

'Bloody FUCK!'

Rahman opened his eyes, and rolled over. It was already light, the sun pouring in through the blinds, casting fine diagonal lines of white across the wall. He stumbled to the bathroom, to brush his teeth and wash his face. He looked knackered; his eyes were bloodshot, and the skin around them was puffy and raw. He stared into the mirror, trying to work out which day of the week it was.

'Bloody fucking BASTARD!' his dad yelled, even louder. He must have stubbed his toe on something, or broken another kitchen utensil. Rahman put a t-shirt on, and went downstairs. His dad was sat in front of the old laptop, hunched forward, his eyes bulging.

'What?' said Rahman. 'What is it?'

'Look at this,' his dad said, seething.

On the screen was a middle-aged woman with pearly white teeth and a cardigan. 'Arianna Clarke', said the caption; and on the line below, 'Programme Co-ordinator, The Victim Within'. An uplifting keyboard track was playing softly in the background, positive chords in a lightly syncopated rhythm. 'There's no such thing as a bully who isn't a victim,' Arianna Clarke said, solemnly. Then, she laid an almond-shaped hand on a boy's shoulder, and the camera panned out, to show Jordan Donaghy looking peaceful and friendly, his face glowing a little, fuzzy at the edges. His skin condition was radically improved; that, or someone had edited out his spots.

'See?' his dad shouted, gleefully poking at the screen. 'It's that bloody Lady Patience boy who videoed you. Victim? Victim my bollocks!'

'I never realised,' said Jordan, doing his most convincing impression of a normal person, 'that I was really lashing out because *I* was the one who was hurting. It's just — it's so hard to talk about.'

The camera cut away to Arianna Clarke, who'd sat down opposite Jordan, and was nodding gently. 'I'm listening,' she said, as the music soared upwards.

'Bloody hell,' muttered Rahman's father.

Rahman wondered what El Jaw was getting out of his ritual humiliation. At least a Youth And Young Adult scholarship, he guessed, if not more. It had to be something big. The shot cut away to an in-school mediation session, teachers and students looking at one another with concerned expressions, still a little fuzzy-edged, still a little glowing.

'The Victim Within programme is all about seeing perpetrators for what they are,' Arianna Clarke's voice said. 'But our sessions aren't just there to help those who've become victims of their own bullying behaviour.'

And then, Jordan Donaghy again. 'What really changed things for me,' he said, 'was when I had the opportunity to sit down with —'

'AAARGH!' his dad roared, and smacked the laptop closed. Then he picked it up, ripping the power cord out, and threw it at the floor. It landed with a soft flump on the carpet, looking no more broken than usual. Rahman watched his father. It looked like he was thinking of jumping on it, or taking a hammer to it; but he was probably thinking about the cost of a new laptop at the same time, and Rahman knew which thought would win out. After a moment, he shouted, 'that bloody fucking school!', and stormed out of the room, slamming the door behind him. 'Victim!' Rahman could hear him snorting in the kitchen. 'Victim!'

Good for you, El Jaw, thought Rahman. He'd never really minded El Jaw; he didn't get to Rahman, not in the same way as God and Thor did. Maybe it was the acne. Or the braces.

Rahman sat down on the sofa, opposite the picture of his mother, her hair forever cascading over her shoulder, her face forever sympathetic to the plight of the Mateen menfolk, permasmile. He tried to locate himself in time, finally settling on Wednesday, because that was the day when his dad left late, the process of slamming cupboards and hunting for keys delayed by an hour. The day of Odin, he thought: Ms. Burton taught them the origins of the weekdays in Reunderstanding European Heritages, explaining how their names were examples of Non-Linear Reunderstanding. She made herself a Viking helmet out of papier mâché, and wore a sack-like grey dress which rolled down over her massive breasts and her baby bump, almost hitting the floor, fastened under the bump by a wide leather belt. She poured out alcohol-free mead, specially ordered, which was claggy, like cough syrup; and all the students had to design their own longboats using the vector app on their tablets, and the best design was thrinted, and put on display in the corridor outside the staff room. Each student then had to write a short passage on what it must have felt like to be a Viking: the girls had to imagine themselves as Viking warrior men, braving the North Sea in their longboats, while the boys had to consider raising children in a patriarchal society. So Rahman had to think of things to write about breastfeeding and powerlessness and child mortality, while Grace Hill drew battleaxes, colouring the edges of their blades blood-red. But he could remember thinking about battleaxes, and how cool it would be to be a Viking, and to own a battleaxe, and go pillaging with it.

Andy Thornton won the longboat contest, so Rahman's longboat was never thrinted; but he could still picture it, the scroll of wood at its prow where it parted the water, ferrying on its crew of marauders. He tried to visualise himself as a Viking, pale and red-haired, taller, broader, more muscular, with a tribe all of his own striding out across the sea, England's ripe valleys in sight.

•

Rahman pulled all of his clothing out of the wardrobe piece by piece, and spread it out across the floor, categorising by colour as he went. To the right, he put the colours that Ibrahim would wear, the blacks and greys and navy blues and olive greens; to the left were the bright colours, the dog-eared Americana t-shirts his dad picked up at car boot sales, the cartoon underpants he should have thrown out years ago, the daffodil yellows and grass greens and Superman blues of his youth. Then, he started bagging up the brightly coloured clothes, one sustain-a-bag at a time, knotting each tightly at the top, until he had half the amount of clothing he started off with. He walked to the recycling compacters at the end of the road, and posted three bulging sustain-a-bags into the clothing bank. Change A Life Today (Please: no underwear, socks or shoes). Immediately, his life felt changed. He didn't want anyone to look at him next to someone like Gray, and think — that. He wasn't a faggot; he knew that much. Faggots had high voices and wore tight trousers, like hipsters from the twenty-tens.

He walked home, and went back up to his bedroom, where his thinned-out collection of clothes was still waiting on the floor. Then, he logged on to Sleazydoesit, and deleted his account, which felt like the right thing to do. For a second, he was sad to see it go; but the internet had dozens, hundreds, thousands of ways to get him off, if he used his imagination. It was much easier than he thought it would be, and he was tempted to keep going, and get rid of the videos he'd downloaded from Thor's Trollr profile as well; but then he realised he couldn't, because that would leave him with nothing, and he wouldn't know what to do with himself.

dad › me
Fwd: BSc Computer Science
The University of Southern Wessex, the... [Read more]

dad › me
Fwd: Assistant Contracts Manager, Southern Health
Applicants should have at least two years of... [Read more]

dad › me
Fwd: Pre-Graduate Internship, Kray & Soubry Plc
A unique opportunity to start your career... [Read more]

dad › me
Fwd: Junior Client Interface Operative, MQB Industries
Are you a natural self-starter? Able to work... [Read more]

buddleia › me
Are you ok? Haven't heard from you in ages. Fabble me.

There were still no Blackfl.ag messages from Ibrahim, the small white circle of the Shahadah logo alertless in the corner of the screen. He tapped, to start a new message, but then realised he had no idea what to say. 'I'm having nightmares?' He'd sound like a girl; and he couldn't trust himself not to fall apart, garbling out the whole mess about the gay pride badge in a confused, breathless splurge. He looked at Ibrahim's friend list, a cascade of avatars, and his feed, where the links and videos piled up on top of one another: news reports and executions, shakily-filmed Imams, crowds gathered in squares, smiling daredevils dodging bombs and drone attacks, marching soldiers, their eyes fixed forward, their bodies unflinching, volleys of bullets, heads breaking like smashed fruit. Thumbnail after thumbnail stretched down into the past, until Rahman and the Bible were no more than thin layers of ancient soil in a cliff face.

He knew he ought to feel bad about Blackfl.ag; he could hear Ms. Waterman-Patterson's voice talking about Global Possession And Dispossession, explaining how today's intra-community conflict could something something something. And he did feel bad for the victims, when they were women; he had to scroll over the thumbnails quickly, because some of them were crying, which gave him a funny feeling in his gut. But it was different with the men. There was something tantalising about that landscape of kangaroo courts and wrecked buildings, where everything was the colour of dirt roads, and the sun was so high up in the sky. He could see himself in it, pointing his finger at the camera, and then to the heavens for divine backup. Maybe he'd make a good jihadi, pure of heart and devoid of mercy, with Ibrahim standing beside him, trusting him implicitly, brothers-in-arms.

Rahman lay on his bed, and thought about hanging Thor. He'd do it tenderly, slipping the noose around his neck without grazing the skin, toying with him, a cat with a bug, letting the sympathy run between his claws. He'd lean in, so close that he could feel the blindfold against his lips, and whisper to him.

'Homo,' he'd say. 'Faggot.'

And Thor would let out a muffled sound, half whimper, half question mark; and Rahman would kick him hard in the pits of his knees, and the rope would fly down after him, whooshing until it stretched taut; and then, there'd be a snapping sound, a twig breaking underfoot, wood splintering into a squelch of leaves, and he'd be gone, taking the bird's nest of blonde hair on his stupid head with him, silencing forever the roaring, startled-donkey laugh. Would Rahman peer over the edge, to see the blood? Or adopt the vigilante's pose, head held high, hands clasped behind his back?

He opened his eyes, and tried to work out if that counted as a Thor fantasy. Yes and no, he concluded. Like everything else with Thor, the answer wasn't certain.

INFORMA/MCKENZIE

The Brothers and Sisters of God in Harmony had been recognised as an At Risk Minority Ethnic Or Religious Group. All the Christians Craig shook hands with, Sunday after Sunday, went through with their threats of demographic suicide, so Craig was at risk. It was worth far more than a stack of qualifications from some dead-end inclusive partnership academy. It was job interview gold. Suddenly, he was an eligible applicant, not just for plucky little English start-ups hoping to be eaten by multinationals, but for the multinationals themselves. In the land of ethical hiring, Craig had changed from peasant to landowner, overnight. And it wasn't a rampaging Germanic god who'd liberated him, but his opposite: a kindly, forgiving, Christian god with clucking, gossipy followers, waiting to cash in their meekness for a worldly inheritance.

So after two whole hours of research, which is more time than he'd ever spent researching one particular career, he decided to be bold, as the Phoenix Programme leaflet advised. He went to Informa/McKenzie's website and tapped *Become A Partner*, scrolling down the list of religions and ethnicities and genders and subcultures and physical statuses which would get preferential treatment; and sure enough, there was 'Evanglican', right between 'Eurasian (mixed non-Turkic)' and 'Exosexual'. Required qualifications, it said, would depend on the individual; for members of endangered species, like Craig, a full complement of grades was desirable but not essential.

So he applied for a job as a tagxpert. It took him five minutes to find out exactly what he'd be tagging, which turned out to be cats, dogs and other small mammals doing funny things, data which would then be sold on to news websites and blogs. Bullet point by bullet point, he worked his way through the Diversity And Mission form, cross-checking his answers with 'Making money in the post-social network' to make sure that he was using all the correct words, replacing 'quota' with 'aim-range', swapping 'keen' for 'driven'. And, within the day, he got an automated message telling him he had a job.

Constable Hudson said it might be an administrative error, and that Craig shouldn't get his hopes up; so Craig showed him the message, and the candidate-centred induction video. The constable seemed derailed. Obviously, he'd planned a trajectory for Craig, one where he had a shelf-stacking job at SupaBuy and was grateful for it. But Informa/McKenzie had 'agreed to hire' him, as Constable Hudson put it; and in the absence of the constable's ideal world, the Social Responsibility Contract would have to be declared satisfied. That, in turn, freed Craig from the arthritic grip of the Evanglicans. His parents' friends warmly congratulated him, nodding and smiling as they pretended to understand what a tagxpert was. The pastor mentioned him, too, not in a nameless reference to 'those of us who have found ourselves cast asunder in the maelstrom,' but by name. People seemed genuinely proud. They could send him out into the bedevilled world, happy that their spiritual support had redeemed him, or whatever it was they thought they'd done.

His parents said that they were happy for him. But rumbling beneath that was a deep suspicion of Informa/McKenzie, which was international, and therefore not English, and therefore liable to overlook, exploit or otherwise mistreat their son. When Craig showed them Informa/McKenzie's website, they were cagey and monosyllabic, presumably convinced that it was a portal through which someone was hacking into the Rupples' living room, for purposes of marketing and research and data-mining and vote-rigging. He liked the idea of working for a multinational, because it was so fertile with opportunities to piss his parents off. He'd be able to wind them up with his new colleagues' provocatively foreign names, or pretend he'd become a gluten-free vegan.

He cycled to work from home, setting off at eight, climbing the hill to the Informa/McKenzie estate perched above the city, icosahedral pods which could be freed from one another and moved around as the management saw fit. The induction video said that Informa/McKenzie prided itself in investing in smaller cities, because it fostered a sense of inclusivity. The tech park was 'only a stone's throw from the heart of the community,' even though none of the senior staff would ever set foot in the suburbs, much less the heart of the community. They all lived in the villages to the north, with the duck ponds and the old red telephone boxes, or in São Paulo-style condos overlooking the sea, and drove to work in expensive electric German cars, overtaking Craig at the end of his commute as he slogged his way up the long drive through the sculpture park. By the time he'd locked his bike up, his socks would be wet with sweat, as the managers and psychologists and ontologists hopped from the cool of their cars to the cool of their offices.

Informa/McKenzie was complicated. He had a highly prestigious position, but the pay was terrible. And even though it felt like he was an employee, he wasn't; he was a creative consultant, and he had to sign a form saying he understood the difference, even though he didn't. That meant that Informa/McKenzie wasn't his employer, but his client, which felt to Craig as though it were upside-down, like someone had made a copy-paste error. He didn't have a boss, but he did have Siobhan, who was a senior creative consultant, and told him what to do. He liked Siobhan, but she wasn't anything like the people in the candidate-centred induction video: she looked tired, like she worked really hard, and she was definitely over forty, even though none of the people on Informa/McKenzie's website were over twenty five. She had her own pod, dangling high up in the canopy of trees, with 'Ms. S. Williams' thrinted on the door. Craig didn't even have his own work cube; Informa/McKenzie liked to shake things up by randomising workspaces on a sporadic basis, as they did with the floorplans of the buildings, so a work cube was a place to squat until shooed on.

Siobhan was nice about it, and told him that they were both in the same boat. But while she waded through the thoughts of a hundred million strangers, identifying cognitive patterns and conversational anomalies as she went, Craig ranked puppies according to cuteness. If they were in the same boat, she was Noah, carefully selecting the last pairs of freakish animals to be squeezed onto the Ark, deciding which to preserve and which to cast back into the waters; he was a deckhand. He tried not to dwell on it too much.

Siobhan peered at Craig's paper-thin Informa/McKenzie branded tablet. 'This one's wrong,' she said, and flipped it around, to show him. It was a video of a recently awoken kitten in the empty drum of a washing machine, which he'd tagged *Cuteness* and *Huggles*.

'Why?' he said. 'It looks cute to me.'

'It's darling,' she said. 'It has cuteness written all over it. But you need to check your stats. Kittens can't exceed eighteen percent. Anything over that, and it's onto the slush pile. People get kittened out.'

'Oh,' he said, feeling a little sorry for the kitten.

She smiled. 'Don't worry. It'll rotate back round, next month. Also, that's not really huggles. Huggles has to have humans in it. To be honest, you're not going to be using it that much.'

'Okay.'

'I know it can feel a bit pointless,' she said. 'Just think of the money.'

'It's not pointless,' Craig said, quickly. 'I'm enjoying it.'

Siobhan leant back in her chair, and smiled. 'Craig,' she said. 'They're all shits. The company's shit, Waldren's shit, the commute's shit, and it's a shitty job. There's no need to be nervous; I'm not going to turn you over to management. Trust me,' she added, 'I'll be getting the fuck out of here as soon as I can. And so should you.'

Craig didn't say anything. There was a chance she was testing him, a chance he estimated at ten to fifteen percent, now that he was surrounded by percentages.

'Seriously,' she said. 'You *need* to be looking for the next thing.'

Why was she trying to get him to look for a different job? He'd only just started. 'It's my third day,' he said.

'That's like a year, in this place. It's fucking brutal, I'm telling you. One market adjustment, and —' And she drew her finger across her neck, an assassin's knife.

'Really?' he said, thinking: but I'm an Evanglican.

'Any one of us. The whole place, if they can get a better deal on corporation tax.' She hit *Slush*, and gave him back his tablet. As his hands touched the glass, the tablet said 'Hi Craig!', and the payment counter in the top right-hand corner restarted at zero. 'Nice break?'

'Don't forget,' Siobhan said: 'hands on. One time, I lost a whole morning's pay because I was still wearing my gloves.'

'Got it,' he said. 'Hands on.'

He went back to his cube, or rather the cube he was in, making his way past the other tagxperts. Somehow, it was clear that they'd never be friends; people at Informa/McKenzie didn't seem to have friends. They had contacts and networks and resources, webs of brains to be exploited, knowledge to harvest. He looked at the clock. It was analogue, and back to front, to discourage creative consultants from checking it too often; the second hand rolled leftwards from twelve to one, sinking back into the future.

•

As soon as his first payday arrived, Craig moved out. He couldn't afford to leave the city — as a lowly tagxpert, that wouldn't happen for years — but he could at least get out of his parents' house. He hated it. He hated how thin his bedroom walls were; he hated the wooden instructions his mother had bought as decorations, DINE in the dining room, COOK in the kitchen, LOVE in the lounge, each guarded by a miniature teddy bear with a bowtie on, a stuffed fascist barking out fluffy commands. He got an apartment on Mavis Road, advertised as 'a bijou living concept', and he had to ask Fabble what 'bijou' meant. It hardly had enough room for his clothes, and the kitchenette was basically a basin; but it was in the right place, not so far east that he could smell the rubbish dump, not so far west that he'd be shelling out two-thirds of his income on rent. The block of apartments had its own kitchen-garden canteen serving fresh soups and kimchi and superfood salads, open twenty-four hours, with body-specific breakfast algorithms designed to charge the stomach up with nutrients. Mavis Road looked newly washed, compared to the browns and greys of his native habitat. He was living in a different country, fifteen minutes of city away.

It happened just in time. Ever since his mother's intervention at the Community Hive, the house was filled with new guests, some of them Martyrs of Albion, some of them fellow travellers, all of them convinced of the need to get organised, and that Craig's mum was the one who should do the organising. Behind the decade of tight-lipped 'hmph' noises she'd been making at the television, his mother had been hiding an entire political programme, a philosophy to be visited on the unsuspecting world in meticulously ordered stages. People came to the door and asked for 'Carla', rather than 'the homeowner' or 'one of your parents'; she was a regular caller on Joey Silver's Quicksilver Phone In Show, so regular that they started calling her, rather than vice versa. Craig was living in alcoves, trying to avoid getting into debates with taxi drivers who'd had it up to here and former school governors who'd been sacrificed on the altar of political correctness, who were colonising the house room by room, spreading out onto the patio and across the garden. His mum was a terrible celebrity; she didn't have the indifference for it. She stayed up until midnight washing teacups and saucers, and making lists of things to get dry-cleaned, so the house would look nice for the half of the city which now treated it as a conference centre. On the day he moved out, the apartment on Mavis Road felt like his own national park. He had whole metres to himself, enough to go for a walk in.

The day after, his dad called to say that they'd been burgled as they slept. His mother's interim conclusion was that immigrants did it, which fitted in nicely with her new hobby; she didn't seem that bothered about the stuff that was stolen.

'It's just the thought of it, Craig. When you're asleep. In your own house.'

'I know,' said Craig.

'This is why,' she said, in her Joey Silver's Quicksilver Phone In voice. 'This is why people want proper sentencing back. There's no deterrent. Even if they did get anyone for it, they'd get two weeks of community service, and be out there the next night, breaking into someone else's house.'

'I know.'

His dad, on the other hand, listed the thefts one by one, in decreasing order of value — the forty inch television, the desktop computer, the pressure washer — leaving a pause after each, for Craig to express his sympathy.

'My set of screwdrivers,' his dad said, sadly. Pause.

'That's terrible,' said Craig. They're only fucking screwdrivers, he thought.

'Yes,' said his dad, 'well. I was going to give them to you, some day, and they were actually pretty bloody expensive. But I suppose you don't care about that kind of thing anymore, what with your flashy new job.'

It wasn't fair, and they both knew it; Craig's new wage didn't allow for the buying of expensive screwdrivers. But that wasn't the point. There were obligations which he'd failed to meet, a war he hadn't been waging while he'd been gallivanting around eating superfoods, leaving his father stood alone on the battlefield, dazzled by an invisible enemy.

'What did the police say?' Craig asked.

His father snorted. 'They were useless. Basically told your mother to stop talking or they'd arrest her for racism.'

'Racism isn't a crime.'

'Not yet, it's not.'

Craig was getting bored. 'So they won't be able to arrest her for it, will they?'

His dad hung up, without saying goodbye. The war that he was fighting was in his own mind, and there were wars going on all over the world, real wars, wars in which Craig couldn't afford to pick sides. He didn't phone back.

•

'We've set aside a little more time than normal,' Mr. Waldren said, 'so we can discuss some of your particular circumstances.' And he nodded at the folder on the table, which said RUPPLE,

CRAIG across the top, and was worryingly fat. 'Don't worry,' he added. 'This isn't an interview; you're already very much a part of the Informa/McKenzie family.'

'Okay,' said Craig.

'We just have a few things to ask you before your talent exploration session this afternoon,' said Mr. Waldren. He opened the folder. 'You were put on something called a — Social Responsibility Contract, is that right?'

'Yes.'

'And that's who this Constable Hudson is? Your — what would you call him, case worker?'

'Um,' Craig said. 'I guess.'

'Right. I see the police here are still using paper,' said Mr. Waldren. 'Quaint.'

Craig stared at the pile of paper in the folder. There must have been fifty sheets, maybe even a hundred.

'There's no need to panic,' Mr. Waldren said. 'I have no intention of reading all *that*, believe me.'

'Oh good,' said Craig.

Mr. Waldren looked down, and pulled out one of Informa/McKenzie's special tablets. 'We have interns for that, if necessary,' he said.

'Hi Daniel,' the tablet purred. 'Let's get started.'

'What I do want to know,' said Mr. Waldren, still looking down, 'is whether this Constable Hudson is brand-compatible with us. I don't want us wasting time on this,' he said, slapping the top of the pile, 'if we're dealing with someone whose values aren't Informa/McKenzie values.' And then, he looked up.

'That's difficult to say,' Craig said, and scratched the skin behind his ear. He knew what Constable Hudson's values were, or at least some of them: they were roughly the same as his dad's values, because the constable was always trying to prove that, in an ideal world, he'd lock everyone up for at least as long as

Craig's dad would. Craig also knew what Informa/McKenzie's values were, because they were thrinted onto the walls, and written on the cups at the canteen, and on the Informa/McKenzie tablets' lock screens. But working out their compatibility was impossible.

'Well,' Mr. Waldren said, patiently, 'let's start with the basics. Where would you place him on a five-point scale for global openness?'

Craig opened his mouth, and looked at the corner of the room for suggestions.

'You did *watch* the candidate-centred induction video, correct?'

'Yes,' Craig said. He remembered global openness, but not what it was. 'It's just — well, he's a police officer, so — I guess — three?'

Mr. Waldren smiled a friendly smile. 'Informa/McKenzie has offices in fifty-seven countries across six continents,' he said. 'Our values are the same, whether we're here or in Hong Kong. I'm not interested in how well he enforces local *laws*. I'm interested in whether or not he shares our vision.'

'Oh,' said Craig. He thought about it for a second, and concluded that Constable Hudson's vision of the world wasn't like Mr. Waldren's at all. 'Maybe two, then,' he said.

Mr. Waldren stopped smiling. 'Creative consultants do *need* to be able to make snap judgements,' he said.

'Definitely a two,' said Craig, quickly. 'He's quite low on global openness.'

Mr. Waldren started tapping at the tablet. 'And on brand autonomy?'

That one, Craig could remember: the freedom our brand needs to flourish in the marketplace of ideas. It didn't sound like one of Constable Hudson's priorities. 'Two. Again.'

Mr. Waldren smirked. 'I see,' he said. 'And on the same five-point scale, mobility?'

Mobility was the one which had something to do with Craig not being an employee, and Informa/McKenzie being his client rather than his employer. He thought about whether Constable Hudson would ever describe the police service as his client, and decided that he wouldn't. 'One,' said Craig. 'Very low.'

Mr. Waldren looked at the top sheet of paper, and the constable's block capitals lining up in boxes. 'Well,' he said, after a pause, 'it seems to me there's very little point in reading any of *this*.' He reached out and closed the folder, nudging it to one side. 'Why don't you give me a precis?'

'Um,' said Craig.

'A summary,' Mr. Waldren said, clasping his hands together on the desk. 'Tell me what happened.'

'Well, it's — it's a bit difficult to describe,' Craig said, eventually.

'Try,' said Mr. Waldren.

'I had a profile,' Craig said. 'Online. A — video profile.'

Mr. Waldren started typing. 'And the content of this profile got you in trouble with the police in this jurisdiction,' he said.

'Yes.'

'And how would you rate the content in terms of its compatibility with Informa/McKenzie values overall?' he asked, still typing.

Craig closed his eyes. 'Probably about a three,' he lied.

'Is the content still in the public domain?' asked Mr. Waldren.

'No. Definitely not.'

'So there's no proprietary issue,' Mr. Waldren said.

'No,' said Craig, trying to memorise the word 'proprietary' so he could ask Fabble what it meant.

'How would you describe the content?' asked Mr. Waldren. 'I don't need to know everything. Give me a headline.'

'Um, well — it was — videos. Just — me and some friends

goofing around, really. Mainly.'

'But nothing that I'm going to run into.'

'No,' said Craig.

'Even if I made an effort to find it online?'

'No. It all got deleted.'

'I see,' said Mr. Waldren. Then, without looking up, he yelled, 'CORA!'

After a couple of seconds, the door behind Craig opened, and a frantic looking girl ran in, no older than he was, her black hair piled up on top of her head and fixed in place with a cable tidy. 'Sorry,' she said, out of breath. 'I was just —'

Mr. Waldren picked up the folder, and held it out. 'Take this back to Serena in People And Personnel, would you? And tell her there's no need to go through it all.'

'I'll do it straight away,' she said.

'Thanks, Cora,' said Mr. Waldren. He leant back in the chair, and smiled at Craig. 'I'm a big believer in moving on,' he said. 'Back here at one thirty, for talent exploration?'

And with that, Constable Hudson's carefully assembled notes disappeared, and Craig breathed out. He could pass the whole thing off as a minor educational issue, a blip in an otherwise confident, upward trajectory. What a bullshitter Constable Hudson was, he thought. 'This is what lands people in dead-end jobs.' 'You have a real mountain to climb.' 'Anyone seeing this is going to think *red flag*.' As though police officers understood a thing about companies like Informa/McKenzie. It was like getting careers advice from a lamp.

Craig went back to the pets who were patiently awaiting his judgement. He started with videos of dogs body-boarding in Cornwall; then, dogs failing to do backflips and somersaults; then more cats sleeping in improbable places, which seemed to be a mainstay. After a quarter of an hour, he was gazing at the screen, watching a depressed-looking chinchilla wearing a miniature tuxedo, trying to decide whether or not it was *Cuteness*. But how could he? It felt like committing treason against a fellow being, allying himself with the forces of fate pushing down on both of them alike.

He hit *Slush*. See you next month, he thought.

•

In his bijou living concept, Craig was using JerkShuffle every night. It wasn't a conscious choice, so much as a natural consequence of having thicker walls, walls which didn't have parents behind them, the kind of walls he'd been longing for since puberty. The guys on JerkShuffle outnumbered the girls five to one, so he had to wait in line; but he didn't care if he had to wait five minutes, even ten. He might hit the jackpot, and get one of the Chinese girls whose connections hadn't been fried by layers of state surveillance. Or twins. Less realistic, but hope springs eternal, as Pastor Colin once advised him over biscuits.

He didn't get twins. But when he persevered, he got his fair share of hot girls: a nail technician from Bristol, who he almost talked into getting on a train to see him; a marine biology student from London, who had blonde hair and kept her thick-framed glasses on the whole way through, even when she was butt-naked in front of him, so she looked like the porn version of a teacher; a quiet-voiced Indian girl in Brussels who kept calling him 'Sir' even though he didn't ask her to, which was insanely hot; a woman in her thirties, who turned out to be a bit weird, but had a vibrator, and wasn't shy about giving a demonstration. Night by night, it got easier; he learnt to handle the feeling of being one in a long line of punters, to be dismissed once he'd outlived his purpose. And with no one else there, he could finally use his normal voice, instead of whispering like some fumbling cuck who was scared of waking mummy and daddy. If he kept at it, he told himself, he'd find the perfect combination: near, hot and young, or at least as young as he was.

And the night after his two interviews with Mr. Waldren, he got paired with a girl only four kilometres away, and his age. All he needed for the holy trinity was hot. As the chat loaded, he realised her camera was already on, a shaved pussy square in the middle of the frame, skin the colour of milky chocolate. He wouldn't even have to coax her out of her clothes. Already half-hard, he angled his tablet down to take his face out of shot, and hit *Accept*.

'Hey,' said the girl, softly.

Was it — ?

'Buddleia?' he said.

And then, there was a rustling noise, and a flurry of blurs passing over the screen as she rushed to close the app. Craig stared at his tablet.

Rate me!
★ ★ ★ ★ ★
★ ★ ★ ★
★ ★ ★
★ ★
★

You bitch, he thought.

Then, he thought: you actual fucking bitch. Who the fuck did she think she was? Someone who hadn't egged him on all those months, telling him how hot his profile was, goading him into wilder and wilder stunts? Someone who hadn't smoked his weed, who hadn't made him buy her vodka even when he was underage, who hadn't lured him into the girls' toilets on the promise of a kiss he never got? What, she could just click close on him, and he'd go away, just like that?

Craig threw the tablet down onto his bed, and dived across the room for his phone. Not this time, he told himself: I, Thor, the hatemonger, the heretic, the pillager of dignity, the messiah, cannot be ignored forever.

After about ten rings, he was about to give up; but then, there was a light click, and Craig could hear breath, and the faint rustling of material behind it.

'Was that you?' he said.

There was a long pause. Then, she hung up.

Fuck that, thought Craig, and pressed *Call* again. He waited, counting the rings, pacing up and down in the tiny space between his bed and the kitchenette, until she finally picked up again.

'I don't want to speak to you,' said Buddleia. At least she sounded embarrassed.

'I can't believe you just did that,' he said.

'I don't want to talk to you,' she said, a little louder.

'Yeah,' he said, 'but you're happy to sit with your twat on show for some random guy though, aren't you?'

'Oh,' said Buddleia, 'and you were doing what, exactly? Playing Scrabble?'

'I can't believe you'd just hang up on me. After all of that shit, and you —'

'I don't want anything to do with you,' she interrupted. 'Not after everything you've done. Stop calling me. You're toxic.'

'Wait,' he said. But she'd hung up, again. So Craig threw his phone at the wall.

Five minutes later, he'd worked out a way to clip his phone back together. The camera wouldn't work, not unless he sent it in to get the casing repaired, but that was okay, because he still had his tablet. The shoelace got in the way of the home screen menu, too, but he could still send a message, which was the only thing he gave a shit about. You're toxic: as though she'd been his timid little victim, locked away in a basement while he terrorised her innocent, captive mind. You actual fucking bitch.

> me › budd
> fuck u 4 saying what u just said, i suppose its true what everyone at school said about u after all, u really r a selfish person

> me › budd
> jokes on u, im working as a creative consultant 4 informa mckenzie now + i have my own place. so it looks like being without u was the best decision i ever made. guess it must be u whos toxic

> me › budd
> tbh i only called u cos i felt bad 4 u. u r obviously a very troubled person. if im honest i genuinely feel sorry 4 u. i hope u find a way 2 become a nicer person + i mean that from the bottom of my heart

> me › budd
> ok well take care of urself, im sure u will u usually do

He waited for the delivery receipts to arrive in his inbox, and then went to the fridge. There were four bottles of Budweiser, which was enough to make a dent in his anger if he drank them quickly enough, but no bottle opener, which is why there were still four bottles of Budweiser in the first place. Briefly, Craig considered throwing one at the wall, but then remembered his phone; so he smacked the metal caps against the stainless steel kitchen worktop, ignoring the scratches he'd promised his landlady he wouldn't make on it. It turned out that drinking Budweiser really fast wasn't that easy, mainly because the openings of

Budweiser bottles were too thin; so he took out the large saucepan which his mum had given him, to make sure he didn't just live on takeaways, and emptied all four bottles into it, and then downed the contents.

budd › me
The fact that you would even speak to me like that tells me everything I need to know. I guess my dad was right about you in the end, you are a bit of a loser. Thanks very much but if that's your version of wanting the best for me then I think I can learn to live without it

budd › me
I've blocked your number so you won't be able to call or text me anymore. Goodbye Craig, enjoy your new life and I'll enjoy mine

Craig went back to the fridge, just to check that there wasn't another beer hiding somewhere in it, even though he knew that there wasn't. Then he sat back down on the bed, and decided that he really hated his new life. It felt like a good decision, because it was at least honest.

He hated the fact that his only friend was his boss, and he couldn't even sit next to her at lunch because everyone else would think he was fucking his way to the middle. He hated the fact that he'd never have any other friends at Informa/McKenzie, because all the other tagxperts had good exam results, and juiced, and swore in Chinese, and listened to New Baroque, and he didn't speak any Chinese, and found New Baroque really irritating, and ate pickled onion crisps at his desk. He hated watching his pointless ratings stacking up, to be sucked across the Atlantic and fed into a prediction engine bubbling away somewhere in the heart of Informa/McKenzie's lair. He hated the peace wall he had to cycle around on the way to the job he hated. He hated his bijou living concept, which he'd already trashed in the space of a few days, and the piles of clothes towering up the walls, and the moulding ValuBred balanced on top of the stack of takeaway cartons in the kitchenette, and the growing mound of underwear wedged between the toilet and the shower cubicle, and the filthy mirror above the sink, stained with crusted water and mouthwash, and the scratches on the worktop from the beer bottles. The only thing he really liked was his phone, and now that was busted, so he'd have to hate that, too.

YOU ARE ABOUT TO SHARE WITH THE WORLD

When Rahman thought about it — really thought about it, separating out each strand of his life and considering it in isolation — it was obvious what he had to do. He had to tell everyone he was a Muslim, and he had to mean it. There were two big problems: Rahman hardly knew anything about Islam, partly because Miss Waterman-Patterson didn't like being too specific, and partly because his father had refused to teach him about it; and he also had a horrible feeling that he might be gay. Still, the advantages far outweighed the disadvantages.

It was the only way that Buddleia and Gray were going to forgive him for the protest in Solar Garden City. No other excuses were available; only deeply held religious convictions would cut it. And they were the only people from either of his schools who were going to the University of Southern Wessex, like Rahman, rather than moving away. Without them, he'd have to start making friends all over again.

It was also the only way he could get Ibrahim back. Ibrahim replied to his Blackfl.ag message, but only with a 'hey', which wasn't very encouraging; Rahman would need something more to offer. He was already sending Ibrahim as many links as he could — videos of Ku Klux Klan marches, footage of the French National Front scuffling with the police — tagging each with #imperialistbullshit or #kaffirpropaganda or #apostateasshole or #kufr or #zio. But that wasn't enough; Ibrahim was a warrior, and warriors didn't waste their time on fence-sitters.

And it was the only way to shut his dad up. Even though

Rahman was going to a half-decent university, and studying a half-decent subject — Communication Studies, a compromise between his father's suggestion and the course he actually wanted to do — his father still had plans, which had subplans, demands with subdemands, and in each of those, a nested list of requirements to meet and standards to live up to. When was Rahman going to learn to drive? How would he meet a nice girl if he didn't? Why wouldn't he go to a proper bloody barber for once, and get that bloody fuzz off his face? Why wouldn't he meet his father's colleague's nephew, who had a business plan? Where was Rahman's business plan? And what *were* Communication Studies, anyway? Islam provided an exit from his father's expectations, a set of values which could be pinned on the Quick Brown Fox, and by extension on one of his dad's Big Decisions. I never *asked* you to send me there.

And, even though he didn't understand it, Blackfl.ag was the only thing which cheered him up after a guilty half-past-midnight fantasy over a white nationalist. Without it, Rahman just lay there, getting angrier and angrier, the ceiling above him swelling with blankness. Somehow, Blackfl.ag was the antidote. So the decision made itself.

He wasn't sure about Allah, though. If Allah was real, why had he chosen to put Rahman through all that shit on purpose? What kind of god would sit back and watch him suffer, measuring his responses, making the whole of his life an endless, pointless, choiceless, gradeless exam? There was probably a good answer to that, something he might have learnt at the Quick Brown Fox if he hadn't been sitting in Miss Waterman-Patterson's class trying to work out what colour best represented the concept of alienation. But it still made Rahman angry, the thought of his whole life scheduled in advance, pencilled in for millennia as the seas boiled and the mountains cracked upwards and the tribes divided and conquered. So instead of deciding what he thought about Allah, Rahman started with clothing, which was easier. He copied the uniforms he saw on Blackfl.ag: the logoless t-shirts, not too loose, not too tight; the multi-pocketed, belted cargo pants; the steel-capped boots.

'Woah, Batman,' Tarek said, 'what's with all the body armour?'

'Go kill yourself,' said Rahman.

'Seriously, what's the plan? Are you going to bring down a drug lord?'

'Go kill yourself.'

'Corrupt police chief?'

'Go kill yourself.'

'Aw, don't be like that. You look splendid.'

'Go kill yourself.'

If he got his outsides right, Rahman told himself, his insides would follow, dragging his spirit up to the surface. He started pronouncing the 'h' in his name, like Mr. Ayoob used to; it sounded harder and drier, and made him think of the cat-faced news reporters on itaqullah.net, with their light veils and melodic voices, or a village in North Africa, with squat white homes built around an oasis. It was the name of a visiting angel.

On the weekends, Rahman took his tablet out into the garden so he could watch TV without his dad suggesting careers, or Tarek taking the piss out of his clothes. He was avoiding his bedroom, which the summer months had filled with a different kind of air, a stuffiness he'd never shift. Outside, there was nothing above him but sunlight, like in Solar Garden City's motto, slowly turning a shabby dusk green, up in the airless October heights. He didn't really listen to his tablet. Instead, he watched the stars coming out, and looked at the moon slicing into the sky: not a full moon, but a thin, bright fingernail. It was the kind of moon he remembered from the front covers of Mr. Ayoob's Islamic Studies textbooks, with their colourless, pictureless chapters, and from Interfaith Studies, where he'd draw out the symbols of the world's major religions, the crescent moon and its giant star one brand among many, jostling for space with crosses and Stars of David and other, more convoluted shapes. The crescent moon, he decided, looked better without a star, like it had a little more space to breathe. Like it could cut skin.

•

Communication Studies turned out to be easy, maybe even easier than the geosociology course his dad put the kibosh on. It was a Lady Patience type of easy, because nothing was ever totally right, nor totally wrong.

In the first week, they started off by learning that everything was a sign, and therefore a potential communicator of information, and that a number of tools could reliably be used to identify and analyse any sign, from a traffic light to a shrug. The lecturers really liked using the overhead beamers, and incorporating bits of cartoons from their childhoods into the classes; so Rahman had to watch a talking dog holding a martini glass and say what type of information the martini glass communicated, and then watch a bar owner with a yellow face getting prank calls and determine which communicative modes were and were not at play. Was the martini glass intrinsic or extrinsic information? Intrinsic, because it was a central part of the character's representation; but also extrinsic, because it wasn't always there. Were the prank calls a type of visual communication? No, because the bar owner couldn't see the prank caller; but also yes, because Rahman was watching it. After his short exile in the wilderness of right or wrong, he was back in the soft green meadows of yes and no. With that, and the fact that Students Against Fascism were busy camping out on school playing fields, the campus was its own little bubble, a holiday in the past. The chaos of peace walls and counter-protests was far, far away, a storm front out in the ocean, which would probably veer north, or south, or somewhere else.

'Take a look at this,' said Suki, his lecturer for Introduction To Signs And Signals. She aimed the clicker at the front of the hall, and up flashed a giant picture of a woman in a supermarket, her back turned to the camera, refrigerated aisles of milk and cream and yogurt stretching away into a blur. The woman was wearing a pink velour tracksuit, with 'In your dreams, honey!' written across the back in diamanté lettering. 'What do you think she's trying to communicate?'

Rahman put his hand up.

'Rahman,' said Suki, pronouncing the 'h'.

'She wants sex,' said Rahman.

A snigger passed around the room; one of the girls sitting on the same row as Rahman said 'oh my God,' and put her head in her hands. But it was true, Rahman thought: she did, and everyone knew it. What was he supposed to do? Pretend?

'Well,' said Suki, 'actually — he is right. It is a bit more complicated than that,' she said, smiling, 'but this is a sexual message, isn't it?'

The girl on Rahman's row put her hand up.

'Olivia,' said Suki.

'She's literally doing the exact opposite. She's saying, *in your dreams*, like — that's a way of saying no, not a way of saying yes.'

'Of sorts,' said Suki. 'But. The signal is sexual nonetheless, no? This is not a woman who is celibate.'

'But it's still saying no,' said Olivia.

'It's saying no to some,' Suki replied, 'but maybe not to all. Maybe she is signalling — yes, but only to a subset of communicative recipients? So, only to a certain *type* of sexual partner?'

Rahman put his hand up again, and Suki nodded at him. 'Like, if you see it, and you didn't let it put you off, then —

that's the kind of person she wants?'

'Which would make it — ?'

'A multi-tiered communicative strategy,' Rahman said, which is what saying two different things at the same time was called in Communication Studies.

Suki snapped her fingers with approval. 'Exactly,' she said. She turned back to the front of the room, and clicked onto the next image, which was a peacock, his feathers splayed in a brilliant arc. 'And this?' she said. 'Could we say the same thing about this communicative message?' She moved her hand in a semicircle across the peacock's tail, her fingers spread out. 'Think about this shape,' she said. 'What is it? Is it a barrier, or an invitation? Or even — both?'

Out of the corner of his eye, Rahman saw Olivia's face aiming a single-tiered communicative strategy at him. Maybe, he thought, Lady Patience wasn't that useless after all; it had taught him how to translate exam words into real words and back again, and that's where the marks were.

It was even better when his lecturers were from overseas. They said that they were going to emphasise the importance of the world beyond the Anglosphere, and raise the profile of the Global South, and then gave Rahman the same looks the teachers at Lady Patience used to give him at Eid, the appreciation-fishing smiles, because Rahman wasn't from the Anglosphere, or at least not properly. For his first Communication And Frontiers essay, he wrote about how communicative signals were less polarised in the Global South, using his dad as a case study. He got eighty-four percent. It would have been even higher, Françoise told him, if he'd included more than three references. He'd made it all up — his dad left Pakistan when he was nineteen, and polarised every conversation he ever had, and Pakistan wasn't even in the southern hemisphere — but it worked. His analysis of the telephonic medium was highly effective. He had clearly grasped the concept of the internalised frontier. His portrayal of a communicative agent was both rounded and nuanced. It only took him an hour.

•

'What?' groaned Rahman. It wasn't even light. Was the house on fire?

'Come downstairs,' said his dad's outline, from the doorway.

'I'm asleep.'

'Come downstairs,' the outline repeated.

Rahman sat up on the bed, and cricked his neck. His dad was holding something, a long black shadow gripped in his hand. 'Why?' said Rahman, shuffling down under the duvet. 'It's like — six o'clock, or something.'

'Stop bloody arguing and come downstairs.'

So Rahman followed his dad out onto the landing; it looked like he was holding a rolled-up poster. They walked downstairs into the freezing living room, where his dad had moved the coffee table into the corner, uncovering the burnt bit of carpet where Tarek had the accident that no one was allowed to talk about. Rahman's dad sat down, leaning the rolled-up tube against the edge of the couch. 'So you want to be a Muslim, do you?' he asked.

Rahman rubbed his eyes. 'Um,' he said. 'Yeah. Maybe.'

'All right then,' his dad said. Then, he unrolled the tube, which wasn't a poster but a thin mat, the colours worn in the middle, and spread it out over the burnt bit of carpet. 'Go and wash your hands, then,' he said.

'Why?'

'Because you have to wash your hands before you pray. If you want to be a Muslim, you have to pray before sunrise.'

Rahman looked at the window. It looked pitch black out in

the street, or almost pitch black; couldn't his dad have waited half an hour?

'If you want to be a Muslim,' his dad repeated, slower, 'you have to pray. Every single morning. Now go and wash your hands.'

Rahman went into the kitchen, and washed his hands with Nectarine Dream washing up liquid. He wondered how long his dad had been hiding the mat, and where; there must have been a stash somewhere in the house, a suitcase of relics from his mum and dad's former lives in the Global Not-Quite-South. Rahman looked down at his fingers, small crescents of orangey pink gathering in the spaces between them. Did Muslims *really* get up at four o'clock in the morning? *Every* morning? No one at the Quick Brown Fox ever mentioned that.

'Done?' said his dad. He was standing at the end of the mat, his toes an inch or two from the fringe.

Rahman stared at him. He was smiling, the same way he did before announcing that Tarek and Rahman had to clean out the garage. 'Sit there,' he said, pointing at the sofa. 'I'll show you.' He closed his eyes, and put his hands up to his ears, holding them out like satellite dishes, as if to say 'I can't hear you.' Then, a voice other than his own — a softer, lighter voice, a younger self — began to sing 'Allah hu-Akbar,' the words slow and clear. As he moved his hands down, clasping them in front of his belly, Rahman realised how automatic it was, like going to sleep or swallowing, an effortless coalition of body and brain. 'Subhanak Allahumma wa bihamdika,' the improbable voice sang from his dad's throat, 'wa tabarakasmuka, wa ta'ala jadduka, wa la ilaha ghairuk.'

Rahman closed his eyes. The sound of it was making him sleepy. But there was also something annoying about it; it felt like one of his dad's performances, like when he made Mr. Nassem look at the photos of the big house they used to live in, or started ranting about how he was an entrepreneur, and how Rahman and Tarek's generation wouldn't know an entrepreneur if it hit them in the face. Why did he still remember how to pray, after all the years, if being Muslim was so crap, and being English so amazing? He couldn't even remember his own Fabble password, and that was only eight characters long. This was a whole song, with choreography as well. But Rahman could hardly interrupt; his dad was in full flow, each note floating up and back down again, the words quivering, lingering in the chilly air. His dad let out the longest note yet, which sounded like the word 'lean', the final 'n' hummed out across the room, the dawn workings of a quiet machine. Then, after a pause, he sang 'ameen', opened his eyes, and turned to Rahman.

'Ready for more?' his normal voice said. 'Because there's a lot more.'

Rahman shrugged.

'You want to do that every morning of your life, do you?' asked his dad. 'Like I had to?'

'Yeah,' said Rahman, weakly.

'So I'll keep on going, then.'

'Yeah.'

'Bloody waste of time, if you ask me,' said Rahman's dad.

•

Rahman assumed that he'd been invited to the Leaders of Tomorrow seminar because of his marks. It was only when he checked his handbook that he realised it was because he was Asian. Leaders of Tomorrow seminars, he read, provided a dedicated space for Black And Minority Ethnic students to explore their potential role in the student community; and sure enough, when he turned up at the main lecture hall, Buddleia was there, exploring her potential role. She was sitting in the middle of the front row, chatting with a Chinese girl wearing glasses with thick red frames, ranks of black and brown and yellow faces filling up the seating behind her.

'Oh my God!' she said, suddenly delighted to see him. 'Come and sit here!'

Rahman edged his way down the row while Buddleia had her new Chinese friend scooch down to make room. 'This is my Muslim friend,' she said, not bothering to introduce either of them by name. 'I haven't seen you in weeks,' she gushed. 'How's communication?'

'Easy,' he said. 'How's maths?'

'Impossible,' she said. 'You have no idea.' Except that he did: he'd already heard Buddleia Mbatha tell her friends how impossible things were, just before she got the second highest mark in the year.

Françoise stood up and cleared her throat. 'Welcome,' she said, spreading her hands out to both sides. 'Bienvenue, bienvenidos, svaagat he, kuwakaribisha, ahlan wa-sahlan, huanying.' She pronounced each version perfectly, and a small murmur passed around the lecture theatre. 'Welcome to the Leaders of Tomorrow. For those of you who don't know me, my name is Françoise Carbonneau, and I'm a professor of Communication Studies. And this,' she said, pointing to her left, 'is Itsuki Akiyama, assistant professor of Mathematics —'

'He's *such* a nice guy,' said Buddleia quietly, leaning into Rahman's ear.

'— and this,' Françoise went on, pointing to her right, 'is David Navarette, from the department of American Studies. And I'm delighted to say today we are graced with the presence of the dean of the Faculty of Humanities, Edward McEldowney — so best behaviour, please —'

And then, a bald man with almost no eyebrows, who'd been sitting at end of Rahman's row, stood up and looked out across the students with a smile, raising his long-fingered hand in a silent wave.

Rahman looked down into his lap. The insides of his head all tilted to one side at the same time, and a pinging noise smacked into his ear so hard that he thought he'd fall off his chair. He looked back up at Françoise, whose lips were moving, but he couldn't hear any words coming out, because of the ping; she must have said something funny, because Itsuki Akiyama and David Navarette both laughed — but there was no laughing sound, only the ping getting louder and louder, and the toppling of Rahman's brain pushing him sideways. He swallowed, and the taste of sick travelled up his throat, turning into a burp halfway up. Slowly, he moved his eyes across to the edge of the room. The dean was still standing up. For a second, he looked right at Rahman; but then, he looked at Buddleia, and then the Chinese girl next to Buddleia.

He didn't even remember. *But then, you people all look the same to me.*

Rahman closed his eyes. For a moment, he thought he might need to piss, and realised he was cupping his hands over his crotch; but then, a second later, the sick feeling came back, this time like it meant it, and his cheeks inflated all by themselves. He doubled over in his seat, steadying his head a few centimetres above his knees, scared to breathe out in case he puked.

'Are you all right?' whispered Buddleia. 'Rahman?'

He focused his vision on his cargo pants, the tiny strands of fabric woven into one another, too grey to be black, too black to be grey.

'Rahman!' she hissed.

She was staring at him, and so was the Chinese girl; except that Buddleia's stare was a stare of concern, and the Chinese girl's was curiosity. He sat up, slowly, pressing his chin into his neck, trying not to breathe, in case something slipped out of him he could never get back in.

'I'm fine,' he managed to say, eventually.

Françoise had her shoulder turned to the room. Beamed onto the great blank expanse at the front of the lecture theatre were the reasons why Black And Minority Ethnic students could trust the University of Southern Wessex to represent their interests. The staff were well trained in recognising structural bias. *Take your clothes off.* The university administration hired its staff from across the community. *Put your hands behind your back.* The dedicated diversity team had three full-time employees, and five part-time consultants, two of them former professors. *Stand with your legs apart, Taliban. I'm gonna give you a proper smack.*

He turned to Buddleia. 'I have to go,' he whispered.

'Do you want me to come with you?' she whispered back.

Rahman looked at her, and thought about it. He couldn't work out what would happen if he said yes, nor what would happen if he said no.

'I have to go,' he said again, and stood up, training his eyes on the floor in the hope that Françoise would keep talking. Student by student, he excuse-me'd and sorried his way down the row; behind him, he could hear Buddleia following, and the rustling of angled knees and shifting backsides.

'What is it?' she said, in the corridor. 'What's wrong?'

Rahman swallowed, and shut his eyes. The ping in his ear still hadn't gone; perhaps it was permanent, a battery alert for a part of his soul that was draining faster than he could charge it.

'That guy,' he said. 'The dean.'

'What about him?'

'He — I —'

Buddleia had his hand in her own, rubbing his skin gently. 'You can tell me,' she said.

'He — assaulted me,' Rahman mumbled. Then, he opened one eye, to watch.

'What? I mean — I believe you,' she said, 'but — *what?*'

Could it really be that simple? Could Rahman bomb an enemy village without setting foot in a jet? That was the kind of justice available only to the rich, to Hollywood starlets and national newsreaders; surely, he'd need evidence. He opened the other eye. She looked so sad, so kind.

'He sexually assaulted me,' Rahman said, a little clearer. It was sort of true, he thought. It wasn't totally true, but it was sort of true. 'When I was a kid,' he added, for good measure, which was also technically true.

'Oh my God,' said Buddleia. 'Oh my *God.*'

'Don't tell anyone,' he said, still trying to work out what he was doing. It was too much information to give up, too much power to cede; he should have kept on walking, out of the faculty, off the campus, and not come back. But it was too late for that. She was giving him the strangest look, like she was halfway between crying and celebrating.

'You know I wouldn't,' she said. 'But you'll have to tell someone. You can't just keep it a secret.'

'I don't want to,' Rahman said, and then realised that she *was* crying.

'What did he do?' Buddleia asked, wiping her eyes on the edge of her sweater, and snivelling.

'I don't want to talk about it,' he said.

'That's okay,' she said. 'I respect that.'

I don't, thought Rahman.

•

Instead of going to seminar four of Communication In Space And Time, Rahman was sitting with Buddleia in her parents' living room. It was vast, the same size as the entire ground floor of the Mateens' house, and almost two storeys high; and out of the kitchen flowed a seemingly endless supply of coffee and bread rolls and cured meats and Spanish cheeses and sun-blushed tomatoes. All he had to do was sit on his arse, and she'd do everything else.

It was day one of Buddleia's crusade against the dean of the Faculty of Humanities, and so far Rahman was getting away with it. When things got too specific, all he had to do was look at his feet and sniff, and say that he didn't want to talk about it, or just say nothing; then, she'd apologise for asking, and say it was okay. He wondered where she found the time for all her accounts and profiles and contacts; as soon as one message went out, another came in, and Buddleia would touch him on the knee, and tell him the name of the latest soldier recruited to her army. Her friend Izzy was going to get her some poster board from Fine Arts. Her mum was bringing marker pens back from work. She'd disappear into the dining room to take phone calls, which she fielded in the voice of someone trying not to startle an animal. Then, she'd come back to the sofa, folding up her knees below her and gazing at Rahman with admiring eyes. She knew that he was going to get through it. She was so inspired by his dignity. Did he want another coffee? He needed to drink. He was so brave; so, so brave.

'Look,' she said, handing him her phone. It was yet another student, calling out Professor McEldowney. 'A breach of trust'; 'exploiting'; 'privilege'; 'wielding.' It was frightening, how ready her new friends were to take up arms in defence of an invisible citadel, how eagerly they loaded the weapons, how quickly Professor McEldowney had gone from teacher to target. None of them seemed to care that the allegation was anonymous. After another dining room phone call, she told him she was meeting with Human Resources; apparently, even they didn't need names.

'You shouldn't come,' she said, biting her lip with concern.

'It's not right. You shouldn't have to talk about this. You're not in any state. I'll go; they can talk to me.'

'If you think that's best,' Rahman said, concentrating on his toes.

'I don't have to. I can stay, if you want.'

'I'm okay,' he said. Fuck that, he thought: go, go and kick up some stink. The trick was to make himself as small as possible, folding up his arms, hunching in his shoulders, pursing his lips inwards to stop the grin escaping. He wondered what Professor McEldowney was doing. Was he barricaded in his office, phone on silent, as Students Against Fascism mobilised outside his door? Maybe he'd gone home. Maybe, at that exact moment, he was being sacked.

Buddleia stood at the front door, her bag slung over her shoulder, readying herself to deliver a tender goodbye before she went off to war. 'I'm gonna come *straight* back,' she said. 'I don't want you to be alone, not today.'

'Thanks,' Rahman said. 'That means a lot to me.'

Then, she paused, her hand on the doorknob. 'I — I just need to say something,' she said.

'Okay,' Rahman said.

'I'm so sorry. For Solar Garden City. I should have thought about putting you in that situation. *We* should have thought about it. I didn't — I mean, I just hope you don't think I'm Islamophobic, because I'm really, really not. And — I just —'

Fucking *hell*, Rahman thought. She looked like she was about to cry again.

'You should never have been put in that situation,' she said. 'I feel awful about it.'

He smiled a sad smile. 'It's all right,' he said. He wasn't thinking about Solar Garden City; he was thinking about the fridge, and what other goodies might be hiding in it, waiting for him to raid.

Once he was alone, Rahman sat at the marble-topped counter and ate a focaccia. Then, he rinsed out his coffee mug in the Olympic-sized kitchen sink, and half-filled it with the cava which he found in the fridge door. She'd already texted him twice: once to say that she hoped he'd be okay, and to call her if he needed anything; then, to say 'he won't get away with this'. The cava was delicious, like nothing he'd ever tasted, summery and light, so he poured himself another half-mugful, and flicked between the tabs on Buddleia's laptop. Why is this shit STILL going on!?!? #enuffsenuff #speakupandspeakout #ditchthedean. Can't believe USW STILL dragging feet on #powerimbalances #nomoresilence #ditchthedean. Boycotting Comms Theory class tomorrow #ditchthedean #enuffsenuff. She had a private message from Gray, whose bio proclaimed 'Genderqueer Activist + Student Against Fascism'; below it, a stack of other messages was growing, the titles decorated with supportive hashtags and links to other professorial indiscretions, scandals ongoing and resurrected. I could get used to this, Rahman thought.

And that's when he had an even better idea. He opened a new Fabble tab, and typed 'Craig Rupple'.

Craig Rupple was a tagxpert at Informa/McKenzie, and part of the creative consultancy team. It sounded impressive until Rahman clicked on the link, and saw the dozens and dozens of tagxperts' names, so many that he had to scroll down to get to 'C'. Craig Rupple's profile was even less impressive, two lines of nothing-saying text and a fatter-faced version of Thor glaring back out at him with a pained smile. Rahman kept on scrolling until he got to the menu options at the bottom of the page, Thor's face moving down with the cursor, characteristically persistent. He read through the options, and clicked *feed/back*.

Informa/McKenzie › me
Hi/there. What would you like to tell us?

Then, in another tab, Rahman logged in to the cloud account where he kept his porn. One by one, he deleted his videos, bidding each a silent goodbye: the Aussies First! politician with the sexy beard; the SayNo2Islam vlogger in the slightly-too-tight tracksuit; the blue-eyed Irishman at the Repeal Gay 'Marriage' rally. It was a purification ritual, like the initiation ceremonies of the eMancipated when they burned their phones. Nothing was left but the Trollr videos, artefacts from a buried empire. It'll be okay, he told himself. He could make do with quick glimpses of the hotter of the weather forecasters.

padl.og › User06188245
You are about to share with the world!
Make http://padl.og/fmm8lpPi public?
Yes   No

He hit *Yes*, and downed the cava. Then, he provided Informa/McKenzie with some feed/back.

me › Informa/McKenzie
this is what your tagxpert craig rupple is up to
http://padl.og/fmm8lpPi

And his shoulders dropped, and his fists unclenched, and the cells of his skin came back to life, and all the winter in his spine rushed upwards into the heavens, and he was finally, finally free.

•

While Rahman was busy destroying Thor, he got a voicemail from his dad. It wasn't the usual level of anger, beneath which could be lying any number of emotions. It was real, undiluted fury, at points lapsing into Punjabi. Rahman called back.

DICE, the Department for Identifying and Combatting Extremism, had sent his dad a letter, and his dad was taking it very seriously. Rahman had never heard of anyone taking DICE seriously, from the Martyrs of Albion to the users on Blackfl.ag. What's the difference between DICE and a dog with its balls on the pavement? The dog has more than one asset on the ground. But Rahman's dad didn't find it funny. He read the letter down the phone: it said that, as a result of DICE's automatic monitoring system, Rahman's dad's bloody internet usage would be subject to further bloody surveillance, and provided him with a bloody address he could write to, should he decide to challenge that bloody decision.

'WELL?' screamed his dad.

'It's Islamophobia,' said Rahman. 'They don't want Muslims using the internet, that's what it is.' It wouldn't work, but it was the only answer he could think of.

'Fucking bloody BOLLOCKS is it Islamophobia!' Then, his dad went back into Punjabi, so Rahman hung up. He wasn't in the mood for warfare. He was too happy.

me › fuckthewildwest
my dad got a letter from dice lol

Ibrahim would understand, Rahman thought. If DICE started sending letters to Ibrahim's parents, he'd treat it as a badge of honour.

fuckthewildwest › me
well done lol

fuckthewildwest › me
whats the difference between dice and a postman
the postman actually duz know where u live

me › fuckthewildwest
whats the difference between dice and a bucket of shit
the bucket

fuckthewildwest › me
u seen this http://www.blackfl.ag/post/088189294

Rahman went out onto the patio, taking the bottle of cava with him, to sit on the sun lounger and wait for Buddleia. It was suddenly warm, more like August than October, the sky bright blue behind the yellow-leafed trees. He couldn't remember the last time he felt so relaxed. The world was his own, to be summoned and dismissed as he pleased. If the clouds rolled in, he could whisk them away with a flick of his wrist.

WHERE ELSE?

As instructed by Mr. Waldren, Craig read down the list of the metrics.

Q   How our decisions relate to our overall QUEST
E   How our decisions interact with the ENVIRONMENT
N   How our decisions shape our NEIGHBOURHOOD
O   How our decisions affect our desired OUTCOMES
B   How our decisions represent us as a BRAND
I   How our decisions impact on you, the INDIVIDUAL

He tried not to read too much into the fact that he, the individual, came last in the list. It felt as though too much emphasis was going on other factors; after all, he was the one being sacked. Surely his life was more important than Informa/McKenzie's overall quest?

'Any questions about that?' Mr. Waldren asked. 'We'll give you a copy of the analysis afterwards, just in case you want to query anything.'

'No,' said Craig, because there wasn't any point.

'All right. In that case, I'm going to run you through the metrics. You get a score between zero and one for each. If the overall average is above 0.75, that means you can continue to engage Informa/McKenzie as a client. Anything below that, and I'm afraid we'll have to part company.'

'So you'll sack me,' said Craig.

'You're not employed,' Mr. Waldren said; 'you're self-employed. But it will mean that we have to terminate the contract you asked us to sign.'

Craig couldn't remember asking Informa/McKenzie to sign anything, but he couldn't be bothered to read yet more paragraphs of stuff he'd apparently agreed to. 'Okay,' he said.

'So the quest score isn't great,' Mr. Waldren said: '0.21, which means that there's a fairly serious compatibility issue between our quest as a company and your —'

Mr. Waldren couldn't find the right word. 'Videos?' Craig suggested.

'Past history,' said Mr. Waldren. Then, he brightened up. 'On the other hand,' he said, 'you cycle to work, so you got 0.84 for environment. That's good.'

'Great,' said Craig, flatly. He started adding the numbers together in his head so he could divide the total by two, but then remembered that he'd never been any good at averages, because he was crap at division.

'The neighbourhood score is — low, I'm afraid. As you know, we're passionate about engaging with minority communities, and you're a — what was it —'

'Evanglican.'

'An Evanglican, yes, so that probably did bring it up a little. But there's the issue of perception, and obviously —'

'You think I'm a racist,' said Craig.

'Well, I wouldn't want to speculate. But it's 0.25. Which is low. As I said.'

'I guess being an Evanglican counts for nothing, then,' said Craig, bitterly.

Mr. Waldren looked shocked, and a little offended. 'Not at all,' he said. 'It's a quarter. That's not nothing.'

So all those Sunday mornings bought him a quarter of a redemption, Craig thought, a fucking fraction. 'Okay,' he said.

'Then there's outcomes,' said Mr. Waldren. 'Again, I don't

want to speculate, but I suspect what's going on here is that there are concerns about your ability to hit targets, if —'

And he tailed off.

'If everyone thinks I'm a racist,' said Craig.

'If other people don't feel that you're enmeshed in the Informa/McKenzie family,' Mr. Waldren said, holding up his fingers to demonstrate enmeshing. 'So that's really *very* low, 0.08. Then for brand —'

'Do we have to do the last two?' Craig interrupted. 'I mean, I'm obviously not going to pass.'

'For brand,' Mr. Waldren persisted, 'we're seeing the same compatibility issue as quest. Basically, it's quite difficult to reconcile what we've learnt about you with the image we want to project as a brand, and that's a big, *big* concern for us. So that's another low one, I'm afraid. 0.07. Although,' he added, 'it should be said that brand is always quite low. It's certainly the lowest metric on average. So I wouldn't be too disheartened by that.'

'Oh good,' said Craig.

'And then, there's the impact on you, the individual, which we've given a value of 0.97.'

Craig closed his eyes. 'Wait a second,' he said, trying to work it out. 'You're saying that not sacking me has a positive impact of 0.97?'

'We're saying,' Mr. Waldren said carefully, 'that we want to consider the impact on you, the individual, and that allowing you to keep us as a client has a positive impact of 0.97.'

'So it's 0.03 percent —'

'Not percent.'

'Okay,' Craig said, and started again. 'So sacking me is 0.03 of a good thing? For *me*?'

'I think you've misunderstood the QENOBI system,' said Mr. Waldren. 'If it's a positive impact for you, it's a positive impact for us, too. We care about our relationships. But that's only a sixth of the overall calculation.'

'So why is it 0.97, and not just one?'

'Oh,' said Mr. Waldren, chuckling, 'no one gets *one*. These algorithms are highly, highly sensitive.'

'Right,' said Craig.

'All of which averages out at 0.4, which is 0.35 below the required threshold.'

'Which means you're sacking me, then.'

'Which means,' Mr. Waldren said, 'that we don't feel that it's in our best interests to continue in a client role when it comes to your consultant services.'

'So do I still have a job?' asked Craig.

'Of course you do,' Mr. Waldren said, cheerfully. 'It's just that you need to find a new client. And premises. And return your access card for the building. You're still a consultant, just not for Informa/McKenzie.'

'Because it feels a lot like you're sacking me,' said Craig.

'Yes,' Mr. Waldren said, thoughtfully. 'A lot of people seem to perceive the QENOBI system that way. We may need to tweak the design.'

'Can I ask you something?' said Craig.

'Of course,' Mr. Waldren said, smiling warmly.

'Who sent you the videos?'

'Oh, I'm afraid I could never disclose that,' Mr. Waldren said. 'We have a strict confidentiality policy. We treat members of the public with the same level of discretion as members of our own team.'

'So, not *that* much discretion, then,' Craig said.

Mr. Waldren leant back in his chair. 'I'm sorry you feel that way. You know, you're not the only one who's disappointed, Craig. You rated those videos at three, in terms of compatibility with Informa/McKenzie values. Three. On a five point scale. It shows a fundamental misunderstanding of the metrics.'

Craig stared at him, trying to decide what to say. Except that there was nothing to say. He could think of something to kick, or to punch, but not to say.

'We will need you to come back in, in half an hour, for your exit interview,' Mr. Waldren said. 'Is that all right?'

'Can't I just go home?' asked Craig.

'Of course you can,' Mr. Waldren said. 'But that would be a violation of your contract, if you check, and there might be ramifications. In terms of pay.'

'So I can't go home, because then you won't pay me.'

'It's *your* contract,' Mr. Waldren said, as though Craig had insisted on it.

Craig went back to the tagxpert zone, to pack up his things and wait for half an hour. And then, he saw that his desk was decorated with tiny strips of coloured paper, neatly arranged to spell RACIST. At the bottom of his tablet, just underneath a puppy sleeping in the pocket of a cardigan, there was an accompanying note.

> Dear prick:
> Enjoy this gift!
> Fondly, your
> former colleagues.

It was quite creative; they'd obviously made an effort, and used scissors rather than just ripping. He'd added to the authentic English experience of his Chinese and German and Canadian colleagues: a real slice of England, far realer than views of the rolling downlands, or the advertised sunshine and showers, or the honest-to-goodness accents of the canteen staff. An English racist getting the sack, to be sent back down into the swamp of alcoholism and illiteracy below, an anecdote to be shared among the

Cambridge and Shanghai and Zürich graduates. He picked up the left edge of the R, and held it up to the light, sideways.

#whitejobsmatter

It was a Martyrs of Albion flyer. He closed his eyes.
'Fascist,' said a voice from behind him.
'I'm not a fascist,' he said, into the darkness.
'Pff,' said another voice, this time from in front of him.

Who were all these people, who'd never said a word to him, who now hated him so much? They were like ants: harmless on their own, but together an army, marauding across the dirt, leaderless and unstoppable. He'd never noticed. He was starting to think that noticing things wasn't his strong suit.

•

Siobhan, Craig decided, was a decent person, so he asked her to be his workplace advocate during his exit interview. He had a right to a workplace advocate, although he wasn't sure why, because he'd already been uncliented, or whatever the correct term was. It was the right choice, because she did things which wouldn't have occurred to him, like activating the frosting on the glass dividing wall so no one would be able to see the meeting, and taking in a notepad rather than an Informa/McKenzie branded tablet. She smiled at him on the way in. 'Sit tight,' she whispered; 'almost done.' The giant plasma screen was turned off, which was a relief. At least he wouldn't have to relive his schoolboy crimes twice in one day.

'Hi again, Craig,' Mr. Waldren said.
'Hi,' said Craig.

Mr. Waldren introduced the man sitting next to him, who was wearing a bowtie. 'This is one of our colleagues, Mr. Campbell, who's here to talk through some of the pastoral and contractual consequences of our meeting earlier.'

And Mr. Campbell leant across the table to shake Craig's hand. 'Hi there,' he said. 'Thinks for coming in. Did you git something to eat?'

'Yes,' Craig said.

'End, ahhh — Siobhan is your workplice edvocate, corrict?'

'Uh-huh,' said Craig.

'Just from a contrectual point of view,' Mr. Campbell said, 'it would be a little bitter if you stuck to yis or no.'

'Okay. Yes.'

'Good. So I just want to sigh, we're really griteful for how you've dilt with this. We do understand that this is a unique sit of circumstances. At this point, our mine priority is to mike sure that you're feeling supported, in the pestoral sinse,' he said. 'It's virry important that you know that Informa/McKinzie is determined to do right by you.'

'Okay,' said Craig. 'Except that you have just sacked me. Or whatever you call it,' he added, as Mr. Waldren opened his mouth to object.

'Will,' Mr. Campbell said, 'yis. But from a liability point of view —'

Mr. Waldren touched his colleague on the arm. 'We want to make sure you've had the opportunity to say everything you want.'

'All right,' Craig said. 'I think you're discriminating against me.'

'In what sinse?' said Mr. Campbell, looking concerned.

'Well, I'm a member of a minority,' said Craig. 'Sounds like discrimination to me.' It was a better argument in his head than it was out loud. Siobhan cleared her throat, and stared at the blank notepad.

'As I explained to you, Craig,' said Mr. Waldren, 'that was

covered by your neighbourhood metric. We did account for that.'

'Yeah,' said Craig. 'My quarter.'

'You can appeal that,' Mr. Waldren said.

'What's the point?' asked Craig.

'Well, that's your choice,' replied Mr. Waldren. Then, he glanced at Mr. Campbell. 'There is something else we want to discuss. We've become aware that one of your colleagues may have phoned the police. About one of the videos. The Qur'an.'

So that was why they'd brought in the next tier of management, Craig thought. They were afraid of the police turning up, impacting their outcomes and brand with pesky questions and fluorescent jackets. That was what 'liability' meant.

'As you know, we try not to get bogged down in local jurisdictional matters, Craig. Our focus is very much international. It's just —'

'We thought we'd give you a hid's up,' Mr. Campbell interrupted, smiling. 'Do you hev inny frinds you can talk to about all this?'

Craig looked at Siobhan. 'Yes,' he lied. The last thing he needed was one of Informa/McKenzie's consumer psychologists playing doctor, poking fingers into his reopened wounds.

'So,' Mr. Campbell said, 'Siobhan's going to contect Jinnifer in People End Personnel — yis?'

Siobhan nodded.

'— who'll take you through the rist of the stips you'll need to follow. Just so you know, we're not expicting you tomorrow or the die after, so you're free to leave as soon as you've tied up all the odds and inds with Jinnifer. Is there innything ilse you'd like to sigh?'

'Yes,' said Craig. 'There's an — abusive message. On my workstation.'

Siobhan closed her eyes, and squeezed Craig's hand. The two

men looked at one another.

'Obviously, we'll get someone to investigate that,' said Mr. Waldren. 'If you want to make a complaint about workplace harassment —'

'I don't,' said Craig.

Mr. Waldren stood up, and shook Craig's hand. 'Best of luck,' he said, warmly.

'Yis, bist of luck,' said Mr. Campbell. And the two of them strode out towards the paternoster lift, chatting as they passed below the glass walkways overhead.

Siobhan sighed. 'Do you want to appeal the neighbourhood metric?'

'No,' said Craig. 'They're not gonna change their minds.'

'You still *got* here,' she said. 'That's saying something. You don't see many other kids from Lady Patience in a place like this.'

So that was the morsel she was throwing him. He could at least comfort himself that he'd overcome adversity. Sorry, didn't mean to be a fascist: bad schooling.

'Will you let me know if I can do anything?' she asked.

'Thanks,' he said.

Craig walked back out into the shared office space, and slumped down in front of the cardigan pocket puppy and the RACIST collage. Somewhere, behind him, or perhaps in one of the pods below, he could make out a voice. 'You're fucking dead, señorita,' it said. 'You're fucking yesterdead.'

He looked at the lettering on his tablet.

Informa/McKenzie
Enabling/Your/Digital

What he really wanted to do was lob the tablet across the office, scattering shards of plastic and metal over the workstations, and roar, roar deep from the surface of his lungs, a roar that couldn't be analysed apart by the algorithms which Informa/McKenzie had been calculating at him all morning. Instead, he looked at the puppy, and, in a bold act of defiance, tagged it *Huggles*.

Then, for the last time, he left Informa/McKenzie, the tagxperts' eyes following him down into the lobby and out into the fresh, autumn air. As he walked towards the bike racks, he passed one sculpture after another, triangular scrapes and spherical blobs, great metal accidents rising up out of the earth. A woman with a hollow oval for a face, studying her hollow hands with an eyeless gaze: Diana, Goddess Of The Hunt, Considers The Hunted. Two irregular cubes of rusting metal, each of which had an ultrathin graphene cone balanced upside-down on top: Romulus And Remus In The Internet Age. A spiral of glass and metal, swivelling up into a climax of geometry before turning into a dove, trapped in mid-flight: Prometheus Regrets. A tide of meaninglessness had washed in, sweeping over the city and up onto the hills, depositing rafts of junk onto the grass, a cast of mythical figures and minor deities, nicked by the digital revolution, a panorama of colourless buildings laid out below them, framed by the shining grey sea.

And then he saw that someone had slashed his tyres.

Craig stood looking at his bike. He only had two options. The first was to walk it home; the second was to leave it as a gift to Informa/McKenzie, in recognition of their dogged even-handedness. He could leave it in the bike locks, but that didn't seem very creative. It'd be much more fun to hurl it at one of the metal sculptures, as a piece of performance art. Maybe he could wedge the handlebars through Diana's hollow face, suspending the bike from her head; then she'd really have something to consider. But then, he thought, it would have to be recorded as a Hate Incident, what with Craig being at risk, and some poor fucker would have to wrestle it back down, and fill out forms.

So he pushed his bike all the way home, past the detached faux-Tudor manorettes which lined the hill road, past soil outlines of the words LIFE and HOPE and LOVE and SPRING, to be planted with daffodils and snowdrops after the winter, hauling it over the pedestrian bridge which crossed the motorway, the tyres shredding, step by step.

What was the point of it all, then? he thought, as he walked. What was the Social Responsibility Contract for, if all his videos could be reactivated all the same? Why did he spend all those Sundays with the Evanglicans, eating up their Old Testament fury, drinking down their New Testament forgiveness? His Trollr account might as well have stayed active, his crimes proudly pasted all over the internet; at least people would've got bored of them, and moved on. He could've been hiring lap dancers and snorting cocaine for all it mattered. He could've been having fun. He checked his missed calls: five from his mum's mobile and two from Constable Hudson, which meant that Constable Hudson knew the videos had resurfaced, and therefore so did his mum.

> mum › me
> Rtying to call you ,Just wanted to say ,try and stay positive ,thinking of you

> mum › me
> Are you there ?Not sure if you're vetting my texts

> mum › me
> Didn't mean vetting Not sure you're getting my texts ?Do hope you're okay

> twat › me
> Pls contact myself ASAP Yours Cons. Jeff Hudson

Craig hit *Call back*. There was a robotic female voice, explaining to him how he could get in touch with a particular officer, other than the way he'd already chosen, before his call connected.

'You've reached Constable Jeff Hudson. Unfortunately, myself is currently unable to take your call at present. Please leave a name and a contact number, and myself will endeavour to return your call, in an ideal world within twenty-four —'

He hung up.

It must have been Buddleia; who else could it have been? All that time, she was downloading his videos and stashing them away, building up an arsenal. And that's what you get, he told himself, for showing off. 'Joke's on you': except that, obviously, it wasn't. And then, he noticed that his fists were clenched, and his mouth was curled up into a snarl, and resolved not to think about Buddleia yet, so he didn't explode.

When he got back to Mavis Road, he padlocked up his useless bike and let himself into his flat, which stank of dirty sheets and discarded washing, the housework he'd allowed to slip, week by week. He sat on his bed, attending to the blisters which bubbled up halfway through the walk, watching the gloop move as he prodded at them with his thumb. Then, he realised he'd have to call his mum.

'Oh, Craig,' she said. 'I'm so sorry. I really thought all that was all behind you.' And she was sorry; he could hear it.

'Me too,' said Craig. He wanted to go out and buy some booze, something with a higher alcohol content and a wider neck than Budweiser; but the bicycle-flinging, tablet-lobbing, smashing-shit-up part of him wasn't done yet, so it was probably a bad idea.

'You know, you can always come home,' she said. 'You know that. We'd love to have you back.'

The teddy bears flashed into his mind. DINE in the dining

room, COOK in the kitchen, LOVE in the lounge, SHIT in the loo. Craig hadn't thought about the flat. He could barely afford it as it was; he'd have to give his notice. And she was right. They would love to have him back, for a day or two, perhaps. Maybe it would even be weeks before they got sick of him. She was offering because he had no other options. He said yes; he was too tired to think what else to do. Then she made him talk to his dad, who she said was worried, and who didn't really have anything to say. Then he hung up.

Craig decided to do the washing up. He had nothing else to do, and there was no point letting it fester just because he kept forgetting to buy washing up liquid. He emptied the stagnant water from the sink in the kitchenette, transferring the forks and spoons and mugs onto the floor; then, he refilled the tiny conical basin, and added shower gel and fresh hot water, watching the bubbles climb slowly up the side. 'Blib blub,' he said to the bubbles, stirring the water with his fingers.

Then, he realised he was making bubble noises, out loud, like a six year old.

And then he thought about Buddleia.

And *then* he started smashing shit up.

•

'This is Celeste,' said Craig's mum, 'who works at Spangles, the nail bar; and this is Calvin, her husband —'

'Hi,' said Craig.

'— who used to work for — who was it?'

'Costello's.'

'Costello's! Oh God, I'm starting to lose track!' And then, she did her for-flip's-sake-I-don't-know-whether-it's-Christmas-or-Easter laugh. 'Calvin's the one who printed me out those leaflets I told you about.'

'Hi there,' said Craig. He pressed his back against the wall, trying to edge towards the window. He only came down for a sandwich, and even that was impossible.

'All right, mate,' said Calvin, and stood up to shake hands. He was wearing a Martyrs of Albion polo shirt: St. George, with his shield, minus the sword and the dragon. 'Wise move, jumping before you were pushed. You were never gonna get a fair shout with that lot.'

Craig looked at his mother. 'I know he'll think this is a very mumsy thing to say,' she said, 'but I think they were lucky to have him.' And she gave Craig a smile, loving and tight-lipped. *Play along.*

'That's not mumsy,' said Celeste. 'It's sweet.'

'Any white man who takes a stand, I tip my hat to,' said Calvin. 'Uphill struggle, mate, uphill struggle.'

'I think you're really brave,' Celeste said. 'It takes a real man to walk out of a job on a point of principle.' And she took Calvin's hand, giving his knuckles a sympathetic rub with her thumb.

Craig had to admit that it was a nicer image: jobless and honourable beat jobless and cowardly. In his mother's version of events, there was no trashed flat, no lost deposit, no angry emails from the landlady, no tears; there was only her son's silhouette, valiant and defiant at the top of a hill, shield in hand, blameless and swordless. 'I just came down to get a sandwich,' he said. 'I didn't mean to interrupt.'

'I read on Fabble that those people in the tech park didn't hire us lot, anyway,' said Celeste. 'It said they only employed foreigners.'

'Positive discrimination,' Craig's mum said, and sipped her coffee. She was getting good at omitting details — the same positive discrimination which got him the job in the first place — pinning him with a warning look for each unspoken fact.

'You should look into self-employment,' Calvin said. 'There's only two types of boss: yourself, and a fool. What's your area of work?'

'Video tagging.'

'Oh,' said Calvin. Then, undeterred, he added, 'you should think about doing it as a sole trader. I bet if you put your mind to it, you could get something going.'

'You're such an ideas man,' said Celeste.

'See, this is the problem,' said Calvin, leaning his elbows on the table. 'If they're gonna start sacking good people, just because some Muslim somewhere doesn't like some video you made, they'll have no one left. And then they'll have no one to blame but themselves.'

'I didn't make that video,' said Craig. 'It was someone else's. I was just in it.'

'Still,' Calvin said. 'It's the same principle. And why should you be ashamed of speaking up for Christian values? Whatever happened to free speech?'

Craig's mum tutted with sad approval, and took another sip of coffee. What had she told them? That he'd started a vlog on religious freedom?

'It wasn't exactly about Christian values,' Craig said slowly, eyeing his mum.

'Aw,' said Celeste. 'Stop being so modest. You know, your mum's very proud of you. And I'm sure your dad is too. You've got so many people rooting for you.'

And Craig thought about the emergency brake in the middle of the road, and how his mother screamed **'SHUT THE FUCK UP!'** at him, and her makeup running in the head teacher's office, and the weeks and weeks of silence which gathered in the corners of the house as the Social Responsibility Contract looked down from the fridge door. It all felt like it was years ago. What a long, long road his mum had travelled in a few short months, and how bendy it was, and how steep. The view of the land looked so different, its once-impassable craters now dimples on sunlit fields.

•

Constable Hudson arrived at four o'clock; Craig walked out onto the landing, to listen. What did he want this time? A nightmarish vision popped into Craig's head: the police roping him into becoming a Victim Within, sobbing out his experiences of tyrannising vulnerable children. 'Take your shoes off, please,' he heard his mother say.

'Oh — yes, sorry. All right then,' the constable said. She was doing it to spite him; it was an assertion of territory. Poor Constable Hudson, thought Craig. No one told him that Craig's mum had turned into a warlord. 'I've come to talk to Craig, Carla. Do you think —'

'Actually, I'd prefer it if you would address me as Mrs. Rupple.'

Brilliant, thought Craig. He walked downstairs, past Constable Hudson's scuffed boots, which were standing underneath the letterbox. Mrs. Rupple, who'd just got out of the bath, was wearing a dressing gown and moccasins, and the facial expression of a woman in a ball gown. They sat in the front room, without biscuits, and Constable Hudson explained what would have happened in an ideal world, and the things he could unfortunately do nothing about in the present circumstances at this moment in time.

'I'm sorry,' said Craig's mother, 'I don't follow. *Why* are you here?'

'Obviously —'

'Don't tell me things which are obvious,' she said. 'If it's obvious, then I'll already know it. I'm not a fool.'

The constable said vowels, a word in the making.

'Why are you here?' she repeated.

'Obv — it's a very volatile time,' he said. 'We're under an awful lot of pressure to deal with this whole — situation. With the peace walls, and these protests at the University, and Students Against Fascism, and — well, we have to be seen to be taking Islamophobic crime seriously.'

'Which means you can't take these videos down from the internet, I suppose,' she said. 'Even though my son has already lost his job over them.'

'Mrs. Rupple, if a video is hosted in a different country, we have to follow a procedure. We can't —'

'Well,' she interrupted, 'perhaps you ought to have thought of that before you put my family through that ridiculous contract of yours.'

'Yeah,' said Craig. He was kicking a man when he was already down, which was even more fun than it sounded.

'We're satisfied,' said the constable, 'that the contract was fulfilled, and all of that's firmly in the past —'

'Except for the videos,' she said.

'As I say —'

'If you've already told me something, don't tell me again. I don't have memory loss.'

'Look,' Constable Hudson said. 'I can see you're upset. I'm just trying to provide you with some reassurance.'

'I'm not interested,' Craig's mum said, 'in what you think you can see. Can you — *reassure* — me,' she asked, her voice heavy with sarcasm, 'that my son won't be dragged through any more of this nonsense?'

'As — erm —' he started. She'd robbed him of every sentence opening he had. He sighed. 'It's a very volatile time,' he repeated, eventually.

'No one in this house is responsible for those idiotic students,' said Craig's mum. 'You don't see me barricading any schools, do you?'

'I understand what you're saying, Mrs. Rupple. And it's very unfortunate that these videos are back online. But the police service has to be seen to be dealing with the legitimate complaints of members of the Muslim community,' said Constable Hudson, 'now more than ever.'

Craig's mother drew herself up in her pink dressing gown, puffing out her breast until it was the size of the officer's stab-proof vest. 'I don't care,' she said, 'what you have to be seen to be doing. I want you to guarantee my son,' — she gestured at Craig with an upturned palm — 'that he won't be facing yet more punishment over something he's already made amends for. Can you do that, or not?'

'In an ideal world —'

'Yes, or no?'

'Mrs. Rupple,' he said. 'I am keen, more than keen, on — reassuring — what I mean to say is —'

Craig's mother stood up. 'Out,' she said.

The constable didn't know what to do. His jaw drifted open, and stayed there.

'You're no longer welcome in this house without a warrant,' she said. 'Go on. Out.' And she bustled him into the hallway, like a cat who'd been sick on a rug.

'Could I just speak to Craig —'

'No. He's under twenty-one, so I have the right to speak on his behalf, unless he doesn't want me to.' She turned to Craig. 'Would you like to speak to the officer yourself, Craig, or are you happy for me to do it?'

'Happy for you to do it,' Craig said, and smiled at the constable.

'Good,' his mother said, opening the front door, banging it against the wallpaper as she stood to one side. 'Leave those,' she said, as Constable Hudson bent down to put his boots on: 'you can do that outside.' She snatched the boots from him and dropped them the other side of the doorframe, where they landed upright, wobbling a little. Then, she slammed the door behind him, rattling the double glazing.

'Fucking *hell*, mum,' Craig said.

'Please don't swear, Craig. You know how I feel about swearing.' And she sat back down on the sofa, putting her mug of tea on the occasional table, making sure it sat with its handle at three o'clock.

How foreign an experience it was, Craig thought, for his mother to fight like that. But perhaps that's what she'd been doing all along, in her own, bewilderingly wrong way. He felt bad for having written his parents off. The poor bastards had actually believed in all the Social Responsibility Contract bullshit; he'd assumed it was all to piss him off.

'What do you think they're going to do?' he asked.

She thought about it for a moment, running her fingers over the handle of the mug, and then straightened her neck. 'I don't know,' she said. 'But —'

And then she stopped herself.

'But what?'

'I think we failed you over that video nonsense, Craig. I don't think either your father or I really understood what was going on at that place.'

He felt like he should say something like 'thank you', but 'thank you' wasn't quite right. 'Okay,' he said, instead.

•

Craig was sitting on the marina wall, trying to decide what to do. On the minus side, there was a chance Buddleia would accuse him of stalking her, and call her dad, or the police; on the plus side, he really wanted to scream at her, and the only way to do it was in person. And it wasn't his fault that she geobroadcasted her every move on Fabble. He hit *Refresh*, and the same purple pindrop reopened its petals across the map of the city.

<blockquote>
Buddleia Mbatha is dining at Where Else?
Where Else? Eco-friendly cuisine with a harbour view
★I'm here too★ ★On my way there★ ★I wanna go★
</blockquote>

Except that he couldn't say that he was there too, or on his way, or wanted to go, because he was still blocked, the silver-on-white words a tactful reminder of his exile. He just wanted to know why she'd done it, really. It wasn't as though getting him sacked did her any good. And she couldn't really believe that he was such a terrible person, no matter what Amelia Brink or Noodle or any of her new friends were telling her. Some part of her must remember him — the real him, the him she'd kissed, whose dick she'd sucked, the beautiful person she said she could see beneath Thor's surface. He walked over towards Where Else? and stared through the glass. Tiny bowls of flower-garnished salads and cream-swirled soups with jumbo croutons trundled along a conveyor belt, so close that they made his belly rumble.

And there she was. She had her back to him, but he could see it was her: the small red snake around the coiled bun of her hair; the colour of her skin. She was sitting across the table from a man in an open-necked shirt with tall, tidy hair and perfect teeth, and twirling her earlobe with her finger. Craig walked up to the glass to give it a good bang, but the man — her date? — had already seen him, and was furrowing his brow, stretching his neck to get a better look. Then, Buddleia turned in her chair, and a smile dropped from her face.

Oh fuck, thought Craig: what was my plan, again?

The man stood up, because Buddleia was standing up, and he

was a gentleman, the prick. And then, Craig had to wait as Buddleia made her way between the tables, smiling awkwardly. Other diners were interested, now, casually looking out at him, the third party of a love triangle, or a suicidal vagrant, or a cleaner who'd lost his keycard, or a Students Against Fascism terrorist, to be confirmed. He closed his eyes, and felt his stomach sinking, one millimetre at a time. There was a soft beep-boop, and Buddleia let herself out through the ePayment doors, walking towards him, rubbing her bare arms with her hands.

'Er — what the fuck?' she said.

'Why did you do it?' Craig asked. 'Just tell me. What was the fucking point?'

'Do what?'

'Fuck off,' he said. 'You *know* what. Why? Why would you do that?'

'I have literally no idea what you're talking about,' said Buddleia. 'How did you know where I was?'

'Because you put it on Fabble, like everything fucking else. And you know exactly what I'm talking about. The videos.'

'*What* videos?' she said.

'*The* videos. The fucking Trollr videos. The videos you sent to Informa/McKenzie to get me fucking sacked.'

'What the hell are you talking about?' she said, raising her hands up into the air. 'I don't *have* any videos of you.'

'Bullshit,' said Craig. 'I told you I had a new job, and you just couldn't stand to see me succeed. All because of International Women's Day, and your dad being a bigoted prick.'

'Why would I care about your job? I don't care about your *job*. I don't care about *you*. What, you think I want to be reminded that I went out with some —' And she looked him up and down like he was a 7G phone, a relic.

'Some what?' said Craig. 'Go on. That you went out with some what?'

'Some no one,' she said. 'And you know nothing about my dad. He's the least bigoted person I know. *You're* the one whose mother was on the radio with the Martyrs of Albion. If anyone's a bigot —'

'Oh, so that's why? Because of my mum? That's why you did it?'

'Listen to me,' Buddleia said, drawing herself up. 'I. Didn't. Keep. Your. Horrible. Little. Videos. All I want to do right now is forget that I had anything to do with you.'

It wasn't going the way he'd imagined. So much for forcing an apology out of her; so much for a showdown. Behind her, Craig could see Mr. Perfect, tapping at his phone, studiously not watching.

'Who's that?' Craig heard himself say.

'That,' Buddleia said, 'is Jay, and Jay is none of your business. I'm sorry, I really don't understand what that's got to do with you. What the fuck, Craig? What are you even doing here?'

'Bit old, isn't he?'

'It's none of your fucking *business*,' she hissed. And then: 'Right, I'm going back inside.'

'Don't,' blurted Craig. 'I —'

And then he realised: it wasn't her. So who?

Gradually, Buddleia's face changed, anger giving way to pity. 'Craig,' she said. 'I'm sorry if you lost your job, but I meant what I said. I don't want anything to do with you.'

Craig tried to focus. There must be some way, he thought, to turn the conversation around. But he couldn't wrangle his mind into action. Who the fuck was *Jay*? A surgeon, like her dad? It had to be something like that, some level of achievement closed off to Rupples. He glared through the glass, willing Jay to look up.

'Goodbye,' Buddleia said, and turned around.

'So that's it, then?' Craig yelled at the back of her head.

'That's it!' she called out, walking towards the doors.

Okay, Craig told himself: Plan Z. 'And what if your parents knew about you getting off on my horrible little videos?'

Buddleia stopped, and turned back. 'Try it,' she said, her voice worryingly calm.

'I didn't mean —'

'Yes you did.' She looked in at Jay, who was fingering the stem of his wine glass. 'You see him?' she asked. 'He's the kind of guy who doesn't make threats unless he's prepared to follow through with them.' As though the two of them had synchronised brainwaves, Jay looked up, and smiled warmly. 'Which is why he's in there,' she said, giving Jay a girly wave, 'and you're out here.'

It was all Craig could do not to launch himself through the plate glass.

'Don't ever follow me again,' Buddleia said. And then, she went back into Where Else?, warming her shoulders with her hands again, like she was putting a coat back on.

Craig looked back into the restaurant. The diners weren't staring at him anymore. Clearly, he wasn't going to propose marriage, or blow them up, or do anything else interesting; his blanket of invisibility, briefly lifted, flumped back down over his head. On the conveyor belt were small black china plates with fondant squares and candied berries, each with an accompanying test tube of fizzing liquid, and a nest of caramelised sugar; then, tiny chocolates hovering in the air, their magnetised wrappers defying gravity. A young waitress, her hair slicked into a ponytail, had spotted him, and was shooing him away with widened eyes, as though he was a pigeon in the road, and the restaurant was a parked car; at any moment, it could screech into action, revving towards him, snuffing him out in a thwack of bodywork and blood-smeared headlights and feathers. If he stood there for too long, someone would call security, and he'd be scooped off the pavement and deposited somewhere he wouldn't spoil the view.

He went back to his wall, the yachts behind him tinkling lightly as they nodded in the water, and looked up at the condos. The wall-to-ceiling windows flaunted their contents: steamed-wood chandeliers; a swimming pool stretching the length of the ground floor, the ceiling rippling with turquoise light. There was a cascade wall just in front of the entrance gates, tastefully uplit, with threads of water trickling down around CASSIOPEIA MANSIONS, written in large golden letters. Behind the gates, a car purred by, its smooth silver body glinting under the Victorian-style lampposts. It swept into a wide parking bay; there was a pause as the number plate was verified, and then the rectangle of dots on the ground faded from blue to green. A man in a sleek black suit stepped out, bipping the alarm. 'Goodnight Rob,' said the car, in a lullaby voice; and Rob looked at Craig, suspiciously.

Buddleia wants a Rob or a Jay, thought Craig, not a Thor: someone with a parking space wired to keep out intruders. On the other hand, the Robs and Jays of the world had to pimp themselves out to Informa/McKenzie, or Massey & Yakimenko, who'd only employ you if you had their logo tattooed onto the nape of your neck as a sign of brand allegiance, or Conscientia, who credit-checked all of your nuclear family members before they'd offer you an interview. Maybe the bullet-nosed talking car came at too high a price.

•

I will spend the rest of my life lying on my bed in my mum and dad's house, thought Craig. Where Else? He hadn't summoned the courage to check, but there was no doubting the tagxperts' abilities: the video must have gone viral. With every passing moment, people in Taiwan and India and Ireland and New Zealand were multiplying him into immortality, and there was nothing he could do about it. No pristine church attendance record was going to save him this time.

Craig decided not to think about it. Instead, he lay on top of the duvet and covered it with crumbs from chocolate digestives, and chain-drank sugary tea, and listened to other people's thoughts rather than his own. He watched a three-hour documentary by the Kaffir Kollektiv on anti-Swedish racism in Sweden. He watched footage of Generation Omega occupying the Bundestag, trying to stop Chancellor Ramdani's party entering the chamber. He watched the #koranban protestors battling the #openösterreich activists on the streets of Salzburg. He watched the livestreamed trial of Tammy Monk and Billy Whitehead for attempting to bomb the Parliament, and the coverage of the mass brawl outside the High Court when they were sentenced. He watched Chromosome Y's vlecture series on feminist microaggressions and verbal self-defence for men. He watched reports on the gated migrant camps in Sicily, with their thumbprint locks and mandatory wristbands. He watched the Serbian police ripping off women's headscarves, and the riots in the filthy banlieues of Paris. He watched as the Martyrs of Albion won control of their first county council, and the Padanian President declared independence from Italy, and Poland closed its border with Germany, and the Men's Rights Alliance marched on Washington DC.

He paid attention, because it felt like the world was changing in some way that he didn't quite understand, but would need to; but he didn't pay *that* much attention, because he'd decided that the things he couldn't understand would forever outnumber the things he could, and that was okay.

INTERNATIONAL MEN'S DAY

Because he was in the middle of the alphabet, Rahman had to wait an hour before he found out whether he'd got through the first round; so he went downstairs to WIRED!, Reifsteck's in-house coffee chain, to drink cappuccinetti and pretend he had messages on his phone. The interview went well, or well enough. The only awkward bit was when Louise asked him why he'd left the University of Southern Wessex, and he mumbled for thirty seconds about how it wasn't what he'd expected, and it wasn't a very good university anyway, and neither of them looked convinced; but they moved on quickly, so it probably wasn't a big deal. Working for Reifsteck didn't look that bad. WIRED! was full of people his age, with ear tattoos and colourful hair, and it had nineties-themed décor and a foosball table and a multiplayer two-dimensional platform game where a hedgehog and a fox had to race one another. On the other hand, he'd actually have to do work, work which would take him a lot longer than his Communication Studies essays, and he started to wonder whether his dad had been right about university all along.

> buddleia › me
> And and and? How's it going? Did you get through?
> ☺

> me › buddleia
> still waiting so far so gd

buddleia › me
Tell me everything. What did they say about uni? Did they ask why you dropped out?

He laid his phone down on the touch-response table; around it, a small rectangle of black swam into view, HANDS OFF MY PHONE, B★TCH! scrawled to the side of it in a graffiti font. He wanted to tell her to mind her own fucking business, but that was out of the question; the longer he refused to explain what happened with the dean, the more it felt like he owed her something. An update on his joblessness was the least he could offer, if he wasn't going to reveal the juicier details of his sexual victimhood. She was getting more and more impatient: 'you know you can tell me' turned into 'I wish you'd just tell me', which turned into 'you'll have to tell me eventually', a silent 'or else' lurking at the end of the sentence. She wouldn't be happy until he was sobbing in Françoise Carbonneau's office, with his hand clutched in hers.

'I don't know,' said a voice from behind him. 'I thought she was good. A bit shy, but good.'

It was Jeremy, from the interview. Rahman was going to turn around, but then he heard Louise say 'she's a fucking field mouse', and decided not to.

'That's a bit harsh,' said Jeremy.

'Seriously, can you imagine?' said Louise. 'I had to ask her to speak up *three times*.'

'Durham University, though,' Jeremy said. 'That's something. And with an enhanced first. Maybe she's just a bit — you know. Quiet.'

'I fucking hate quiet people,' Louise said. 'Quiet people can suck on my tit.'

'So what, then?' asked Jeremy. 'The one with the birthmark?'

'Oh *God* no,' said Louise. 'English Lit? He won't be able to string a sentence together without having a crisis about it. And think about having to look at *that* all day.'

'Honestly, I felt like it was watching me. You know, like one of those paintings where the eyes follow you around the room wherever you go?'

'A portrait of Dorian Gray,' she said. 'Minus the portrait.'

'Well, it's that or the dropout,' said Jeremy.

'Don't write the dropout off too soon,' Louise said. 'We put him through, we get diversity off our backs for a whole week.'

'Cynic.'

'You know I'm right,' she said, laughing. 'Jesus, he was weird.'

'What do you think was wrong with him, anyway? He was so — shifty.'

'Ugh,' she said. 'He was a bit runty, is what was wrong with him. Did you see the shoes? They literally looked like children's shoes. Tiny.'

'You're such a bitch,' said Jeremy.

'Don't knock it,' Louise said. 'You don't pay VAT on kidswear. My aunt's four foot nine; she reckons it's saved her thousands, over the years. I guess there's less material, in fairness.'

'D'you think he really thought he had a chance, though?' Jeremy asked. 'I mean — he can't seriously have expected to get through.'

'Sympathy vote,' she said. 'Asian, dwarf, school burned down, couldn't hack it at uni. Multiple oppression. It's a narrative. We all need a narrative.'

'You can't be serious,' Jeremy laughed.

'I fucking am,' said Louise. 'I mean it. A whole week without diversity. I'd take that over a Caribbean fucking *cruise*, at this point.'

And then, Rahman turned around.

'Oh God,' said Jeremy, and clapped his hand over his mouth.

'Oh, *shit*,' said Louise.

Rahman picked up his phone, the black rectangle and its graffiti label bubbling back down into the faux-formica. He stood up, pressing his chin into his neck, the skin of his cheeks hot with blood, and walked out of WIRED!, past Jeremy and Louise's widened eyes. Behind him, there was the sound of someone standing, and Louise's voice saying 'Rahman! Rahman!' But he kept on walking, out into the cool of the atrium, the vast tropical plants swooping overhead, and towards the glass doors, *Reifsteck* spelled out across them in solar wiring. He could hear a scurry of feet following him along the polished concrete; as the doors parted in front of him, there was a hand on his shoulder.

'I'm — I'm so, *so* sorry.'

Rahman turned to look at Louise. Her face looked painfully contorted, possibly sorrow but probably guilt. She looked scared as well, which was nice. 'Will you — come back in?' she asked.

'Go and fuck yourself, you flat-chested whore,' he said.

'Yup,' said Louise. 'Totally deserved.'

Rahman walked to the bus stop, and stood in line beside five people taller than he was, one of whom was a child, and tried not to think. Instead of thinking, he closed his eyes, the November sun beaming down onto his eyelids, spilling a warm red-orange across the darkness, and listened.

Runt, he heard. *Paki runt. Taliban Paki runt.*

He leant down, adjusting his trousers, just in case anyone was watching. Just in case it showed.

•

Rahman opened the front door to find Noah, and a bored-looking policewoman beside him, short and overweight with spiked black hair.

'Rahman, my man,' said Noah, shaking Rahman's hand way too hard. 'How goes it?'

'Ra-H-man,' said Rahman.

'Oh right. I guess I should say Noa-H, eh?' And Noah grinned at his own joke. 'Don't worry about her, mate. She'll wait out here. She's just here to make sure I don't get lost. You're the human GPS, eh?'

The policewoman said nothing.

'Mind if I come in?' Noah asked. 'Super quick. Five minutes. And no note-taking, I promise.'

'Am I allowed to say no?' asked Rahman.

'Not really,' said the policewoman.

'Ah, just ignore old misery guts here,' Noah said, smiling. 'No but seriously, you should probably let me in.'

The three of them stood for a few seconds. Finally, Rahman moved to one side, and Noah bustled into the hall.

'Cheers, mate,' he said, as Rahman closed the front door. 'It's bloody nippy out there! Wouldn't wanna be her, eh, stood out there like a garden gnome?' He clapped Rahman on the back. 'Anyone else in, or just you?'

'Just me.'

'Great. Let's go through here, eh?' Noah suggested, showing himself into the lounge.

Rahman stood in the hallway. Why did Noah have a policewoman with him? Anti-bullying counsellors had nothing to do with the police; at least, that was what he remembered from Bully Free Fridays at Lady Patience. He walked into the lounge, where Noah was already set up on the sofa, looking around at the walls with a chirpy smile. 'Right, mate,' Noah said. 'Let's take a seat, eh?'

Rahman sat down. Then Noah breathed a little puff of air out of his nose, as though he was about to start a speech. 'So why'd you drop out of uni, dude?' he asked.

Rahman blinked. What did that have to do with anything?

'Bit concerned, fella,' Noah said. 'I mean, it seemed like you had a plan, and now — well, what's the story? What are you gonna do?'

'What's it got to do with you?' Rahman said. He'd crossed his arms, and could feel himself scowling. 'I thought you were an anti-bullying counsellor.'

'I am,' said Noah. 'But I'm a community cohesion specialist, too. After that — video, they thought you needed — you know. Just someone to look out for you.'

'You mean spy on me,' Rahman said.

'Don't be like that, mate. I want what's best for you. Uni is a good move. Don't chuck it away.'

'That place is full of perverts anyway,' Rahman said. 'Shouldn't you be asking *them* the questions?'

Noah leant back. 'Sorry, buddy,' he said: 'no sale. I don't buy it. No way did you drop out over that ditch the dean thing, no way.'

Rahman said nothing.

Noah sighed. He started to speak a couple of times, but aborted. Finally, he asked, 'You're on Blackfl.ag, aren't you?'

And then, Rahman felt a prickle of hairs on his neck. It was the same prickle he used to get when God came into a classroom: not fear, exactly, but readiness. He raised his eyebrows, and still said nothing, tightening his folded arms.

Noah hunched forward on the edge of the sofa. 'I'm not gonna shit you around, my man. That is *not* good. Especially not if that's why you dropped out. Those people — they're — they're pretty hardcore. I mean, serious hardcore. Real extremists: Sharia, the Caliphate, you name it.'

Rahman looked at Noah, his arse parked on someone else's couch as though it belonged anywhere in the world. 'How do you know *I'm* not a real extremist?' he asked.

Noah smirked. 'Because you're not,' he said.

'Maybe I want Sharia. Maybe I want a Caliphate.'

'Except you don't,' said Noah.

'You know fuck all about me.'

Noah drew his breath in between his teeth. 'I know you're unhappy,' he said. 'I know your mum died, which must have been fucking impossible. I know you had a hard time at Lady Patience, and that Brewster lad dicked you around. I know you're friends with Ibrahim Awad. And I know Ibrahim Awad is not the kind of guy anyone should be friends with. So yeah, I do know you, a little bit. And I know for a fact that you ain't no Islamist, man. Trust me: I've dealt with a few of 'em.'

Rahman's heart was going too fast. He was trying to remember what he'd reposted on Blackfl.ag, and work out how legal or illegal it was. He looked at the policewoman's outline in the centre of the window, hair glued into a peak, the cold sun streaming in either side of her, lighting up the curtains and the room beyond. If he'd broken the law, she'd be in the house, not stood out on the street.

'So tell me why you like Blackfl.ag, then,' said Noah. 'If you're into Islamism now. Gimme an example.'

'It's for Muslims,' Rahman said. 'And only Muslims.'

'So you're a Muslim. A practising Muslim.'

'Yeah.'

'Okay,' said Noah. He spread his arms out wide. 'So teach me. What's the Ummah?'

The Ummah, said the Miss Waterman-Patterson in Rahman's head, *is the Muslim concept of siblinghood*. 'The Muslim concept of brotherhood,' Rahman said.

'Not exactly,' said Noah. 'But close enough. What's Al-Baqi'?'

'I'm not gonna sit here and be tested by you,' Rahman said to Noah and Miss Waterman-Patterson at the same time.

'Right,' said Noah. 'So you don't know what Al-Baqi' is?'

Rahman didn't answer.

'Cos you're not really a Muslim,' Noah said. 'Look, mate. Let me give my dude at the USW a call. He can get you back in. You can catch up on all your work, and forget all of this Blackfl.ag crap. You've got a real opportunity here. Don't blow it.'

'I don't want to,' said Rahman.

'Then what? Hang around with Ibrahim Awad until you wind up being an *actual* Islamist? Is that what you want?'

'Maybe,' Rahman said.

And then Noah laughed, right from the belly, the laugh rising up into the room, a long chuckle rising up after it. 'Right,' he said. 'I mean, that's obviously — well. Bollocks.'

Rahman thought about bullshitting. He could've been the victim of discrimination; he could've been spat on in the street, for example. But Noah was smiling at him as though he were nothing but a child in mid-tantrum. There was nothing to say.

'Look,' said Noah. 'You're a bright lad. So I won't beat around the bush with you. What you're doing with this Blackfl.ag thing — it's just not on, man. Just not on at all. What do you think it'd be like, living under that lot? Getting bumped off for listening to music? Come on, dude.'

Or for jerking off over Martyrs of Albion, thought Rahman; but that wasn't an idea he wanted to pursue. He burrowed his eyes into Noah.

'Just think about it, will you?' he said. 'This militant bullshit — it's gonna cause you *way* more problems than it solves.'

Rahman pushed his shoulders back. 'The only militants are the Martyrs of Albion,' he said, trying to keep his voice low and steady. 'Go annoy them.'

Noah stood up. 'Funny you should say that,' he said. 'That's where I'm off to next, actually. But I'm coming back to see you next week, for a longer chat. Something a bit more — formal. If that's okay.'

'Any point saying no?' Rahman asked.

Noah grimaced. 'Ugh,' he said, frowning. 'Not really.' He walked into the hall. 'Don't wanna keep the GPS waiting!' he said, brightly.

'Piss off,' Rahman said, from the couch.

'All right, mate,' said Noah. 'If that's how you wanna play it.'

Noah and the policewoman left, leaving Rahman alone in the house, listening to the neighbours' dog barking, and thinking about Noah. Maybe he was working for DICE all along, and would come back with a Restricted Movement Order in his hand, minus the beard and the clownish clothes. Rahman's fantasies about being a jihadi didn't extend to Restricted Movement Orders and courts and media coverage and prison time and a patriotic fork in the ribs. So he deleted Blackfl.ag from his phone. But it didn't feel anything like deleting his Sleazydoesit account, or his secret videos of bulky-armed skinheads. He wasn't sure how many more bits of himself he could cut off. There'd hardly be anything left.

Rahman decided not to tell Ibrahim about Noah. He was going to, to begin with; but the longer he thought about it, the worse the idea seemed. Instead, he called his dad, to see if Noah had spoken to him, too.

'What?' his father answered.

'Hi, dad,' Rahman said.

'What?'

For fuck's sake, Rahman thought. 'Just calling to see how you are,' he said.

His father hesitated. 'Why?' he asked.

So Noah hadn't called him; that made things simpler. Since the massive yelling match the day he dropped out, Rahman and his dad had managed to re-establish communications, of sorts; they texted one another in the day, careful not to say anything that might restart hostilities. Rahman wrote things like 'am here all day looking for jobs not going out,' and his dad wrote things like 'tell me when driving licence forms come,' and Rahman wrote back things like 'fine,' and left printouts for job applications in places his father would see them. DICE wasn't mentioned. Rahman had wandered into a surrender, and his dad, an expert in two-man combat, knew when he had the upper hand.

Tarek, however, had other ideas: one son's failure was another son's opportunity. 'Why should I have to pay rent?' he said, over dinner. '*He* doesn't.'

'He's not working,' said Rahman's dad. 'You have an income, you pay rent.'

'I work in a phone shop,' Tarek said. 'It's twelve quid fifty an hour. That's not an income.'

'It's a hell of a lot more than I had at your age. You have an income, you pay rent.'

'So maybe I'll quit, then,' suggested Tarek. 'Then I won't have to.'

His dad slammed the table with the palm of his hand, which made it wobble on its shortest leg, the leg which was only there because of the palm-slam after the carpet incident. 'He's eighteen, and you're twenty,' he growled. 'You know what I was doing between eighteen and twenty?'

'Tell me,' said Tarek. 'I might forget, without the weekly reminder.'

And then, Rahman's dad slapped Tarek in the side of his head. But it didn't look like much of a slap, not for that level of sarcasm; and when Rahman looked at his dad, he realised that it wasn't Tarek who was in trouble. His dad was glaring at him. 'You didn't even last a month,' he said.

And with that, the ceasefire ended.

Rahman had a list of excuses lined up and ready. Communication Studies was useless; he'd never have been accepted onto a real science programme; the university was full of perverts; he'd never be able to pay off the student loan. Together, they seemed fairly robust, but none of them was strong enough to lead with. He also had a backup plan, which was to say that he wanted to be an entrepreneur like his father; but that wouldn't wash, because all three Mateens sat around the wobbly table knew that Mr. Mateen was a contract worker, and far from an entrepreneur, and the whole idea behind Rahman going to university in the first place was to stop him winding up as a contract worker who couldn't afford a new table.

'I'll get a job,' Rahman said to his tray of lasagne.

'Show me what you applied for today,' his dad said.

'I — applied to the car dealership you told me about,' Rahman said, reaching for the printout strategically positioned on the kitchen counter.

'That was yesterday,' his dad said. 'Today.'

'It's mostly online,' Rahman said.

'Show me,' his dad said. 'You have your phone, don't you? Show me.'

So Rahman opened up Fabble Lifepaths, scrolling as far as he could to the right of the page so his dad wouldn't see the date stamps for his latest applications, and handed over the phone. As his dad squinted critically at the screen, Rahman looked at Tarek, who was grinning. 'What's Reifsteck?' his father asked.

'They make solar panels,' Rahman said. 'Like the ones that go on car bumpers.'

'And they want *you*?' asked his dad, with incredulity. 'How are you going to make solar panels? You didn't even do chemistry.'

We all need a narrative, thought Rahman. 'It's not to make them,' he said. 'They make them in China. It's branding. Anyway, they're probably not gonna —'

'Bollocks job,' his dad interrupted. 'Low paid bollocks job.

How do I get back to the last screen?'

Rahman leant across, and swiped back to Lifepaths. His father did more squinting and sneering, his eyes tracking slowly from line to line. 'What's a social influencer?' he asked, finally.

'It's — difficult to describe,' Rahman said.

'Fashion,' said Tarek. 'Like, what's the newest thing to wear, and what your hair should look like, and stuff.' He smiled at Rahman, and stared pointedly at his plain black t-shirt. 'Which shade of black is the new black.'

'Pff,' said his dad, and swiped back again. This time, Rahman could see his finger moving too far across the screen, revealing the date stamps. 'That was a week ago,' his dad said. 'What — where's today? Where are today's?'

'I — I was — there aren't —'

Rahman's father smacked the phone down onto the table, so hard that Rahman and his brother both winced. 'Careful,' said the phone, its edges lighting up red.

'What have you been doing all day?' he snarled.

'I —' Rahman started. And from the other side of the table, just out of his dad's view, he could see Tarek's hand making the wanker gesture, his tongue stuck out in pre-orgasmic joy. 'Changed the beds,' he finished.

His dad thumped his elbows onto the table, and put his fingers to his temples. 'You're both useless to me,' he muttered. 'Useless. The things you have that I never had.'

It wasn't fair. There weren't jobs, or at least not jobs that Rahman wanted. What did his dad expect him to do? Get a job in a phone shop? He had rights.

•

As part of his punishment, Rahman had to sit and watch television with his dad every night, to prove that he wasn't wasting his bloody youth on the bloody internet. It was easy to see why no one under fifty watched TV, because you couldn't pick the bits you wanted, and had to sit through someone else's idea of interesting: people selling one another homes, and antiques, and third-hand cars, then buying them back at a loss, grinning at the cameras; people guessing the prices of farmhouses in France; a live-action telenovela where the viewers decided on the plot, texting in suggestions of twists and diseases and pitfalls and murders, communicated to the burnt-out actors by earpiece. There weren't even clickable links.

The television news turned out to be a lot like the news on Fabble; the graphics were cheaper, and slower to get out of the way, but the footage was exactly the same. Lines of migrants outside the Passport Office, with heavy-handed hints at terror plots and sex trafficking; then, appalled residents who weren't racist, but had lots of things to say about *how* they weren't racist; a clump of young black men sitting around in a football field, burning rubbish, baffled passers-by gazing at them through a chain-link fence; the Student Union in Solar Garden City which had been declared a safe space, with hired security guards standing at the entry points, checking ID cards to keep out Martyrs of Albion; a crowd of passively-resisting students flooding across tarmac in the twilight, the sound of their singing rising and falling below the anchor's voice.

'Bloody communists,' his dad muttered. 'Wash your bloody clothes. Bloody joke.'

On the left of the screen was a commentator, her blonde hair cut into a furious bob, demanding to know with whose money the security firms had been hired, and on whose authority, and how the data on membership of the Martyrs of Albion had been leaked, prodding the air in front of her, pink in the face, refusing to let the anchor speak. Then, the caption slid into view.

Carla Rupple
Southern Region Convenor, Martyrs of Albion

Rahman sat up, with a start. There was no doubt about it; she looked just like him, right down to the tumble-dried hair. So, he thought, that's where Thor got the xenophobia from. It was horrible: he wouldn't even be able to file 'Rupple' under pornography anymore.

'*Nothing* about this is civil,' Mrs. Rupple half-yelled, '*nothing* about this is passive, and *nothing* about this is resistance. They're denying our members access to university buildings —'

'But what we're hearing from the students is —' started the anchor.

'You *keep* interrupting me! I'm here to speak on behalf of my members, our members, and you won't let me! This is absolutely typical, typical biased media. This is exactly the kind of thing people have been complaining about for years. Our members have the same right to use these buildings as anyone else. If *we* started blockading buildings with these so-called safe spaces, you'd be saying, oh, what awful racists, oh, someone has to put a stop to it. It's double standards, as usual, with you people. You ought to be ashamed of yourselves.'

'And I'll put those points to the students' representative, but I'm speaking to *you*, now, and what I'm trying to get at is —'

'Well,' Mrs. Rupple interrupted, 'you'll have to, won't you? Because they're refusing to debate me.'

'The truth is,' the anchor said, patiently, 'you may not be racists, but your organisation, let's face it, is — unpalatable. To some people, a lot of people, it's unpalatable, isn't it, Carla Rupple?'

'That's all beside the point,' said Mrs. Rupple. 'How can you defend English students being denied entry to English schools, English universities? How can you defend that?'

'It isn't up to me to defend —'

'You *can't*, because it's *indefensible!*' she yelled. 'We've had reports today, four different reports, four unrelated reports, of students being asked what faith group they're part of. Faith! My challenge to the minister — who I notice hasn't bothered to show his face yet — my challenge to the minister is to explain in person — in person — explain to my members, and not just to my members but to the public, how this is being allowed to happen. If people are being asked to declare their religion, it means some religions are allowed, and others aren't. Which religions? *Which religions?* Your viewers will be watching this and thinking, like me, oh-hoh, usual suspects —'

'But wouldn't the students say these are isolated cases?' asked the anchor. 'You do accept that the vast majority of —'

'That's crap, and you know it,' said Mrs. Rupple.

'Please,' said the anchor, 'just, it's still before the watershed, if we could just please keep the language —'

The screen went dead. Rahman's dad had turned off the TV. 'Communists,' he said, and went off into the kitchen, taking the remote with him.

A silence sank across the room, floating down into the space left by Mrs. Rupple's indignation. A car drove past, slowing for the speed bump, then revving up, then braking for the next one, then revving again. Rahman looked at the picture of his mother, casting her frozen gaze over the furniture, the roots of her jet-black hair pulled back tightly, the pink of her dress sharp against the dappled blue-grey flecks behind. He looked at the wallpaper around her, scrolls of cabbagey flowers twisting around one another, and at the crease where the back of the sofa met the armrest, the pleather puckering, and the too-thick carpet, and the yellowing ceiling, and the lopsided dado rail, and the thousand other things which hadn't changed, and never, ever would, squashing down into the dark, history to be fossilised.

He closed his eyes, and pictured a Martyr of Albion strapped to a chair, with black eyes and busted lips, his head groggy, nodding down, lost in the deep sleep of pain; or lying dead in the sand, a tap of blood spurting from the crown of his head; or knelt down on the nothing-coloured carpet, begging for Rahman's forgiveness, desperate and snivelling.

Except that he couldn't picture it, because Mrs. Rupple was a Martyr of Albion, and she was as far away from a skinhead as he could imagine, and it made him feel worse, not better, and the whole thing was ruined.

Carla Rupple, the Martyr of Albion. It was like a joke, and he was the punchline.

•

It was International Men's Day, and Buddleia was delighted. A female geosociology student had come forward to accuse Professor McEldowney of tying her to a bed and having anal sex with her, and had a trail of Sleazydoesit messages to prove it. It was helpfully specific, especially because Buddleia was writing an article for Fash Off, Students Against Fascism's online zine, and said she was calling it *Victim-shaming doesn't work: Here's why*. Now she had a real victim, her article didn't need 'Amir (not his real name), who is of Muslim heritage'. It was hardly a great disguise, especially when she kept referring to Rahman as 'my Muslim friend' in her daily Fabble posts, implying that she only had one.

Rahman looked at Buddleia's placard. True to form, it was better than his, #DITCHTHEDEAN stencilled out in immaculate capitals, with each letter given a spangled outline. He looked down at his own offering, islands of dried-out marker pen in a cardboard-brown expanse. The Mbathas probably had a whole stationery cupboard dedicated to Buddleia's political protests; his placard had *Huawei* printed on the back, upside down.

'Here we are,' said Mrs. Mbatha, pulling up at the edge of the Faculty of Arts car park and hitting the handbrake button. She turned to Buddleia. 'Five o'clock, unless I hear otherwise, then?'

'You won't,' Buddleia said. 'We're staying all afternoon.' She opened the passenger door and swung her legs out, manoeuvring her placard out of the foot-well after them.

'As long as it doesn't get out of hand,' said Mrs. Mbatha.

'Mum,' Buddleia said. 'It's already out of hand.'

Mrs. Mbatha reached into the car door for her sunglasses. 'Remember, I was a student once,' she said, smiling. 'I know how these things can escalate. Phone on, okay sweetheart?'

'Obviously,' Buddleia said.

'And you, Rahman.'

'Okay,' Rahman said, checking his phone.

tarek › me
did u nick my black trainers u twat

'¡Viva la revolución!' said Mrs. Mbatha from behind her sunglasses, raising a not very serious fist. Rahman opened the improbably heavy door; the car was so tall that he had to jump down from the seat, the seatbelt clip automatically retracting behind him, burrowing down into the cream-coloured leather.

'She's such a bitch to me,' Buddleia said, as the car swished quietly out of the car park.

Placards in hand, they walked together towards the black ziggurat of the Student Union, the shadows of cloud moving across its sloped glass. Rahman could see a clump of students already gathered by the steps, #ditchthedean posters at the ready, a few of them with giant foam hands pointing skyward. He started to feel a bit nervous; how many of them would recognise him? How many times would he be asked why he left?

'*There* she is,' Buddleia said, pointing to Gray, and sped up, striding across the tarmac; and Rahman trundled after her, scanning the crowd in the hope that he wouldn't see any friendly faces. He couldn't bear the idea of Françoise pleading with him not to quit, again, especially not in public.

Gray was even more embellished than usual, dozens of badges pinned all the way down the edges of her top. One said something about Las Malvinas; another declared that she was moving beyond gender; a third, larger badge announced that she was heterolesbian and proud of it. It must be exhausting, Rahman thought, to be attached to so many causes, to have so many different interests to juggle, so much identity to manage, such mental gymnastics to perform, the badges clacking against one another with every swing of a philosophical hip. She hugged Buddleia, one of the badges briefly snagging on Buddleia's pink and black kaftan, and then gave Rahman a cautious half-hug, which meant that Solar Garden City was never going to be forgotten.

'Hey,' she said, and then turned away before he had a chance to answer.

These are my friends, then, thought Rahman: two girls, neither of whom was facing him, neither of whom he'd ever sleep with, nor wanted to. With every passing moment, his alter egos — Rahman the fighter pilot, Rahman the jihadi warlord, Rahman the drone-proof photojournalist — were becoming less convincing. His job was to stand around on the campus of a university he no longer attended, and admire the application of glitter to paper. What made it even crazier was that #ditchthedean was only happening because of him, the one person who didn't want to be there.

'That's so much better than mine,' Gray said to Buddleia, miserably. 'I couldn't get any glitter.'

'Mum got me some, from this kids' outreach thing she does at work,' Buddleia replied, looking down modestly. 'I just thought it was worth making the effort.'

And then, out of the corner of his eye, Rahman saw Noah. He was sitting alone in the passenger seat of a police car, its wheels mounting the kerb, wearing a bobble hat and aviator sunglasses. It looked like he was losing a fight with an All Day Breakfast Burrito, the filling leaking out of the bottom of the tortilla and plopping onto the front of his shirt. Rahman ducked behind Buddleia, but it was too late, because Noah had already seen him, and waved.

Crap, Rahman thought. He considered bolting into the Student Union to hide in the toilets, but Noah was already folding the burrito back into its wrapper, ready to ambush. He'd want to introduce himself to Rahman's new, non-hazardous friends, and ask them what they were up to, in the squeaky *hiya-mate-how-ya-diddling* voice he put on when he was fishing for information.

'Gimme a second, okay?' Rahman said to Buddleia, and walked over to the police car.

Noah opened the window, and squinted out at Rahman. 'Hiya, fella!' Noah said. 'What's going on?'

'Are you fucking following me?'

'Dude,' said Noah. 'Why would I be following you?'

'Why else are you here?'

'Well,' said Noah, picking at a dull pink clod of burrito sauce on his bright pink t-shirt, 'you're not the only buddy of mine, as it happens.'

'I'm not your fucking *buddy*,' said Rahman.

Noah sighed. 'All right then,' he said: 'case. But I don't wanna call anyone a case. It's a bit — cold, man.'

'You're lying,' Rahman said. 'You're following me. You're spying on me.'

'*Dude*,' said Noah. 'I'm serious. We're expecting your pal Ibrahim to turn up.'

The ping from the Leaders of Tomorrow came back into Rahman's ear. 'What?' he said.

'Ibrahim. Awad.'

Rahman stared.

'What, you don't think Islamists are against perverts on campus?' And Noah chuckled to himself as he inspected the blob of burrito sauce under his fingernail.

'Here?' Rahman asked. He looked back towards the students, and the forest of demanding placards bristling over their heads.

'What's the biggie, man?' said Noah, grinning. 'You worried he won't like your new friends?'

'Fuck *off*,' growled Rahman, his teeth gritted.

'I did tell you,' Noah sang.

Rahman turned around, and started to walk back to the ziggurat, the ping still ringing in his head. He'd have to make up an excuse, and leave; but he didn't have enough credit for the bus, and the university was miles from home, far too far to walk. 'We still on for next week, yeah?' called Noah, from behind.

You fucking idiot, Rahman thought. He'd seen Ibrahim's Blackfl.ag vlogs on sex, where he sprayed out his disgust at bum bandits and shirt lifters and pillow biters and dykes. How could Rahman explain it, if Ibrahim saw him standing next to a girl wearing a rainbow badge? He wasn't even sure he could explain it to himself. He stood at the edge of the crowd, keeping a healthy distance from Gray, and looked up at the clouds, willing them to burst.

•

It did rain, but Buddleia wouldn't let anyone go home; instead, she gave out dopamine-mango Squish-Es, to keep everyone going. At the top of the ziggurat, Student-Staff Liaison Officers were twitching the venetian blinds running down the diagonal windows, looking down into the stubborn crowd and biting their lips. More and more students turned up, and vloggers and activists and a reporter, and soon Rahman couldn't see anything but other people's shoulder blades, and was lost in the nylon and the rucksacks and the hair and the padded straps of camera cases, having to use his elbows to stay in place. Finally, Buddleia screamed 'SHUT UP!', because Student-Staff Liaison had posted something on Fabble, and she wouldn't be able to read it out unless people stopped talking over her.

And Professor McEldowney had resigned.

The students around them whooped and hollered, raising their phones up into the air for selfies; and then, Buddleia screamed 'SHUT UP!' again, so she could tell them that while strongly maintaining his innocence yada yada yada, atmosphere of consent yada yada, would be stepping back, and that they'd won, and that this was only the beginning, and the roar sprang back up into the air around Rahman, twice as loud again.

And then, in the middle of the small clearing which had formed around her, Buddleia knelt down in front of him, and bowed her head, arching her back until her nose was halfway down to the tarmac. For a horrible moment, he thought she was going to kiss his feet. She looked up, a saintly, love-struck smile on her face, and took his hand in hers.

'You're so brave,' she said.

Rahman fleetingly considered kicking her in the face. But he didn't. 'Thanks,' he said.

Then Gray gave him a mesmerised look, and hugged him, clutching his ribcage with mother-tight arms. She whispered something into his ear, something he couldn't make out; then she pulled him into the centre of the circle of students, crushing his fingers in her grip.

'Rahman,' she called out, 'Rahman is the proof that victims need allies!'

'YES!' screamed an unseen voice, 'THIS! THIS!'

'This is who we're fighting for!' she shouted; then, she beamed at him, and hugged him again, even tighter.

Rahman was breathing too fast, the blood rushing in his forehead, glancing from one pair of wide, friendly eyes to the next as Gray raised her face to the sky triumphantly. A pair of strong hands grabbed him from behind, squashing his clammy t-shirt around his waist, as if to lift him up; as soon as he'd wriggled out of their grip, he saw dozens of people, all looking back at him, and couldn't think what to say.

'EQUALITY!' he yelled, because that was a nice, safe word, and was as good as anything else.

There was an explosion of noise around him, clapping and cheering, hands waggling in the air, phones aloft. Rahman felt dizzy, like a bus had just driven past him too close, threatening to topple him into the road. And then, as soon as he'd got his breath back, he saw Ibrahim, and all his warring parts turned their guns on one another at the exact same time.

Rahman stared at Ibrahim. He was saying something, but Rahman couldn't make it out.

'What?' yelled Rahman, hardly able to hear the sound of his own yell.

And Ibrahim repeated the silent thing, but angrier, and with pointing.

'I can't hear you,' Rahman yelled.

And then, Ibrahim hurtled towards Rahman, and punched him in the nose.

Rahman fell, his back smacking into the ground, a jet of blood snorting out of his nostril. He scurried backwards on his arse and elbows until a knee hit him in the ear, and he keeled onto his side, grazing his cheek on the paving; then he saw Ibrahim's trainers pushing their way towards him, and hauled himself up by grabbing someone's pocket. He squeezed through the crowd limb by limb, ducking between the students, with Buddleia screaming 'Rahman! Rahman!' behind him; as soon as he could, he ran, bombing across the plaza between the faculty buildings, his nose streaming with blood, a weird feeling spreading across his face as though bits of it had been moved around, the freezing air whipping in through the gaps, stinging in his eyes. As he skidded around the corner, he checked over his shoulder.

No Ibrahim.

Rahman stopped, and doubled over, his wrists and fingertips caked in red-brown blood.

I'm two people, he thought. I'm two different people, and they can't both live in the same body. His worlds were bleeding at their edges, their beauty and their agony fizzing where they met, noisy and volatile, a roaring chemistry, threatening to burn him from the inside out.

He checked around the corner again. Still no Ibrahim.

Slowly, Rahman started to walk back home. At the edge of the campus, he stopped at a bus shelter; but then, he looked at his phone, and realised that he'd need to identify at least four hundred pictures with cars in them to get enough credit for the bus. So he kept on walking, wiping the blood from his face onto the back of his hand, ignoring the constant ringtones throbbing against his leg. He was crying, because it wasn't fair, any of it, and because of how Ibrahim had looked at him, as though he was less than nothing, and because of the snake tank, whose lonely inhabitant Rahman, in his self-pity, suddenly pitied.

buddleia › me
where r u

buddleia › me
where r u r u ok

gray › me
where r u

buddleia › me
pick up ur phone

unknown number › me
Hi Rahman, this is Buddleia's mum. Can you get in touch with her please?

unknown number › me
Hi Rahman we're trying to call you, are you getting my messages

At the next bus stop, there was a bin, NO DOG WASTE printed in bright red around its side. Rahman looked at its whale-wide mouth, which gawped right back at him. For a second, he considered chucking his phone in it, because having a phone pointed at him all the time actually wasn't that great, and seemed to be causing him a lot more problems than it was solving. But then he decided not to, because everyone knew it was better to keep your phone with you, in case something happened. So he kept on walking along the bus route, an occasional bus whooshing past him, to emphasise how long it would take him to get home. No one stopped to ask him if he was okay, but they still stopped, to get a good view of the blood, and point him out to one another. As he got to the Gymnothèque, he rolled up his sleeves so he didn't have to look at the blood; but it was still all over his wrists and knuckles, and still dribbling onto his top lip.

And that's when he saw the Martyrs of Albion walking towards him, their jackets puffy and black, their heads bald and stubbly, placards resting on their shoulders, SAVE THE DEAN and SAY NO TO PC and NO TRIAL BY MEDIA and STOP THE WITCHHUNT. And leading them up the hill was Carla Rupple, a Viking god at her side, striding towards the battlefield.

Rahman stopped, and looked at the Viking god. He was so handsome; there was something about his eyes, sea-blue, glinting with mischief. And he was so *big*. So *tall*. What must it be like, to be that tall? Rahman wondered. And what would it feel like to be taken into those great, strong arms?

As the Martyrs got closer, Rahman realised he was staring, but it didn't seem to matter. It felt a bit like his head had been cut loose from his body. His nose didn't hurt at all anymore; it just felt different, like it was in a different place.

'Heh,' sniggered Thor, as he walked past. '*Good*.'

'How's Informa/McKenzie?' Rahman asked Thor's shoulder.

Thor stopped, and turned around. 'What did you say?' he asked.

'I said, how's Informa/McKenzie?' said Rahman.

And then, Thor punched Rahman in the nose.

THE AMISH

The noise Noodle made when he hit the pavement was all wrong: not a thud, but a crack. And then Craig saw the weird angle of Noodle's neck, and the blood, and how it was glugging out of the back of Noodle's head, and how Noodle's eyes had gone all funny.

'Oh my God!' Craig's mum screamed. 'Oh my GOD!'

Craig looked at his mum. She was staring at Noodle, her hands covering her mouth and nose. Then she looked at Craig.

And then, someone else screamed, this time from the other side of the road.

And then Craig ran. He ran off the pavement, straight into the road, and then kept on going, sprinting along the wall and diving right at the edge of the viaduct, and pelted straight down the path along the railway line, on and on, past a woman, then another, past a flash of fluorescent yellow on a bike, head down, feet roaring. He lurched to the left at the end of the path, and ran into a stream of steady traffic, and a car had to brake, hard, and only just missed him by a few inches; then, the car behind braked dead, and beeped, and he only just made it to the other side without the van in the next lane hitting him. He kept running, past the golf club, past the steps up to the station, past the new estate and all the way along the side of the park, past TyreLand and the Baptist church and the Chinese all-you-can-eat, past the pool hall and the whitewashed Jobcentre and the polyclinic and the thrinted tower block, past the betting shop and the tax office, and round a corner, across the rapid bus transit, around the edge of a carpark, and then his shoe came off. He stopped to pick it up, and then ran underneath a motorway underpass, resting his hand against a mural so he could shove his foot back into his shoe, and started running again, along the underpass and out into the light, past banks of cars and hedges and parking meters, right into a man who was looking down at his phone, which he dropped when Craig body-slammed him.

'Jesus —'

Craig fell onto his elbow, his own phone clattering out of his pocket and onto the ground. He looked at the two phones together, and, until he saw the bits of wood glue around the edges of his screen, couldn't tell them apart. 'Sorry,' he whispered, barely able to breathe, and picked his phone up, and put it back in his pocket. Then he started sprinting, and then running, and then jogging, because he'd never heard his heart beat so loudly before, and jogged along the edge of the Supabuy until he got to the tiny pedestrian footbridge which led to the old council offices on Ottawa Square. He jogged up the first staircase, and walked up the second, and yanked himself up the railings of the third, and then walked across the bridge into the pedestrianised plaza suspended above the road, the air rasping in his lungs. He limped down the side of the brown-windowed buildings, until he saw someone in a sleeping bag at the other end of the plaza, and dived into the revolving doors, which were locked. So he stood in the outward-facing quarter of the revolving door, pressing himself flat into its corner.

Shit, he thought.

Then, he saw another sleeping bag; but this one was in the lobby of the council building, which meant that there was a way in. Craig shoved at the door, and it budged by an inch. So then, slamming his shoulder into it over and over, he nudged the door inwards, until finally, when his shoulder was so sore that he had to cover it with his hand, he was neither facing in nor out, but in an airlock, the reflection of Queen Elizabeth II's iron back shimmering on the glass, a seagull hopping down from her plinth.

And then, for the first time, he realised he'd changed a disabled person's name to 'Spacker' on a register, and what a shitty, shitty, shitty thing that was to do.

•

Craig was never any good at plans. The problem with plans was that they required him to pick between options, which meant evaluating, and it never seemed as though there was enough time to evaluate stuff when it mattered. He'd been sitting in the revolving door for what felt like five hours, but might also have been five minutes; and for all he knew, busting his way into the building was just as risky as busting his way back out. He'd need to make a decision, sooner or later, but there was no way of knowing which was the dumber of the two options, and his track record on such choices wasn't great.

Who were those people from Geography And Spatial Belonging, with the bonnets? Craig asked himself. The Amish. He could remember the video Ms. Masood showed in class, the year before the Crackling Bacon NuHome Scent. She said that the Amish had a unique identity, and a strong sense of spatial belonging which resisted external influence. They went around in horse-drawn buggies rather than cars, and wouldn't sell stuff to outsiders if it was going to be used for decoration. They took it way further than the eMancipated: no electric hobs, no TV, not even a radio; just crops and wooden houses and candlelight and sex in the missionary position. That would be nice, Craig thought. Maybe he could become Amish. He'd have to wean himself off Jerkshuffle, though. How did Amish guys hook up with girls? Barn dances?

There was a thump on the glass. He looked up: it was Constable Hudson, hands on knees, his face bright pink.

'Out,' he yelled.

Craig did nothing.

'If you go in, I'll come and get you.'

Craig gazed out at him. 'How did you find me?' he asked, eventually.

Constable Hudson cupped a hand behind his ear. 'Say again?'

'How did you find me?' Craig said, louder.

'Your phone,' the constable shouted. 'You've still.' And he heaved for breath. 'Got it. On.'

Craig took out his phone. The giant cow's eye of the camera was still there behind the shattered surface, its lens still awake, still slightly wet-looking, still watching the world beyond. There was something about it he no longer trusted. It was like it had done something wrong, but he couldn't work out what.

But then, he couldn't have just left it there, lying on the pavement. Everyone knew it was better to keep your phone with you, in case something happened.